The
MOZART
CONSPIRACY

Praise for The Musician's Daughter

"... this book is a rip-roaring adventure with music, murder, and espionage. It's clearly well researched, and the level of detail in the narrative makes readers believe that this story might have actually happened. Theresa's first-person narrative reveals her to be a quick-thinking, courageous, and likable individual."

– School Library Journal

"...a gutsy, sympathetic heroine who remains true to her friends, in a fast-paced historical adventure that offers a hint of romance."

– Kirkus Reviews

ALSO BY SUSANNE DUNLAP

Listen to the Wind

The Spirit of Fire

Émilie's Voice

Liszt's Kiss

The Musician's Daughter

Anastasia's Secret

In the Shadow of the Lamp

The Académie

The
MOZART
CONSPIRACY

A THERESA SCHURMAN MYSTERY

Susanne Dunlap

Susanne Dunlap
88 Crescent St.
Northampton, MA 01060
susanne-dunlap.com

Revised Edition

ISBN 13: 978-0-578-56597-2

Dedication

For my readers, who have stuck with me over the years.

I thought my life had gone back to normal—or as close to normal as life for someone who is really two people all the time could be. But my relative calm was shattered one day shortly before Michaelmas in the autumn of 1781 as I was on my way home from performing in a concert in the Augarten, the park in the Viennese suburb of Leopoldstadt. I had thought about sharing a *Fiaker* with two of the other musicians. But it was almost October and I feared I would miss the opportunity for a walk on the last fine night of the season.

Besides, I wanted to save my money to purchase a new gown.

Although it was not late, it was fully night. The moonless expanse of the heavens was sugared with stars over the dark, empty road to Vienna. Cottages dotted the distant countryside, marked by the light of candles that glowed through their windows, and the tendrils of wood smoke rising like ghosts from stoves lit to take the chill off the evening. But as I continued on the route, coming to the stretch between the edge of the pleasure park and the first dwellings of the suburb, something began to make me feel uneasy.

Mirela, who despite opportunities to better herself still lived in the Roma camp by the Danube, had taught me how to slip noiselessly through the night, how to hear and feel the approach of danger and avoid it. I hadn't much needed to use that knowledge in the nearly two years since my father's murder. But it's always a good idea to have resources to call upon, especially if you're in my situation and must ensure that your two identities are kept entirely separate.

What had alerted me to possible trouble was the sound of footsteps behind me, keeping pace with mine. I continued for a while—as Mirela had taught me—as if I had heard nothing, all the time letting my eyes alone take in everything I passed, looking for escape routes and hiding places. The road curved up ahead, and in its crook stood a copse of Linden trees, still leafy and obscuring at this time of year. One of them I knew from having passed that way many times before had a low branch that was easy to climb on. I believed, too, that I could scale almost to the top of the tree very quickly if I ever found it necessary. I crossed myself mentally in thanks that I was wearing my man's uniform, donned so that I could play in the orchestra since women were not allowed. Forcing myself to keep a steady pace, I mentally counted the steps it would take me to round the curve and put the trees between me and whoever was following me.

I came to the curve, and as soon as I was confident that I would be hidden from sight, I slung my violin case across my shoulders with the strap my little brother had fashioned for me in Herr Goldschmidt's workshop and hoisted myself into the tree. The case knocked softly against the trunk once, but I continued to scramble up into the sheltering leaves until I reached a place where I could see the road in both directions.

I was right. Someone followed where I had recently walked. In fact, I was surprised to discover that there was not one, but two someones. Odd that I had heard only one set of footsteps. The man in front carried an instrument case tucked under his arm—not a violin or viola, but something much smaller. He marched along steadily, possibly unaware, or perhaps not caring, that anyone was behind him. The following man had kept exact pace with him until he was within a short distance of the trees, then hastened his steps as though trying to catch up. I thought for a moment how foolish I was to have been so frightened and suspicious. Doubtless the second man was trying to reach his friend so they could chat while they hurried back to their apartments before the porters locked the doors at ten-of-the-clock. Now I would have to wait until they passed to climb down from my lookout post, and I gazed with not much more than idle curiosity to see how they would greet each other.

It happened that they met almost directly beneath my tree. My view was blocked a little by the leaves and branches, but I could see that they both wore wigs and appeared to be wearing musicians' uniforms, and I was able to hear everything that passed between them.

The man who followed reached out and tapped the first one on the shoulder.

"Grüss Gott!" said the one in front as he turned, apparently recognizing the other and greeting him politely.

I thought at first that the second one returned the greeting by wrapping his arms around his friend in an embrace that temporarily squeezed the breath out of him, but as I watched I began to think that the embrace lasted an unusually long time.

Too long, in fact. The first fellow dropped his instrument case and began to gasp and grunt.

They weren't embracing, they were struggling.

The second man had set upon the first with the intent to harm him—perhaps kill him.

I couldn't simply stay where I was and watch this happen. Two people could overcome one, I thought, and I had not seen a flash of steel or any other indication that the assailant carried a weapon.

Before another instant passed I slid through the branches, tearing my coat and buffeting my violin case, until I dropped onto the ground a pace away from the struggling men.

"Stand back!" I yelled.

The element of surprise had the desired effect. The attacker at once released his hapless victim and fled at a crouching run, unfortunately before I could get a good look at his face, or even have a sense of his size and build.

I knelt down beside the injured man, who lay sprawled on the ground in an unnatural position as if he had no control over his limbs. His eyes flicked from side to side. He was alive, but clearly in extreme distress.

"I will go for help!" I said.

"No use," he gasped.

I realized only then that a puddle of something dark and warm had spread out on the ground beneath us. The other fellow must have had a knife after all and plunged it into the musician's back. I shivered, despite the mild weather.

"Who was it?" I asked, and began to stand, convinced that if I acted quickly enough I might yet be able to bring him aid.

He lifted one hand and grabbed hold of me so I could not move. The man breathed more quickly and shallowly. "Need to tell . . . No . . . Not that . . ."

"What? Tell me quickly, so that I may get help!"

With great effort, the man lifted his head off the ground. The autumn moon began to rise and cast an eerie, soft light across the landscape, catching the expression in his clouding eyes. I will never forget that look, or the sound of his voice.

"Mozart!" he breathed, then his head lolled back and he sighed as though letting go of the world's entire weight.

That's when I knew he was dead.

CHAPTER TWO

I should have been more terrified than I was, but the entire event seemed so unreal. The man had said the name Mozart with his last breath. Could he have been naming his attacker? Surely not! Wolfgang Amadé Mozart, who had been in Vienna since the spring and was rumored to be composing an opera, had not been at the concert in the Augarten as far as I knew. And in any case, I could not imagine the diminutive, fastidious composer—whom as yet I had only glimpsed from a distance—a violent man. But I did not want to waste a moment in that isolated place.

I would have to report the attack to someone. It pained me to leave the musician's lifeless body where it was, yet I dared not try to move it. And it reminded me much too clearly of that other murder, the one that had robbed me of my father. I felt the bile rise into my throat, and looked away.

I had recovered from that horrible time two years ago, but at a cost. I was younger then and not so experienced in the ways of the world. I took the task of solving my father's murder upon myself, and endangered others in the process. I would not make the same mistake again. It would be best, I told myself, to run to the guard station at the city gate no more than a mile off and tell them what happened. They would know how to fetch the police, who at this hour would have begun to patrol the streets on horseback. After that, I could walk away and forget all about the poor man. He was none of my affair.

I took up my violin case and slung it across my back so that I could run unimpeded. As I covered the ground between that fateful spot and the fortified *Bastei*, the broad, high wall that surrounded the center of Vienna, I considered what I should say, how I might explain that I happened to be hiding in the branches of a tree and witnessed this violent action. I would have to give my name, and that might cause some difficulties. Even my mother was unaware of the fact that I turned into young Thomas Weissbrot for the purpose of playing the violin in the smaller local orchestras. I told her—and she believed—that I had found more work copying music for the legions of ambitious composers who flooded the city from the provinces and abroad, and that it kept me from our apartment at all hours. She did not know that I had a selection of uniforms and men's clothing in a room tucked at the back of the Esterhazy Palace, and that the porter was accustomed to letting me in as a lady and seeing me leave as a young man—and vice versa. My godfather Haydn had arranged it all for me.

As I approached the guard's station by the gate, I slowed my pace to catch my breath. The cool air grated in my lungs and brought saliva into the back of my throat, and I thought I would not be able to speak. I bent over and rested my hands on my knees, letting my head hang and trying to slow my breathing to normal.

That's when I saw the blood, all over my knees and on one of my sleeves. *Gottverdammt!* What would the guard think? Would it look as though it had been I, in fact, who had set upon someone and killed him? How could I avoid such a suspicion, especially as I was so suspiciously disguised?

Leaving the poor man's body in the open, however, perhaps to be eaten by wolves, would be unthinkable. Alone I could not move him, even if I dared. Presenting myself before the guards in this state would result in questions I was not prepared to answer.

There was only one solution.

I turned my steps away from the city, this time to the east. I needed Mirela's help. She of all people would know what to do.

I had walked so often to the Roma camp by the Danube that I could have done it with my eyes closed, through the snows of winter or in the swirling dust clouds of hot, windy summer. Still, the wan moonlight distorted everything and created shadows where I never knew them to lurk before. An owl startled me with a coarse hoot from its perch on the branches of a fir tree. A fox darted across my path nearly causing me to shriek and run away before I realized it was not a wild boar. By the time I saw the crazy shapes of the wanderers' wagons and huts ahead of me and the dull glow of a newly doused fire, my heart raced.

I did not have time to go through the elaborate process of greeting everyone in the camp so as not to hurt any feelings. I had discovered in the past two years that the Roma (they preferred not to be called Gypsies, as almost everyone else named them) held etiquette to be extremely important—perhaps even more so than our emperor did, whom I had seen often in my guise as a violinist, and who appeared to differ little from an ordinary nobleman if one were to judge by his dress and easy manners.

In any case, I decided it would be best to go directly to Mirela's hut and enter by the way she had shown me, through a hidden door Olaf had fashioned for her that led out not to the center of the camp, but toward the woods. She said that the secret doors in the Hofburg, the emperor's palace, had given her the idea. We'd had cause to use them in pursuit of my father's murderer. She wanted to be able to come and go without anyone knowing, so that she could meet me in town to go to the coffee house or the market without censure.

For that had been the peculiar thing: the Romany were all grateful for the service I had rendered them in helping to protect them from unwarranted harassment by the guards, but I was still an outsider. Mirela had been urged many times to give up our friendship and return to the old ways.

As I approached my friend's hut I began to worry that perhaps she would not be there, it was so dark. But then I heard sounds from within, at first thinking she was humming some old melody to herself as she fell asleep. The closer I drew, though, the stranger the noises sounded. Mirela's voice was unmistakable, yet the tune she uttered was no melody, just a random assembly of short sounds of different pitches that grew and waned in intensity.

I crept to where I knew the door was located and felt for the latch that would trip the spring.

As Mirela's secret door opened into the darkness of her hut, I heard an unearthly noise, like a wolf preparing to howl. Just as I drew in my breath to call for help, Mirela's voice stopped me.

"Rezia! What are you doing here?"

"*Scheiss!*" said someone else in a deep, groggy man's voice.

I heard Mirela fumbling for the match bottle and soon the obscurity of the hut was illuminated by a single candle. I have always found it remarkable that a tiny point of light can be blinding in certain circumstances, and this was one of them. I just caught the flash of a man's naked back before it was covered with a coat. When he stood and I recognized Olaf, I was glad the light was not bright enough to reveal my deep blush. How foolish of me!

"*Entschuldigen-Sie, Mam'selle,*" Olaf said with a note of amusement as he pushed past me to disappear out the same, secret door through which I had entered.

"So, I expect you came here to lecture me, although it could have waited until tomorrow."

"No, but I hope he has asked for your hand," I said, immediately feeling prudish and wishing I had not burst in as I had.

Mirela stretched one shapely leg out along her pallet on top of the rumpled blankets and gave a long, luxurious yawn. Of the two of us she had been the one to grow into a comely woman, with a figure that drew stares wherever she went. When we met two years ago, she was smaller and thinner than I was. I watched fascinated at her consciousness of her own, voluptuous power as she pulled the disordered pile around herself, covering at least some of her nakedness.

"I have come for your help." I quickly told her the story of my night's adventure so far.

Mirela at once stood and before I could turn my eyes away I caught sight of her taut, brown body. I heard her open her wooden trunk and shuffle around a bit. "It's all right," she said after a moment or two, "I am covered." She had managed to pull on a skirt and a blouse and was digging around for more clothes when I turned back to her. "We must ask for Danior's help. But first, you should change out of those ruined breeches."

I had been so distracted about what I'd seen only moments before that I had forgotten the reason I had made the detour to the camp. Mirela tossed a colorful lump of clothing in my direction, and I soon shed the silk uniform that was not only stiffened with blood in several places, but torn beyond repair from my scramble down the tree. Mirela's blouse was loose on me and the skirt did not cover my ankles. When Mirela saw me she doubled over in silent laughter.

"This is no time for mirth!" I hissed. "A dead man is waiting for us."

"Then there is no hurry," Mirela snapped back. "What do you know of this dead person? What business is he of yours?"

What did I know? I had not even picked up his instrument case to see what he played, or looked closely at his uniform to see whether he was employed by a princely house. All I could recall at that moment was the look in his eyes, and his fervent whisper of *Mozart!* just before he expelled the last breath from his body. And I did not want to tell this to Mirela. I feared she would not understand why it had all distressed me so.

I followed Mirela out into the camp. She hitched up her skirts as she led me over to an old nag tied to a tree, its eyelids half closed and bits of hay hanging from its mouth. She unlooped the horse's lead and in one smooth movement leapt from the ground and swung her leg over the creature's back. Its head jerked up in surprise and it glanced around as if to say, *What do you think you're doing at this hour?*

"Sit behind me," Mirela said.

We were not wealthy enough to own horses. I knew them only from riding in a carriage or jumping out of the way as they clattered toward me over the cobbles in Vienna. I had successfully avoided having to learn how to ride. Fortunately, this beast seemed either still half asleep or too old to care, because it stood patiently as I clambered up behind Mirela, my fiddle still slung across my back. If he could have looked down from heaven then my father must have been holding his breath worrying about the beautiful Amati inside the case. But I had padded it well. Toby had fashioned special straps and grooves for me so that it wouldn't rattle about.

Danior lived in the center of the town now, in the Trattner House. He and Alida had moved there recently. The Varga estates had proved profitable enough to furnish Alida a decent dowry, and her court connections helped Danior get steady work in the best orchestras. "No doubt the doors will be locked by the time we get there," I said. I had a few *Groschen* in my money pouch and hoped it would be enough to bribe the porter—the only way to persuade him to let us in after curfew. I feared that, looking as we did, he would think the worst of us. It was the hour when the lowest class prostitutes lurked in the shadows, looking for stragglers to help them earn a crust.

"Don't worry," said Mirela, in that voice I knew meant that we might end up doing things that were not exactly legal, like the time she "borrowed" some jewels so that we could go to a masked ball. I wondered what she had in mind, starting with how she planned to get us through the city gates, which were no doubt now closed for the night as well.

Soon my question was answered. We crossed the bridge over the river Danube at the point where it came closest to the Bastei and rode boldly up to a guard who, although it was not very late, already yawned with boredom.

"Brishen!" Mirela hissed in a loud whisper.

Could it be? The guard walked into the pool of light shed by the torch near the entrance he guarded. It was indeed Brishen, one of the Romany who had helped me before. I knew he had been given a position with the Imperial Guard for his bravery in bringing my uncle's conspiracy to light, but I never realized he had found such a convenient posting.

"Well, Mirela! What brings you here? You know I should not allow you to pass. Do you have your papers?"

"Papers. Pah!" Mirela tossed her head, threw her leg over the horse's neck and slid down gracefully to the ground. *Don't leave me up here!* I thought, and did my best to dismount as well, getting my skirt caught up and revealing my legs up to my thighs in the process. Once I stood on my own two feet I meekly fished my papers out of the pouch I carried concealed near my waist and flashed Brishen the one that was stamped with my Viennese citizenship. He barely glanced at my passport.

"If I let you in, I will lose my job," Brishen said, slipping his arm around Mirela's slender waist.

"Who will know? I shall be but an hour." She pressed herself against him.

"Olaf wouldn't like you to do this."

"Do what?" she asked, leaning away from him. "I am just greeting my friend, and asking him to look after my docile Dobra while we continue on foot."

Dobra. So that was the obliging horse's name. I wasn't sure whether this was better or worse. We would be more noticed on horseback on the cobbled streets, especially the two of us mounted on one beast. But dressed as we were, it would be easier for us to be mistaken for common prostitutes if we were on foot, hugging the shadows. I pitied the man who ever approached Mirela for such a purpose. I thought perhaps my fiddle case would make me look like a Gypsy musician who had been hired to work at a party.

I appeared to have little to say on the matter, though. Mirela grabbed my hand and pulled me through the gates into the quiet lanes of Vienna.

CHAPTER THREE

We had slipped completely unseen through the back streets to reach the Trattner House, an elegant apartment building, only spotting a policeman on horseback making his indolent way down Schweden-platz as we darted across. The building was on the Graben, not far from the one that used to be my uncle's mansion but that had been turned into a house like any other, with shops on the ground floor and apartments above. As in all such dwellings in Vienna, the door was ruled over by a surly porter who made most of his money by being bribed to let residents and guests in after curfew. I had not called on Danior and Alida since they moved there six months ago, but apparently Mirela was well known to old Steinert, whose red eyes revealed that he had been drinking.

"Was ist los, Fräulein?" he asked. I started to reach for my money pouch, but Mirela clutched my hand and stopped me.

Her action irritated me. We needed to get in immediately. There was no time for games. A man lay dead on the road from the Augarten, and I must notify the authorities so that inquiries could be made.

"Herr Steinert, we are here on important business. I know you will let us in." As soon as the porter turned his key in the heavy lock and eased the door open a crack, Mirela slipped her fingers around it and wedged the rest of her body through, towing me along behind her. Steinert put out his hand to receive the customary payment, but Mirela simply took hold of it and curtsied, then rose on her tiptoes,

13

leaned forward from the doorway and pecked him on the cheek. I expected him to growl after us to call us to account, but to my surprise a huge smile cracked open his grizzled face and he made a mock courtly bow to us. We lifted our skirts and ran up the three flights of stairs.

From behind Danior and Alida's door came the sounds of laughter and music. A pang of envy shot through me. How I wished I were already within, enjoying what appeared to be a beautiful string quartet. Instead I was about to invade their happy home with my dirty face and ill-fitting apparel bringing news of violent death.

Mirela knocked softly but insistently until a lackey opened the door. Far from being surprised or put out, on seeing us he maintained an expression of complete nonchalance. "Whom shall I announce?" he inquired.

But Mirela did not respond, slipping past him, her eyes darted around the room until they alit on Danior, who was playing the first violin part in the quartet. I gave the lackey an apologetic shrug and followed her.

Standing a little to the side, arms crossed and wearing an expression of suppressed delight, was the short fellow I knew to be Wolfgang Amadé Mozart himself. I felt all the tension in my body subside at once, to the point where I was afraid my legs would give way and I would find myself sprawled on the floor. *It can't have been Mozart,* I told myself. He was here, standing before me, looking not in the least ruffled or as if he had run away from the scene of a murder.

"Rezia! Mirela!" whispered Alida, who must have been sitting among the ladies and spied us. She looped her arms through both of ours and drew us away to an anteroom so that our conversation would not interrupt the music.

I was struck by how beautiful their apartment was. The decorations were comfortable and elegant without that stiff pretension I had seen in some of the palaces where I performed. The paintings on the paneled walls were ancient, except for one, a glorious portrait of Alida herself, doubtless painted soon after her wedding. I knew that she was pregnant, not realizing how soon the baby was due since I had not seen her lately. She wore an open gown of gold brocade and no stays, a sort of compromise between dishabille and evening dress. The diamonds on her fingers were set off by a plain, hammered gold band, the ring Danior had made for her.

"What brings you here at this hour?" she asked, "But I don't mean to say you are unwelcome. Indeed, I have expected you to call these past six months, Rezia."

The invitation had been extended at the wedding, which had taken place a year ago. I had called on them in their old quarters, and assumed that was all Alida had expected, that the invitation had been for form's sake only, and so I had never presumed upon it after that. Now I felt that I had misjudged Alida.

"Rezia has something important to tell you."

As quickly as I could, I explained what had happened earlier that evening.

"Why did you not go directly to the authorities?" Alida asked.

What was I to say? That I did not want to compromise myself, and so decided to sneak around like a coward until I could inform them in perfect anonymity? Or that the dead man had breathed out Mozart's name as he died, and I did not want to bring the taint of criminal proceedings against the greatest musical genius of our age?

"I was afraid . . . they would think the worst."

"What Rezia means is that she was covered in blood and didn't dare go to the police, for fear that they would arrest her." Mirela, as always, cut through propriety and went straight to the point.

"Come with me," Alida said. She led us both into her dressing room. "You have grown so tall, Rezia, that I think some of my old clothes would fit you quite well." She opened a wardrobe and selected a grey satin gown, then took petticoats, a shift and stays out of a chest before ringing a tiny bell to summon a maid. "I must return to my guests. I'll speak to Danior and he will come to take you to the police captain so that you can make your report."

I longed to stay and hear the music. The maid helped me into the dress quickly and I washed the dirt off my face. Danior came in soon after, and when he asked, "Have you brought your violin?" I thought he was going to invite me to stay and play with them.

I pointed to the case, which I had placed by a chair.

"Could I show it to Monsieur Mozart? It will take only a moment, and you must finish dressing anyway. Then we can go."

I sighed. So, he thought only of my father's beautiful fiddle, not of me playing it. "Of course."

The maid tried to comb the tangles out of my hair, which had been stuffed into a bag wig as part of my musician disguise. I watched with longing as Danior and Mirela left me there to be rendered respectable. The sweet sound of that beautiful Amati, perhaps played by Mozart himself, tortured me as I sat and submitted to the maid's efforts. When Danior returned, he did not bring the fiddle.

"We'll come back afterwards. Amadé is still playing Antonius's instrument, and I said he could try it out in the next quartet, while we are gone."

"Oh Danior! You know I don't like to let the Amati out of my sight for anyone."

"But this is Mozart! How beautifully he plays! And we will be gone for only an instant. I'll present you to the maestro when we get back."

I wondered if Alida had told him the nature of our errand. I hardly thought he would be so breezy and casual about a murder.

I heard Mozart executing some brilliant passages as the door to Danior's apartment shut behind us. The silvery sounds rattled in my head all the way out to the street.

CHAPTER FOUR

As we walked, Danior tried to start a conversation, but he did it awkwardly, as if he was afraid of offending me. "Things have been quieter since your Papa died," he said, stating the obvious. "I fear we have been neglecting you since our marriage—and of course you know our news."

"Of course! I wrote my felicitations in a letter to Alida. But I am not unhappy with my life. I have a great deal to do, with playing the violin, teaching a few young children, helping Mama with little Anna—you know."

He smiled. I was struck by how much Danior had changed. He did not hide his black hair beneath a powdered wig, but it was tidily dressed and pulled back with a silk ribbon into a long, curling tail. He wore a brocade coat, velvet breeches, and silk hose, and the lace on his shirt was very fine. He spoke more carefully, too. Only his eyes still flashed with the same spirit I remembered from the time when the Roma camp was attacked, and when I saw him at the trial where he was condemned to death, defying my uncle to the last. Alida had tamed him, with her goodness and serenity—and her money.

"What I mean is, you could have come to visit any time, and with Mirela too. We can return to the apartment now, if you would like. No one aside from the four of us knows anything."

I stopped short. At first I didn't comprehend what he was saying. Then I realized why everyone had acted so strangely, why no one aside from me had any sense of real urgency about the matter—except possibly Mirela. "You don't believe me, do you!" I said. "Mirela saw the blood on my clothing herself. She believes me!"

Danior shook his head. "It's just not very likely, is it? Why would a musician be murdered by someone he apparently knew on his way back from a concert in the Augarten? And you could simply have fallen and scraped your knees."

"It could happen, and it did. My Papa was murdered, and he was a musician!" I said, now walking swiftly in the direction of the guard's station. Danior caught up to me and grasped my arm firmly. I yanked it away. "You think I want attention? That I would make such a thing up just to create drama? You are much mistaken!" By now I was quivering with anger, and the guard's station was just ahead.

"I have to wait for you out of the way, *Kushti*," Danior said. I understood. He might have married a member of the Hungarian nobility, but he was still a Gypsy to those who didn't know him, and very uncomfortable about the police and the guards. Besides, his skepticism would not have been helpful in this instance.

Danior withdrew to the shadows and I approached the officer who sat inside a small kiosk. Now I was even more nervous than I might have been. If my closest friends didn't believe me, how would I persuade a policeman to go out beyond the Bastei to look for a dead body?

I cleared my throat and the guard opened his eyes wide in the manner of someone who was accustomed to pretending that he had been awake all along when really he had been profoundly asleep. *"Entschuldigen-Sie,"* I said. "But I wish to report a crime."

"Did someone steal your purse? You shouldn't be out, a young lady like you, at this hour. Should be home in bed."

"This matter cannot wait. I witnessed a murder."

At that, the guard stood up so fast he staggered before catching hold of the frame of the kiosk to steady himself. "A murder you say? Where? Who?"

I quickly gave him the details.

"Did you report this to the guard at the city gate?"

I paused. How could I answer? "I—I did not. I was afraid. I was afraid the murderer would see me, if he had followed me, and I wanted to get right away from there."

My explanation seemed to satisfy him for the moment at least. "Wait here," the guard said, motioning that I could step inside his kiosk if I wanted to.

"I'm all right," I said and stayed where I was. He walked to the end of the lane, looked left and right, and gestured to a policeman on horseback who passed by on his evening rounds. I saw rather than heard them talking to one another. The mounted officer trotted off in the direction of the police headquarters in the Hofburg. This was one of the new measures our emperor Joseph II had taken to increase the security in the city. There had always been guards, but now the police force was more organized. The officers were mostly retired soldiers, though, and not much use for pursuing young criminals. I hoped they would be able to take my information and investigate the matter without me, once I told them everything I knew.

Or almost everything. I hadn't yet decided whether to mention the murdered man's last words. Especially now that I had seen Mozart at Danior's apartment.

Soon the guard returned, and within a few minutes four mounted policemen appeared. Their horses pawed the cobbles and snorted while I described to them where the murder had taken place. I gave them my name and told them where I lived, so that I could answer their questions in more detail once they had recovered the body and the investigation began.

"You will need an escort home," said one of the guards, a grizzled older man with a look I didn't quite trust.

"Oh, no, that is, I shall be quite all right. Friends expect me at their apartment in the Trattner House."

I watched them trot away in the direction of the Leopoldstadt gate, thanked the guard in the kiosk and turned to go.

I walked only a few paces around the corner before Danior joined me as if we had been walking along together all the time. "So, you told them everything?"

"Yes," I answered, conscious that I was lying to Danior, and that I had omitted something important in my report to the guard.

By the time we returned to Danior and Alida's apartment, everyone had gone from the party. Even Mirela was no longer there. Alida stifled a yawn as she invited me to enter and have some tea. "No, thank you, I should go home," I said. I was bitterly disappointed not to have been able to meet Mozart properly, instead of simply seeing him from a distance as I played in an orchestra at a grand ball. "Might I return your dress tomorrow?"

"No need. It suits you so well, and it will be some time before I can wear such a gown," she said.

I was relieved. If my mother awoke, or Greta stirred when I came in and saw me in Mirela's ill-fitting Gypsy clothing, I would have had to make up quite a tale to explain myself. A dress given me by Alida, on the other hand, was quite believable, as she had been similarly generous to me several times before she was married.

Against my protests, Danior fetched a Fiaker to take me the short distance to the apartment I shared with my mother, my two-year-old sister Anna, and faithful old Greta.

It wasn't until I arrived home that I realized I had made a terrible mistake. My normal practice after performing as Herr Weissbrot was to return to the Palais Esterhazy to change into my lady's clothing and transfer my violin to the old case that had belonged to my father. Since I had gone to Danior and Alida's apartment instead, the Amati was still in the newer case Toby had made for me. I prayed that Mama would not notice, and that I would have an opportunity to remedy my slip the very next day before anyone who might recognize the fiddle case would be able to make the connection between my two very separate lives.

CHAPTER FIVE

I received a message the next morning while I was still drinking my breakfast chocolate, before my mother had emerged from her room. She had taken to spending a long time at her toilette of late, and often if I had an early engagement I would not see her until I returned for supper just before curfew. There had even been a time when I arrived home only to be told by Greta that Mama had gone to a card party and would not return until late. It was strange behavior, to be sure.

That morning, though, I was quite glad my mother was still asleep so that she would not see me leap to my feet, grab my light cloak and dash out the door without even helping Greta clear up the breakfast things. The note had come from a captain of the police, who requested my immediate presence at the office in the Hofburg to discuss the matter upon which I had consulted them the night before. I blew a quick kiss to Anna, who was busy miming to her rag doll that she must eat her porridge or she would be spanked, and flew out of the door.

It was early, and the sunlit streets teemed with women wheeling their barrows overflowing with flowers and vegetables to the *Hohmarkt*. Shopkeepers were just opening their doors and sweeping the litter of the previous day off the cobbles out in front while they tried to keep a path clear so that patrons could come and go. It was a constant battle between the more affluent shopkeepers and the merchants thronging the streets with their wagons and tables and baskets set up on the busiest routes. I wove through them as quickly as I could, catching my cloak on a cartwheel once and leaping over a steaming pile of horse dung another time. By the time I reached the door in the small, rear courtyard of the Hofburg I was a little disheveled, but nonetheless intact.

The guard's eyes lit up in that way I had almost become accustomed to, now that I was nearly seventeen and fully grown. Still it disturbed me, to have men cast their eyes up and down my body as if they could see through my dress, my stays—even my shift. I tried hard not to blush, but I could feel the warmth creeping up from my shoulders into my neck. Soon it would spread over my face, and the man—an old fellow with grey hair and watery eyes—would think he had made a conquest.

It was maddening that I had not yet learned how to control this reaction. Life was so much simpler during those times when I was disguised as one of the thousands of musicians in Vienna, wearing either a court uniform or a simple, black coat and breeches. I had to wrap linen cloths around my breasts, but my hips were slim without petticoats to pad them out, and I passed well enough.

"Excuse me," I said, "I received this message telling me I should come here and ask for Rittmeister Bauer." I handed him the folded paper. He peered up and down at it and then at me several times, then scratched his head. "This is a military rank, a cavalry captain. And there is no one named Bauer here." He returned my message to me.

"But as you see, it clearly says I am to meet this Captain Bauer, immediately, here at police headquarters." I hated myself particularly when I took advantage of the weakness men seemed to have for the face and figure of a young woman, but I decided I had better do something to make this fellow find the person who had written the message to me that morning. So I widened my eyes and adopted the most perplexed and innocent expression I could muster.

It never ceased to amaze me how such a blatant tactic could work. Every time. Without exception. The officer puffed his chest up importantly and said, "Wait here," before turning and disappearing behind the door that led from the outer office to the warren of cubbies and corridors where the business of the police took place.

I turned and gazed out of the open door at the scene framed within it. The sky was a startling blue, unbroken by even a puff of clouds. The sun slanted against the limestone buildings and gave them a golden tinge. It was a day to put a smile on anyone's face. But I could not enjoy it. Standing there in the dingy office, waiting to give what information I could about a poor soul who had met a violent end only the night before, I couldn't help but feel that life was not always just. I knew nothing about the fellow, but I could still feel the imprint of his fingers on my arm and hear the rasping words he had spoken just before he died.

I was so lost in my own thoughts that at first I had the impression only that a cloud had obscured the brilliance of the day, until my musings were interrupted by a voice. "Mademoiselle Schurman?" said a gentleman—and I knew he was a gentleman because of his respectful tone and refined accent—and his use of the French *Mademoiselle* instead of the German *Fräulein*.

I didn't have to turn away from the direction I was looking in order to find the source of the voice, I had only to focus my eyes on what now occupied the doorway and blocked my view. A tall figure was silhouetted there, little more than a dark blob in front of me until he took a step into the office and I could see his green coat with its polished brass buttons, his black riding boots and white breeches. His sheathed sword hanging from his belt made one of the tails of his coat fling outward at a jaunty angle. He removed his tricorn hat and swept me as much of a bow as the space we occupied would permit.

When he rose, the greeting I had prepared caught in my throat and nearly made me choke. This fellow, whom I assumed because he knew my name must be Captain Bauer, was so perfectly handsome that my breath failed me. His eyes were either a deep blue or dark grey, I couldn't immediately tell which and later I kept changing my mind about them. Whatever they were, they were lined with thick lashes and accented by eyebrows that were neither too heavy nor too thin and that angled slightly upward from the inside corners, giving him a pleasantly quizzical look. He had a neatly trimmed, black mustache and full, rosy lips. His head, with its chiseled cheekbones and perfectly straight nose, sat atop a sturdy but not thick neck. He was as perfectly proportioned as a symphony.

"Yes," I said. "Yes, I mean, I am Mademoiselle Schurman."

"Allow me to introduce myself. I am Captain Adelbert Bauer of the emperor's Hussars. Would you kindly step outside with me? I have a few questions to ask you."

He could have said, *Will you kindly step outside with me? I'd like to cut you into tiny pieces and feed you to the rats* and I would have done it. It was a foolish way to respond to him. I had seen plenty of handsome young captains, even been courted by some of them under the watchful eye of Alida before her marriage. But mostly they were ignorant and silly, caring only about their guns and swords and how dashing they looked in their uniforms. None of them understood about music. Of course, I didn't know whether Captain Bauer cared for music either.

He took me over to a quiet alcove a short way down Augustinerstrasse, near the imperial stables. He stood so close to me that I was certain those who passed by thought we were having some kind of lover's tryst. If they could have heard our conversation, they would have been shocked.

"Tell me exactly what happened. Sergeant Hirsch told me some of it, but I wanted to hear it from you directly."

"Sergeant Hirsch?" I asked.

"He was the guard you reported the . . . incident to last night."

I explained everything—again omitting the part about Mozart. By now it was too late to correct my original statement without either sounding guilty or risking being dismissed outright as a liar.

"And you say it was under the stand of Linden trees? Just outside the Augarten?"

"Yes," I said, beginning to suspect that he wasn't telling me something. "Why? What did the police find?" I thought he might possibly tell me about the fellow, who he was and where he might have been going.

"That's just the thing. I'm afraid, Mademoiselle Schurman, they found nothing at all. There was no dead musician. And now, they are wondering what you might have been doing there yourself at such an hour, alone, without an escort."

"I–I . . ." What could I say? I didn't want to tell him that dressed as a young man, I was relatively safe. And where had the body gone? "Someone must have moved the man! The police did not get there quickly enough."

"What time did you witness this alleged murder? And from where?"

Now I was in a real mess. I could see no easy way to make this handsome Captain Bauer understand. "I cannot explain it unless I show you," I said. "I realize you all think that I fabricated this gruesome tale, but I assure you, I would do no such thing." I felt embarrassing tears rising into my eyes and struggled against them. Tears would only reinforce what I could now see was the general opinion of me, that I was a silly young woman with an overactive imagination who fancied she saw something.

"I know. I have some knowledge of who you are. I was one of the guards that escorted the Gypsy away from his execution nearly two years ago, when you were still a girl. A brave one, I realized then."

I had to turn away from his eyes, which in the shadows resembled smoldering charcoal. "How can I persuade you that I saw what I saw?"

"I would be willing to accompany you out to the spot itself, as you suggested. Perhaps you will recall some detail that will shed light on the matter."

He offered me his arm. I slipped my hand into the crook of his elbow, noticing that beneath his uniform his arm felt like steel. He handed me gently into a Fiaker, but I was always conscious of his hidden strength as we jostled out beyond the Bastei to the road that led to the Augarten.

The stand of Linden trees was just where it should have been, casting elongated shadows across the road, their leaves looking a little tired and dusty after a hot summer but clinging to their greenness nonetheless.

Of course, there was nothing beneath them besides brown grass and dirt. I didn't expect that suddenly the body I had left there and that no one else had apparently found would reappear in the daylight. I jumped down from the Fiaker as soon as it stopped moving and before Captain Bauer could help me.

"See! See here, how the grass is crushed, and there's a shape in the dirt that must have been made by his instrument case hitting the ground." I pointed. Although the evidence of last night's struggle was clear to me, my heart sank as I realized the defects and marks around the trees could just as easily have been made by horses or simply people walking past as I was.

I circled the trees to get to the limb I had climbed, and without thinking gathered my skirts into a knot and held them fast so that I could clamber up. I realized that my lady's attire would prevent me being able to scramble up to where I had watched from the night before, but as I considered what to do I hit upon an explanation for Captain Bauer, who had walked over to stare up at me with amused wonder.

"You see," I said, "The reason I did not report the murder immediately was because I did not think anyone would understand that in my fear, feeling that someone was following me and thinking they might set upon a young woman alone at twilight on the way home from the Augarten, I climbed this tree, trusting to the shadows to hide me. When I saw what was going on below, I came down so fast I tore my clothing, and did not want to go to the authorities in such a state, looking like a peasant." I surprised myself with how reasonable my explanation sounded. Of course, as a young woman I would be more concerned with my dress than anything else. Captain Bauer had little reason to think that I would be any different from other girls like me.

"It is a pity you showed such scruples, in this case. But I am sad to say that, without a body, there can be no investigation. Are you certain you did not hear anything that could reveal the identity of the victim, or his assailant? And you are sure that what you witnessed was a murder, not just a scuffle?"

"It was a murder. I knelt by the man and heard him breathe his last."

Captain Bauer paused and rubbed his chin. "And you say he said nothing to you?"

"Nothing." Nothing that I was willing to tell Captain Bauer, who, despite protests to the contrary, clearly thought just as everyone else had and was merely humoring me for some reason of his own.

"Perhaps we should return to town," he said, holding out his hand to help me down from the tree. "I think it would be wise for you to forget all about this occurrence, whether or not it actually happened as you say."

A smile tugged at the corners of his mouth. I began to think he wasn't quite so handsome as I'd originally thought and I really didn't want to accept his help. Yet I realized that whether I wished to or not I could not descend from the tree without his assistance without risk of exposing my legs to him in a very unladylike manner. I took his hand and started to jump, but he grasped me around the waist as I did so and set me lightly on the ground, with hardly any strain at all.

"Shall we?" he said, gesturing toward the waiting Fiaker.

I had spent enough time with this fellow, now thoroughly disabused of my initial infatuation, and hoped I would never see him again. "If you don't mind, I'd prefer to go on to the Augarten. I had intended to walk there today in any case."

Captain Bauer swept his sword to the side and bowed deeply to me. "Were I not obliged to report to my barracks for duty, nothing would give me greater pleasure than to accompany you. Please permit me to give you my card. If you discover anything at all, or need assistance in any way, I beg you to send someone to fetch me."

I took the thick pasteboard card he handed me. It was beautifully engraved with his full name.

Graf Adelbert von Bauer, Rittmeister des Hussars

He had already climbed into the Fiaker and was headed back toward Vienna by the time I recovered sufficiently from my astonishment upon reading the card to look up. This infuriating person was not only a handsome captain. He was a count!

I tucked the card away in my reticule. If nothing else, I would simply keep it as a souvenir. Clearly Captain—or rather, Count—von Bauer would likely be of little help.

Rather than continue on toward the Augarten, I immediately began to make a more thorough, minute search of the area around the trees. *There must be something,* I thought. At the very least, if I could discover an identity, or some detail that would suggest where to begin to look for an identity, I could start the process of tracing the poor fellow, perhaps see if he had been missed at his lodgings. As in that other time in the past, when I had persevered in the effort to discover what had happened to my father, this time clearly everything would also be up to me.

I circled the trees, looking, thinking, wondering. I'm not certain what it was, but something drew my eyes to the trunk of the one I had climbed. Down very low on it, almost covered by the grass, I spotted a scratch that looked quite recent. I crouched to look at it more closely.

I soon discovered that it was more than just a scratch. Someone had quite deliberately carved lines into the trunk down where they might never be noticed unless one expected them to be there. At first they seemed randomly arranged, but on close examination I discerned that within the shape of a triangle was a crude, staring eye, and next to it, four lines that were almost joined to form the letter "M". I peered at the scratchings for a long time, wishing I had a quill and paper so that I could copy them down exactly. Instead, I burned them into my memory, measuring the design with my fingers, tracing over it and thinking about it until I believed I would be able to reproduce it, and then set off home. Although it had been too dark to see anything on the tree trunks yesterday, I could tell by the color of the wood where it had been scratched away that these marks were new. If they had not been made within the last twenty-four hours, I would have been very surprised.

CHAPTER SIX

I arrived home to an astonishing sight that nearly drove all thoughts of the marks on the Linden tree out of my head. Three stout workmen were struggling up the three flights of stairs of our apartment building carrying a large, muffled-up object that I knew by its size and shape to be a pianoforte. To my knowledge, the only musicians who lived in our building were a poor trumpeter on the top floor who didn't play well enough to perform very often in any of the regular orchestras, and an Italian soprano who spoke no German whatsoever and lived on the first floor, just above the ground floor shops. The singer might have purchased a keyboard, but the men had already passed that level and continued up.

Imagine my confusion when I found that their destination was our apartment. While I waited for them to pass through the door with their burden I could hear my mother's voice instructing them.

"Just over there. I think it will fit," she said.

I followed the men into the room, which had certainly not grown larger in the past two years, and indeed often felt smaller with little Anna's toys spread about and the general chaos of a toddling child who is always getting caught between one's feet. She was an exuberant little girl, frequently laughing and keeping up constant, childish chatter. *So strange,* I often thought, *to have been born in the midst of such sorrow, mere months after the father she never knew had been murdered and not to be conscious of it.* Her undaunted good cheer, and the wide-eyed innocence with which she viewed the world, had acted as a tonic on all of us. I wondered if we'd have been able to overcome everything so quickly were it not for Anna.

"Ah, Theresa!" my mother said. "You are here just in time. See what a lovely gift we have been given."

A gift? Who would be so bizarrely generous with us? "From whom?"

Then the oddest thing happened. My mother blushed. "You know, Theresa, I told you about that kind Baron van Swieten, the one I mentioned to you before and who has been so helpful since . . ." As always, she couldn't bring herself to mention Papa.

I couldn't question Mama closely while the men were there, so I waited patiently while they affixed the legs to the case of the pianoforte and righted it upon them. A gift from Herr van Swieten. He was nearly fifty years old as far as I knew, and after a life of wandering around Europe as an ambassador and physician had returned to Vienna to be the imperial librarian. Or so my godfather Haydn had told me once when I mentioned him. My mother said that he had been at a card party she attended, but hadn't spoken about him much. I had never met the man, and what she had said made little impression on me. Now this.

Once my mother had given the sweating deliverymen a few coins and a smile and they had clattered back down the steps to the street, I said, "Greta, I think that Anna should go for her walk." I didn't want Greta listening in to the conversation I was about to have with Mama. Our cook and housekeeper had a habit of standing quite still when anything important was being discussed as if she hoped I would forget that she was there. She shot me a sour look. We had maintained our civil standoff since the days after my father died when she sold my viola on my mother's instructions without telling me. Somehow I couldn't forgive her for not realizing that my mother was in no fit state to make such decisions then. But I made up for it by being certain to practice the violin assiduously with the door to my room open so that Greta could not escape the sound of monotonous scales.

I heard little Anna giggle in the next room as Greta put on her harness. "That tickles!" she said. They passed through the parlor, Anna nestled in Greta's beefy arms. "I'm going to walk now," she said in her tiny, distinct voice, and then opened and closed her pudgy fist in a little wave as the door closed behind them.

My mother started talking before I had a chance to ask her a question. "Isn't it lovely? It's not new, of course, but it was made by Herr Walter, who Gottfried—Baron van Swieten—says is at least as good as Herr Stein."

"But Mama, you don't play the pianoforte!"

"I used to play the clavecin, and just because I disapprove of the violin doesn't mean that I think a lady should be unmusical. Besides, Anna will be of an age to start learning soon."

Only if she were an astounding prodigy, I thought. Music lessons for her were at least two years off by my reckoning. "But we don't need it! See how it takes up all the room."

"The baron has said he will bring friends and make music here, bring joy back to our home."

Her words were a slap across my face. Hadn't I been making music? Getting better and stronger at playing the violin every day? I was now good enough to pass for a young professional in many of the pickup orchestras around Vienna. And what about the music of Anna's laughter and my laughter as we played baby games together? Yet I knew that the sound of the fiddle depressed rather than cheered my mother. It was the sound she most associated with our Papa, whom she still grieved for, and she had never wanted me to play anyway.

My face must have expressed more than I wished. Mama came over to me and placed her hand on my cheek, her large, sad eyes peering into mine. "You know I don't mean to hurt you. But it is so very doleful to hear the violin all alone. It's like a baby crying, never to be comforted."

I could not remain angry. What right had I, after all? Didn't I do my utmost to stay away from my home as much as possible, for reasons not dissimilar to those that made my mother dislike the sound of the violin? I could not look at Mama without remembering the expression in her eyes as she gazed at Papa, and seeing how very different she had become. She was still pretty, but it was a studied prettiness. She set her smile, which rarely extended to her eyes, except when she gazed at Anna, and then they always seemed about to brim over. She wore rouge, too, giving her cheeks false roses in place of the ones that had always made her appear so young before.

"Of course, I'm not talented, like you, but it will comfort me to play some of the airs from the opera and the theater."

I kissed her and left her sitting at the pianoforte where she spread out some sheet music on the desk and hesitantly plunked out the notes of a dance tune. I could hear her tentative fumbling as I sat at the little table in my room, trimmed a quill, opened the ink pot and took a piece of paper from the quire.

I stared at the blank sheet before me, trying to recall the design I had seen scratched into the trunk. It was fairly simple, but when I drew it, something seemed missing from it, some connecting line or other that would hold the design together. I took the card Captain Bauer had given me out of my reticule and stared at it for a long time until the letters became gibberish. Should I bring the design to him? Would he think I was just being silly, attaching meaning to something for the sake of getting his attention? I shook my head, wrapped the paper with the design on it around the card, and put the little package back in my reticule.

I was grateful, in a way, that I would not have a lot of time to brood on what had happened in the last two days. I had some actual music copying to do that afternoon, for the elderly Ritter von Gluck, who had been kind enough to employ me while the Esterhazy court was in the country for the summer. All he asked me to do was to set down his alterations of a few notes here and there for the German versions of operas that had originally been written in French. He paid quite well for almost no work.

After spending an hour with Gluck that afternoon, I was to give a violin lesson, then go to play in the orchestra at a ball at the *Redoutensaal* in the Hofburg. Although I had not been much beyond that room since the old empress died a little over a year before, I had heard that the vast imperial palace was a much changed place. That businesslike attitude I had noticed when I went before the emperor with Alida, Danior, Haydn, Zoltán and the rest had extended to the entire establishment. Joseph II hardly maintained enough servants to keep the floors swept, it was rumored, with more luxury and care taken over the imperial stables. Gone were the parades of carriages for grand receptions. Instead, the emperor took his entertainment in the houses of the Viennese aristocracy, or spent his time traveling around the empire.

Thinking about that day when all had been revealed, when my father's involvement in bringing justice to the Hungarian serfs and my uncle's criminal activities had been exposed, invariably started me thinking about Zoltán. Aside from a few moments at Alida's wedding, I had not seen him since that time two years ago. I assumed he was simply busy putting his family's affairs in order and rehabilitating his estates far off in Hungary. And at the wedding he had appeared preoccupied, always looking as though he was needed elsewhere. He greeted me kindly, but spent most of the time discussing some business matter with an elderly noble. Since then I had had a few letters, mostly soon after he had seen my godfather Haydn at the prince's summer palace in Esterhaza. I had the uncomfortable feeling that unless something happened to remind him of my existence, he would forget me altogether.

I shook my head to clear it of the vision of Zoltán's kind, green-grey eyes and lanky frame. It was no use thinking about the way he had kissed me that once. And yet I did—time and again. I clung to the memory of that sensation, his lips on my cheek, but not like the perfunctory, affectionate kisses of a brother. There was something in the careful pressure that made me wish I could have dared turn my head and let his lips meet mine.

Yet he had, after all, only kissed my cheek, even if he had enfolded me in an embrace and let his fingers touch the back of my neck. That act—and I as well—probably meant nothing to him. Clearly he thought of me only as a child, a friend from his youth, the little girl who used to hide in the miles of corridors of the Esterhazy palace. I tormented myself by imagining that he was laughing at me. Or worse, that he had truly completely forgotten me.

And if I were honest with myself, that was the primary reason I hadn't been to see Alida since I had heard that she was expecting. I was afraid I would not be able to prevent myself asking about Zoltán. I didn't want to know if he had met some Hungarian countess and become betrothed to her. Best just to avoid her, so that my own fantasies would not be spoiled. I realized that even a handsome, mysterious captain could not supplant Zoltán for me, at least not without proving himself much more than handsome. As yet, Captain von Bauer hadn't even come close to measuring up.

And besides, for the moment at least I had more important things to think about. It occurred to me that the elderly Herr von Gluck might lend his still-acute mind to the task of helping me figure out the significance of the marks scratched on the trunk of the Linden tree.

I had been careful to keep my drawing in my purse, and to hide the purse away in my drawer when I untied it from around my waist so that Greta would not see it when she swept in my room.

I picked up my violin in its glaringly new case and put on my hat and cloak, taking care to sling the case over my shoulder so that it would be almost hidden from Mama as I left the apartment. I passed through the sitting room and bent down to kiss her on the cheek as she leaned forward to peer at the music in consternation. "It's a C-sharp," I said, plunking down the key with more force than I intended. Greta and Anna were just coming up the stairs as I left. "I won't be home for dinner or supper either," I said to Greta, knowing that, despite our disagreements, she would doubtless keep a plate of food warm for me to eat at the end of the evening.

Gluck was quite a wealthy man. His operas had always been popular and were still performed frequently. I entered his elegant apartment near Prince Kaunitz's palace and gave the serving girl my cloak. I brought the Amati with me into the music room, though; I never trusted servants with it, even if they didn't know how valuable it was—or perhaps for that very reason. I felt there was little chance the case would give me away to Herr von Gluck, as he did not frequent the sort of concerts and balls I performed at.

Unlike Haydn, the Ritter von Gluck treated me with great formality. Aside from the fact that he didn't know me very well, I don't think he was quite comfortable with a girl as his copyist. He had agreed to engage me out of respect for Haydn, I thought. I had a feeling there were many more tasks for which he could have used my services, but that he tried to get me out of his apartment as quickly as possible—while still justifying the three Florins he paid me to come to him each week.

"Grüss Gott," he said with a bow. He was still in his dressing gown and soft cap, but I could see by his smooth cheeks that his barber had been there before me. He sat at the fine pianoforte and gestured me to take my place at the desk, where sheets of paper that had already been lined with staves, three quills that had already been carefully trimmed, and a full bottle of black ink stood waiting. As was his custom, he played a few measures several times, telling me what he had changed, and I wrote the notes down in piano score. He had someone else do the orchestral arrangements. Gluck believed—like the vast majority of Viennese, perhaps even the vast majority of people—that while ladies could enjoy a knowledge of music and serve a certain function, the serious business of performing in an orchestra was best left to men. I tried not to judge him for it. He was old and set in his ways, no doubt not realizing that the world was changing rapidly.

He was old—yet also very intelligent and knowledgeable. That was why, when our hour of transcription had ended, I cleared my throat and dared to broach a different subject with Herr von Gluck. "If you will forgive me, I have come across a bit of a puzzle and wondered if perhaps you could help untangle it for me."

"Of course, Mademoiselle Schurman. Speak."

I reached into my pocket to get the paper where I had drawn what I saw on the tree trunk, forgetting that I had wrapped it around the captain's card, which fluttered to the floor just at Herr von Gluck's feet. He bent down to pick it up. I saw that he glanced at it as he returned it to me, and his face registered instant disapproval. Naturally he would assume I had a noble suitor—or rather, seducer, since I was not of a class to be a serious marriage prospect to a count. I don't know why he made me so nervous, but I began to babble like a child.

"It's not—he's not—it's a police matter—you see, I saw something—" I didn't know what to say, and so I stopped speaking and handed him the paper.

At first Herr von Gluck appeared puzzled as he turned the paper this way and that. Then his face went slightly pink, then a little paler than usual. By the time he looked up at me, I felt as if he had purposely locked down his eyes so that I would not be able to see inside them. "I'm afraid I cannot help you. These appear to be the meaningless scribblings of a child." He smiled his kind but patronizing smile and set the paper aside before ringing for the maid to bring my cloak.

He held my cloak for me and stood politely by while I tied my bonnet. I thought that at any minute he would fetch the paper I had given him and return it to me, but he showed no signs of doing so. "*Entschuldigen-Sie,* Herr von Gluck," I said, "*Das Papier, bitte?*"

The elderly composer struck his forehead lightly with the heel of his hand. "How foolish of me! But wouldn't you prefer that I simply dispose of it for you."

I smiled and lifted my violin case. "No, I think I'll puzzle over it a while longer." I took the paper from his hand.

"Are you taking lessons?" he asked, nodding toward the fiddle. "Most ladies don't attempt it, but I suppose with a father who used to be such a fine violinist . . ."

He did not finish his sentence because there was no need. The meaning was clear enough. "I take lessons when I can, when my godfather is in Vienna. I give lessons as well, to quite a number of young ladies who are very willing to attempt it, and I also play chamber music when I have the opportunity."

I enjoyed the look of surprise that crossed Herr von Gluck's features. I curtsied to him before I left.

CHAPTER SEVEN

I wasn't entirely certain why Gluck's response to my crude drawing made me think he was hiding something from me—or if not consciously hiding, withholding. But I couldn't dismiss that impression as I went on to my next appointment that day. It seemed very odd to continue about my business when I knew that somewhere, a man lay dead and no one knew about it or at least believed it—except obviously the murderer, and the man himself if the dead can be said to know anything.

I had a bit of a walk to my next appointment, which was to try to teach a girl by the name of Sophie von Eskeles how to play the violin. I will confess to the workings of both curiosity and ambition in taking on this unpromising pupil. She was distantly related to a family—the Arnsteins—that was very well known in Vienna for being among the wealthiest and most influential—as influential as any Jewish family could be. It had been less than a year since Jews were no longer required to pay the *Leibmaut,* the toll only they had to forfeit whenever they entered the city gates, and since Joseph II had abolished the *Toleranzgelder* payments Jews had been forced to pay for the privilege of living in Vienna. Likewise, I no longer saw the telltale *Judenfleck,* the yellow patches on their clothing that identified Jews to all. And although I had never seen him, it was rumored that young Nathan Adam Arnstein lived as free and easy a life as any wealthy noble in the city and was welcomed in all the most distinguished households as a guest. They could not afford to turn him away, I had heard through the vindictive whispers of gossip: over half the first families in Vienna practically owed their souls to the Arnsteins.

In any event, in taking on my pupil, I hoped that somehow I might be able to gain entrée to the very musical and artistically inclined circle inhabited by the Arnstein and von Eskeles clans. Since Sophie and her parents lived in a modest apartment on the fourth floor of a building in a not very fashionable part of town, I realized my chances of encountering their exalted distant relatives were very slim.

Still, I always enjoyed going there, despite Sophie's lack of industry. She made up for the assault on my ears each week by being unusually amusing and bright for her age, and I thought that hidden somewhere in her exuberant mistakes lay talent that might eventually burst forth. At eleven, she was a year older than Toby, and although he was away from home and slaving to learn a trade, she was also much more aware of the world than my awkward brother.

"We have been invited!" Sophie said before I had even removed my cloak. She hopped around their sitting room on one foot while her mother kept a watchful eye on the fragile porcelain bibelots that decorated every surface in the small space. Adding to the clutter was a fine pianoforte by Stein, which had already been opened for my use during Sophie's lesson.

"That's very exciting I'm sure," I said. "Invited to what?"

"To Aunt Fanny's to hear Mozart. Tomorrow night! Do you think he will listen to me play?"

First, a pang of envy shot through me. A moment later a wave of horror took its place, as I contemplated the possibility that Mozart himself might be subjected to Sophie's squeakings and scratchings. "Best to wait until you are more accomplished," I said. "One should only consent to perform when you are prepared to play without making a single mistake."

Her face fell, but only for a moment.

"Where is your violin?" I asked. She skipped off to the other room to fetch it, leaving me alone with her quiet mother for several moments. Frau von Eskeles looked up from her knitting to smile at me. She had beautiful, dark eyes ringed with thick lashes. Her face looked young, but her hair was streaked with grey. Not all through, just in three or four distinct hanks separated by perfectly black, glossy locks, as though they had been placed there artfully simply to complement each other. She wore her locks in a simple bun at the back. I must have been staring, because she shifted in her seat and cleared her throat.

"Do you play an instrument, Madame?" I asked her, aware that to remain together any longer without speaking while we waited for Sophie would soon become awkward, if not rude.

"I?" she said. "I was taught the clavier as a girl, but I no longer have the time to play."

"It's a pity. You have a lovely pianoforte."

I wanted to ask her about her husband, whom I had only seen in passing once. He had bowed to me, but did not meet my eyes. When I asked my mother about his apparent reticence, she had said, "Oh, it's their Jewish way. I expect looking at women's a sin to them, unless they're married."

I had no clear idea about what "Jewish ways" might be. There was no temple in Vienna, and the Jews—with the exception of the Arnsteins—kept largely to themselves and their businesses. This arrangement to give Sophie her lessons had come not through Haydn, but through Danior, who knew Herr von Eskeles through some connection he did not explain. I had the impression, in fact, that my kindly godfather was not entirely comfortable around Jews.

Sophie returned, eager as ever to get through as much of Leopold Mozart's violin method as she could, and lacking the patience for the necessary repetition to master the lessons one at a time. I always felt enervated at the end of the lessons with Sophie, and quite relieved when it came time to show her once again how to put her violin away so that it would not be damaged.

The Eskeles's paid me handsomely for the lessons, the money always discreetly placed on the table by the door so that it did not pass from their hands into mine directly. I was tying the bow on my cloak and preparing otherwise to leave when I heard whispering behind me. I turned and saw Sophie speaking into her mother's ear. Before she noticed me looking, Frau von Eskeles mouthed the words, "Ask your Papa," to Sophie, who skittered away. "If you would wait just a moment before leaving, Mademoiselle Schurman, my daughter has something for you."

I could hear Sophie running through the apartment. That girl did nothing slowly and quietly. From a few rooms away came the sound of her excited voice chattering and being answered by the deep bass of her father's. Soon not just Sophie's footsteps, but the slower, heavier footsteps of a man approached. To my surprise, Sophie entered the room again dragging her father by the hand. I felt awkward, dressed to depart and unable to greet him with adequate respect. Herr von Eskeles had his spectacles in his other hand and had clearly been interrupted at some business. I curtsied.

"My daughter wishes me to extend an invitation to you, Mademoiselle Schurman, to attend a gathering at my kinswoman Madame Arnstein's apartment tomorrow evening, where we shall have the inestimable pleasure of hearing Mozart perform. I warned my daughter that your wish to enjoy an intimate concert with one of the greatest geniuses of our age might not be strong enough to overcome your aversion to sitting in a room full of Jewish people, with a few brave souls of other persuasions."

He smiled when he said it, but I could see the challenge in his eyes. My own went involuntarily to the pattern on his waistcoat, which was very unusual, not unlike some of the designs on the rugs I had seen in the Roma camp. "I can think of no greater pleasure than a quiet concert among intelligent connoisseurs," I said. "I have no other engagements, and would be delighted to accept."

Sophie's leap for joy only echoed what I felt, and was exactly how I would have responded at her age. We settled that I would find my own way to the Arnstein apartment—since the von Eskeles, being Jews, were not allowed to keep a carriage—but that whichever of us arrived first we would wait to enter all together.

My delight over the prospect for the next evening nearly drove away all thoughts of the poor fellow whose body had mysteriously disappeared from where I had seen it. Perhaps I ought to forget about it, I thought. What responsibility was it of mine to discover what had happened? It was not like that other time, when my own father was killed. Then I could not rest until I had unraveled the complicated threads that led to such a tragic event. This musician, whoever he was, had nothing to do with me.

And yet, perhaps he was someone else's father. Perhaps he had a wife and children somewhere nearby who were waiting for him to return, desperate to know why he failed to come at the usual time. I could not help feeling what they must be feeling. I had at least been able to bury my father.

My joy over the unexpected invitation that would let me at last be presented to Mozart instead of simply seeing him from a distance was completely dampened by the time I arrived at the deserted Palais Esterhazy. I had decided to take advantage of the a little free time I had to practice a string quartet between the end of Sophie's lesson and the beginning of my next engagement. Only a porter, a few maids and an under cook were in residence during the times when the prince's court was still miles away in Hungary at Esterhaza. The porter knew me well, though, and let me into the cabinet room at the back of the ground floor behind the stables where I kept my performance clothes, and where I knew I could practice uninterrupted for as many hours as I wished—provided I returned home before curfew.

To my surprise, a note had been tacked to the door. The note was addressed to Thomas Weissbrot. Work, I thought, grateful that the jobs kept coming and that I was able to supplement our household income in a way that gave me such pleasure. I opened it as I passed into the dark space, fumbling for the match-bottle and a candle.

Monsieur,

Your services are needed in the second desk of a small orchestra to perform tomorrow evening at Adam Arnstein's apartment. There will be a short rehearsal at four, and the performance will take place at seven of the clock. Double wages, as this is the residence of a Jew. You will be expected unless you send word to this address saying that you decline.

At first, I felt like leaping around for joy. But soon, that impulse recalled to me my student Sophie's actions only a short while before, and I felt as if someone had burst a bubble in my head when I realized I had a terrible choice to make. I had already accepted the von Eskeles's invitation to that very same party. I would attend as a listener, a connoisseur, dressed in my finest attire. I would be presented to Mozart, who would no doubt bow to me and kiss my hand. He was not a typically handsome man, but there was something intriguing about him, perhaps his prodigious talent. That something made me wish to be introduced to him as a young lady.

And yet, would it not be preferable to meet him on his own ground? To help him recreate his superb music, be a part of the ensemble that sent the beautiful sounds out into the room to embrace everyone and everything in it? And once I had played in an orchestra for him, would he not suggest that I do so again? I heard he was working on an opera. I would give almost anything to be a member of the orchestra in the Burgtheater for that premier—although I knew that performing in the Burgtheater was no more than a fantasy.

Yet how could I tell the von Eskeles's that I could no longer accompany them to this party? They would surely think only one thing: that I had reconsidered the invitation because I did not want to be seen to associate with Jews, even ones of such wealth and distinction as they and their kin.

My head hurt from thinking. I had some time before I would have to dress in performance clothes for the ball at the Redoutensaal. I decided I could postpone my decision while I practiced for a while. There was nothing like practicing in solitude to help me arrange my thoughts, to remind myself of what was truly important. Nothing made it possible for me come to terms more with my strange life and its conflicting demands than nestling the beautiful violin between my ear and my shoulder, the Amati that had been my father's legacy to me—along with the talent to play it.

I stood in the center of the dimly lit space, drawing my bow across the strings one at a time in slow scales, concentrating on the quality of the sound and the exact pitch. It pleased me to work my way up from the lowest notes to the highest, step-by-step, then in broad arpeggios. I still possessed the dog-eared copy of Leopold Mozart's Violinschule my Papa had used in teaching me, and referred to it now and again to remind myself of the basics. Even if Amadé Mozart had not been a genius in his own right, I would have wanted to meet him for the sake of his father's work. I had hated it and loved it by turns when I was a child, and now that I had my own students, I realized that nothing could equal it.

I turned from exercises to practicing a particularly difficult passage in a string quartet by Hofmeister. I hoped to be able to play it with Danior and his friends sometime. He had sent me the music, and promised that would be the outcome if I could learn the second violin part. It was kind of Danior, but I couldn't help feeling disappointed at my core. My disguise was adequate when I sat in a large group of musicians. I dare say some of them realized what was going on, but no one much cared to make a fuss over it. There was—and still is—plenty of that sort of work in Vienna to go around.

Yet when it comes to the more lucrative performance opportunities, the chamber music among true connoisseurs in the grandest princely palaces, or the opera houses and theaters where tickets are sold at an exorbitant price, it is an entirely different matter. My identity and qualifications would be closely scrutinized, and without the cooperation of someone in a very high place, I would never have a chance to participate, no matter how skillful I was.

It struck me as odd, though, that ladies could appear as soloists, alone in front of the orchestra for everyone to stare at, and be celebrated for it. I could understand the singers, whose high voices could not be duplicated—except for those strange creatures known as castrati, of which only one remains according to whispers among the musicians. But even instrumentalists, mostly those who played the pianoforte, were acceptable in such a role. I had heard of an Italian lady, a Signorina Abruzzi, who traveled all over Europe performing dazzling violin concertos with orchestras in front of royalty and in public. In my heart I knew I was no virtuoso, but I felt the music so deeply! And I thought perhaps those great soloists needed some man to take their part, to put them forward and act as protectors. On my own I would never be able to do it, even if I had such astounding abilities. If my father had not died, perhaps he would have been that protector.

As it was, the work that came my way was all through either Haydn or Danior—who had taken the Varga surname, lacking one of his own.

I gave up practicing after a short while. I was too distracted to concentrate, and realized I had played so by habit that I didn't even recall what I had done. That kind of practice was no good.

I changed into my man's clothing, brushing my hair smooth and tying it back before tucking it into the bag wig. I also transferred the drawing and the cavalry captain's card into my breeches pocket, for no clear reason, just as a precaution against its being lost, I supposed.

I made my way through the bustling, evening streets during the hour when office workers returned home to their dinners, and when those who lived lives of leisure ordered their carriages to take them to whatever evening entertainment lay in front of them. I always felt so much freer dressed as a man. I did not draw stares the way I did when my hair was done up and my figure exposed in a dress. I tried to match my stride to my disguise, taking longer steps and letting my arms swing a little. Sometimes I pitied girls who could not do as I did, but were always imprisoned in flounces and hobbled by dainty shoes. I pitied them on a fine day like that one, when I could mingle unobserved with all conditions of people and yet feel myself apart from them, carrying the secret of my real identity safely within the external trappings that no one ever looked beyond.

The Redoutensaal was in the Hofburg, not far from the entrance to police headquarters where I had met Rittmeister von Bauer. Dressed as I was, it would have been foolhardy to stop in and make any inquiries because it would necessitate having to explain how I knew about the incident. But I could not resist straying as close as possible, just to see if the handsome count was anywhere nearby. I had toyed with the idea of showing him what I had found scratched into the base of the linden tree, but feared that, without any other information, he would dismiss it out of hand as yet more of my fanciful imaginings.

As I passed the open door of the office I heard something that nearly caused me to stumble, I stopped so suddenly. I had to forcibly restrain myself from leaping in to listen more closely to the conversation within.

"I tell you, it is not like my Abraham not to come home. He is no man to go out drinking with his friends. He is only a humble musician, and we make barely enough money to pay our rent and our taxes."

I tried to make it look as though I were examining a speck of something on my breeches as I listened closely to what the lady was saying. That she inquired about her husband or some other family member who had not come home—and who was a musician—was clear. Her voice quivered with emotion. Apparently her plea with the officer was meeting skepticism at best. I could not hear all of the officer's reply, only a few words: come home . . . give it time . . . reasonable explanation.

I barely had time to step out of the way before the petite figure of a woman in a simple dress and a black shawl, a plain cap covering her dark hair, bustled out of the office in a fury.

I was early—I generally tried to arrive at my playing engagements before the appointed time so that I could wait and enter at the moment when people would pay least attention to me, so I often gave myself extra time to stand around nearby. But that day, I did not hesitate before rushing after the woman, who moved so quickly I had to run a little to catch up with her.

I was out of breath by the time I reached her. She had paused to wait for a carriage to clatter by. "Entschuldigen-Sie, Madame," I said, reaching out to tap her on the shoulder.

She whirled around, her eyes wide and frightened. I grabbed hold of her arm as she tried to hurry away from me.

"Please!" I said, "I heard you in the police station, and I know something that might help you."

She yanked her arm free from my hand, but did not run. Her skin was smooth and her eyes clear. She had a serene face that was beautiful in an unusual way. But up close I could see that her cheeks were sunken like those of someone unaccustomed to adequate nourishment, or for whom worrying was a daily—if not hourly—occurrence. "What do you know?" she challenged.

I glanced around at the crowds. One or two people had stopped to stare at us, thinking we were quarreling, perhaps. "This is not the place." I spotted a coffee house nearby. "Allow me to buy you a cup of chocolate and we will see if what I know has anything to do with your difficulty."

I saw the hesitation in her eyes and expected her to refuse, but she nodded once and preceded me to the door of the café, where she stopped. For a moment I had forgotten that, since I was dressed as a young man, she would expect me to open the door for her, but I recollected quickly and we passed through.

We took a table in a quiet corner. "I prefer coffee," she said. I ordered her a coffee and myself a drink of chocolate. "What do you think you know? What interest can you take in my affairs? You don't even know who I am."

She was right, of course, and it was possible there was no connection at all between her missing person and my unfortunate musician. "Forgive me," I began, "but a deeply disturbing event occurred the other evening when I was on my way back from performing at a concert in the Augarten."

The look in her eyes intensified with interest. "Go on," she said.

"First, perhaps we should introduce ourselves. I am—" I almost called myself Theresa Schurman, forgetting for the moment that I was on my way to work. "I am Thomas Weissbrot, violinist." I bowed my head to her.

"And I am Dorotea Bachmann. My husband is also a musician. He plays the flute."

I searched my memory for a flute player named Bachmann and could come up with no one.

"I see you are puzzled. My Abraham does not perform in the fashionable orchestras. He scrapes together a living on the street, although he is a very talented man, and plays when the occasion arises at the Arnstein's home."

Now I understood. This Abraham Bachmann was a Jew. He would be unable to perform in the theaters or the Redoutensaal, and therefore unlikely to be invited to perform in most of the orchestras attached to the princely households during the season. And this mention of the Arnsteins for the third time that day, so closely touching my own concerns, seemed prophetic. "Madame Bachmann, would your husband have been walking home from the Augarten last night, at twilight, after the concert?"

Our hot drinks arrived. Once the waiter had gone, Madame Bachmann stared into the steaming black liquid before her. I thought perhaps she hadn't heard me and was about to repeat my question when she began to speak. "Perhaps you are unfamiliar with the difficulties of living in Vienna without converting to Catholicism? You must know that until a year ago we had to wear yellow patches on our clothing so that good Christians could avoid us at all costs. Such yellow patches were not part of court uniforms in orchestras, and no matter how talented, how brilliant, a musician could not get work. We thought the persecution had come to an end when the wearing of patches was abolished by the emperor after the old empress's death. But still there are many restrictions, and Abraham is no longer young. He could not get work, except of the meanest kind. We live on the top floor of a house in the poorest quarter, just inside the Bastei."

Her voice had become increasingly bitter and raised to the point that several people turned in their seats and looked at us. "But Madame," I whispered, "was he in the Augarten last night?"

She looked up at me. There were tears in her eyes. "He might have been. Sometimes he would walk. Sometimes he went places I did not know where. He was contemplating conversion, for the sake of our children, if we ever have any, so that they might have a future. And yet, he is a devout man. We keep the holidays as best we can."

I had no idea what holidays the Jews kept, but if my murdered musician was this poor woman's husband, I would be very distressed. I did not know how to tell her what I suspected had been his fate and so remained silent a moment.

"Do you think you saw my Abraham?"

The pleading look in her eyes as she said those words, barely loudly enough for me to hear, was almost unbearable. I recognized the yearning—the knowing the worst yet hoping for the best—that shone from them. "I don't know. But I saw someone, a musician."

All the while I told her about what had passed that night, she kept her eyes down toward the coffee in her glass. I saw several teardrops land in the black liquid. Her shoulders shook. She was sobbing silently. I reached out and touched her arm. "It might not have been Herr Bachmann."

"You say you reported this . . . event," she said, with difficulty regaining control of her voice. "Is there an inquiry under way? I wonder that the officer did not mention this to me."

"There was a difficulty," I said, not knowing how to tell her that after all that, there was no body. "I went back this morning, with a Rittmeister von Bauer of the Emperor's Hussars. He wanted me to show him where the act I witnessed had occurred. You see, they had not found a body there."

She looked up again, her eyes now glittering and hard. "Rittmeister—" She stopped herself for a moment, then continued. "Then the person you saw might not have been killed! He may yet be alive, and hiding. Take me to this place," she said.

"I cannot, not this evening. I am expected to work at the Redoutensaal. But tomorrow? How will I find you?"

"Best that you let me find you. Can we meet somewhere?"

I suggested meeting at the city gate that led to the Augarten road, at nine of the clock, when the streets would be busy enough so that we would not be noticed.

"Until tomorrow then, Fräulein Weissbrot," she said.

Before I could recover from the shock that she had guessed my secret, she rushed away. I paid for our drinks, uncomfortably aware that if she had seen through my disguise, so might others. But there was no time to worry about that. I would be late for my engagement if I did not hurry.

CHAPTER EIGHT

I was one of the last musicians to take my place in the orchestra at the front of the large, ornate hall, and had to sit on the end of the third row of second violins. I much preferred to be near the middle, where I could more easily hide myself from scrutiny in the event of seeing someone I knew—a rare but worrying occurrence.

Guests already promenaded in the galleries and hopeful young officers and dandies clustered in corners, waiting for the ladies to arrive so they could claim their dances. There was a side of me that would have preferred to be out there too, tripping through the steps of a lively Mazurka with a handsome partner. For a moment I allowed myself to imagine Zoltán as that partner. But soon it was time to get to work.

The old man who led the orchestra was nearly blind—with the result that his wig never sat straight on his head and his uniform was frequently buttoned incorrectly. In any case, he simply kept time, leaving the players he could only vaguely see to come in at the appropriate moments, frowning if he heard any glaring mistakes. The music was not difficult: German dances, polonaises, and contredanses mostly, with an occasional march thrown in for good measure. Now that the empress was no longer around to hold court, a wide mix of society patronized these public balls, from wealthy burghers to the most exalted nobility. The Redoutensaal was the last remaining place in Vienna where one could meet people outside of one's close circle of friends.

Of course, I realized as we struck up the first dance that no matter how free and easy the mixture of social classes, Jews would not be allowed here unless they had converted to Catholicism. That one act freed them from all the restrictions upon them, but they had to renounce their beliefs and attend church regularly. Whispers abounded that ambitious converted Jews were among the most faithful, going to noon service every day at the Michaelerkirche and confessing every week. I attended church as necessary with my mother on Sunday, and with pleasure on those occasions where a new mass by a good composer was to be performed. The prayers and incantations were as familiar to me as nursery rhymes. I believed it all—how could I not? I wondered, briefly, how it would feel not to believe. It was beyond my power to imagine it.

We began a quiet serenade, and as the room filled, I started to recognize faces. I knew many of the eager dancers by sight, and some were acquaintances. Danior and Alida would not be here, I knew, because of Alida's condition, so I would not have the benefit of Danior's ability to deflect notice from me if it ever became necessary. Yet most other people I might recognize would know my face purely from having seen me in my guise as Thomas Weissbrot, so I was fairly certain that I was not in danger of being found out.

While I was watching the couples whirl around in a waltz, I noticed a highly comical sight, of a heavy, older man with little grace partnering a pretty young girl with golden ringlets. When their path took them quite close to the orchestra, I looked forward to seeing the disgusted expression on the girl's face at being made to stand up with someone who might have been her uncle—or even her grandfather. But I was quite surprised to see her flirting and fluttering at him as if he were a handsome young blade.

"Who is that oaf?" I asked my desk mate when we shuffled through to find the music for the next dance.

"Where?" he asked.

"There." I quickly pointed my bow in the direction of the fat man, who was busy mopping his brow after the dance.

"That 'oaf,' as you call him is Thorwart."

"Thorwart?" The name was familiar, but I couldn't remember where I'd heard it.

"Only one of the most powerful men in the musical world of Vienna. They say no one can perform, or have a work performed at the Burgtheater unless he approves. He holds the purse strings."

So that was it! The girl must be a singer, trying to get on Thorwart's good side. I chuckled to myself throughout the next dance.

I had quite settled into my counterfeit identity and lost myself in the music by the time our first respite came, when the revelers went in to the banquet room for refreshments. The musicians stood and wandered away, instruments tucked under their arms or leaned against their chairs. One or two of them nodded to me, although I cultivated a shy aloofness that I hoped they would attribute simply to youth and never engaged in conversation with them. I stood too, unfortunately feeling the need to relieve myself, and headed toward the back passage that led to the latrines. I laid my violin carefully in the case by my chair. There was an unspoken honor among the musicians that one's livelihood would never be compromised by theft of a musical instrument. Although leaving the Amati out like that made me nervous, I had little choice. I could not take it where I was going.

It was always particularly difficult to carry off my subterfuge at times like those. The rough camaraderie of men exposing themselves as they pissed against the wall was something to which I could not accustom myself. Yet to show squeamishness would open me to teasing, and from there it might be a short distance to being too obviously exposed for a fraud.

I had no doubt that some of the men knew I was a girl and turned a blind eye. As long as I did not rise too far or the work become too scarce, I supposed they would continue to do so. But I hurried past the row of musicians and guests facing the wall and holding their members and went into the water closet, reserved for other needs. I always made certain to stay long enough so my real purpose would not be guessed, and by the time I emerged, the pause was almost at an end and an entirely new selection of men had taken the places of those that had been there when I entered.

That moment, that instant of recognition, is one of the moments that will forever inspire a feeling of the deepest shame and embarrassment in me. For who stood at the farthest end of the wall, nearest the door that led back into the Redoutensaal, but Rittmeister von Bauer, even more impressively handsome in his dress uniform than he was when I had met him that morning.

I might have gotten past him without incident, but in my haste, I did not see an uneven stone in the floor. I tripped. On my way down I reached for the nearest support I could, not wanting to damage my hands against the rough stones, and found myself being steadied by Captain von Bauer himself. I did not look, but I prayed he had completed his business before being called upon to come to my assistance.

"Steady on young fellow!" he said.

I let my voice fall to its deepest register and spoke as I bowed, hoping he would not recognize me. "Thank you, sir."

But as I was heading for the door that would take me back into the crowd and thence to safety, I felt a strong hand grip my wrist.

By this time, the men had generally left the latrines and returned to the ballroom, either to play or to dance. Captain von Bauer and I were alone. "I beg your pardon, Monsieur, but are we not acquainted?" he said, words I lived in fear of hearing when I was in my musician's garb.

"No, Rittmeister, Entschuldigen-Sie." I pulled away as insistently as I could, but he held my wrist tight.

"Stay a moment. I am certain I know you." He raised his other hand to my chin and turned my face toward him.

I tried to avoid looking into his eyes, but I could not. I recognized their lively expression and felt myself blush. When, when! I asked myself, would I master that embarrassing tendency? I could do nothing but remain silent.

"Yes. I do know you. But you were dressed a little differently this morning." I did not like the way he looked me up and down as he said this. He was taller than I was by at least a head, and could easily have overpowered me if he chose to. Now I wished we were surrounded by other men taking their time over their bodily functions.

To my immense relief the door opened to admit an old gentleman clearly intent on relief and Captain Bauer had to let me go. I slipped through the door and ran to take my place moments before old Stahlmeister returned to the clavier and we struck up the next dance tune.

I glued my eyes to the music on the stand, only pulling them away when it was absolutely necessary. At one point, I allowed myself to steal a sidelong look at the dancers, and noticed that the handsome captain-count had maneuvered his bejeweled partner up to the front of the room. Why couldn't he go and rest up in the galleries that ringed the grand room, and give me at least a little hope of escaping that night without having to confront him again? I should be thinking of what to say to him, I thought, but too many other things claimed my attention. I would have to explain everything to him eventually, but I really would have preferred it to be not there, not then.

The moment came when the ball ended and guests began to move toward the doors at the opposite end of the hall, as if it were a funnel that had been gradually, imperceptibly tipped on its side to empty every-one out. The orchestra members dribbled spit out of their flutes, clar-inets and horns and loosened the hairs on their bows before nesting their precious instruments in their wooden cases. At the same time the purser passed among us and gave us our wages for the evening.

It was while I was tucking the two Gulden into my pocket that I felt the dreaded tap on my shoulder. There was no getting away now.

"I wonder if you would permit me to accompany you for a short distance, as I believe our paths continue along the same route for a while?"

I drew myself up as tall as I could, having decided that trying to shrink away would only make me appear more guilty, and nodded my assent.

I don't know what people must have thought to see the dashing captain escort me from the Redoutensaal, unable to resist a touch on my elbow every now and again as if I were a lady and not a young man. I suspected I would be a lively topic of conversation and conjecture for a while, until the captain told his own story to amuse his cronies and the entire fabric of my life was torn to shreds. What would I do? I desperately needed the extra money I earned from these regular en-gagements.

He nodded and tipped his hat to numerous acquaintances as we passed. I wanted so to run, to dive down the nearest alley, but I knew he would find me easily and put his questions to me anyway. I might as well face them that evening. Thankfully, he waited until we were beyond the sight and hearing of the ball goers.

"So, Mademoiselle Schurman, perhaps you would care to explain yourself to me. I ask only so that I may determine the motives for your fruitless report yesterday. You must realize that if all you said is a fabrication—which is what this peculiar circumstance leads me to believe—then I could have you fined or imprisoned for your wanton lack of regard for the time and resources of the Viennese police."

He said all this without altering the pleasant expression on his face.

I was tempted to lash out with some biting response, but I held my breath for a moment. It would not do to make an enemy of someone who yet may be able to help me, but only if he were so inclined. "The story is a long one, but I assure you, it does not reflect poorly on my character. Suffice it to say that finding a way to earn a living was a necessity for me after the death of my father. My ability to play the violin and my skill with music opened a few doors. I teach some female pupils and copy music for Herr von Gluck. But my friends realized that I could earn more money and gain more satisfaction from performing in the orchestras, and as a girl, I would not be permitted to do so."

"Don't you see, Mademoiselle, that such a deception against the entire machinery of society leaves you suspect now?"

I knew what he said was true, but I would not back down. "Whether you believe me or not, I saw what I saw the other day. I am convinced that a man lies dead somewhere, that he was murdered. I have even come upon more things that might lead to the discovery at least of who he is, if not who killed him. I cannot force anyone to do anything about it, to investigate when they cannot even find a body. But that does not change the truth." We had arrived at the place where I would have to turn down an alley to get to the back of the Palais Esterhazy. "I have done nothing wrong, only wished to protect my ability to put food on my family's table by not advertising this dual existence of mine, even to the police."

I gave him my most courtly bow and turned away from him. I actually felt a sense of relief that he knew the truth, whatever use he would make of it.

"Mademoiselle Schurman, wait!" he called after me.

I didn't much care to wait. The night felt heavy on my shoulders, and all I wanted to do was to change into my dress, transfer my violin to its old case, and go home to my bed. But my determination to bring this murder I had witnessed to some resolution was not so easily set aside. I stopped and turned. The captain advanced toward me.

"You said you had discovered something today. What was it?"

"Are you asking me because you believe about the murder, or so that you can see if what I say will compound my lies?" I had passed the point of feeling I must be polite to the captain-count. "And I'm not altogether certain what you think I would gain by calling attention to myself through reporting a murder I witnessed. It should be apparent to you now that I wish nothing less than to be noticed."

"I simply would like to know. It is my duty to investigate until I am completely satisfied with the result."

"After you left me this morning, I did not continue to the Augarten. I stayed a while and looked closely at the area around the trees and the trees themselves to see if I could find anything—a uniform button, a scrap of paper—anything that might give some hint as to the fellow's identity.

"I'm not certain why exactly, but I examined the trunks of the trees and discovered, quite close to the ground, a design scratched into one of them." I reached into my pocket and removed the now creased scrap of paper, still folded around the captain's card. I showed the card to him and held out the paper. "As you see, I had intended to seek you out tomorrow to ask if you understood the symbols."

He took the paper from me and walked a short distance to stand beneath a street lamp. At first he frowned. Then his expression changed in an odd way. It was not unlike that of Herr von Gluck when I had shown him my crude drawing earlier in the day. And like the elderly Gluck, by the time the captain turned toward me he had bolted a neutral expression on his features and said, "I am afraid I have no idea of the significance of these symbols, but I doubt they would have anything at all to do with a murder." And, again like Herr von Gluck, he absently folded the paper and instead of giving it back to me started to tuck it in his own pocket.

"Please, might I have my drawing back—if it is indeed of no signif- icance?" I held out my hand. He could hardly keep the drawing and maintain his assertion that it did not intrigue him. "I would be glad to show you tomorrow where I found the marks."

He returned my paper to me, I thought reluctantly. "You said you had discovered several things that were giving you some ideas. What else was there?"

His response to the symbols on the paper made me wary. I decid- ed I did not want to tell him about Frau Bachmann, not yet. "I only meant . . . the symbols. There are more than one, as you have seen." I thought I sounded evasive and he would see through me instantly, but perhaps that was only because I knew I was hiding something.

"Very well, I shall meet you to return to the Linden trees at nine- of-the-clock. By the Kärntertor gate, tomorrow." Captain Bauer clicked his heels smartly together and gave me a sharp bow before whirling away into the night.

Nine tomorrow. Nine tomorrow! I could not do it. Not if I wished to keep Frau Bachmann a secret from the captain. Now what? It was too late to call Captain Bauer back and change the hour.

I hurried to my cabinet room in the palace. The back door had been left unlocked for me. As I went through the ritual of transform- ing myself back into a lady and replacing my violin in my father's old, battered case, all that had occurred that day began to haunt me. The symbols. Frau Bachmann. And that decision I had not made, about the Arnstein's party. I had much to think about, much to decide ere I slept that night—if indeed I managed to close my eyes.

CHAPTER NINE

By the time I reached our house and crept up the stairs to the apartment, curfew was about to ring.

"Just in time, Mademoiselle Schurman," said the porter, old Joseph, who often let me in without demanding his usual *Groschen* tip when I returned home a little late. I smiled at him but hurried on, not wanting to delay acting on my resolve, which I had formed on the short walk back from the Palais Esterhazy.

My reasoning went like this: First, I would have other opportunities to meet Mozart in my identity as Theresa Schurman. If Danior and Alida had already become friendly with him, they would see to it, I was certain. Yet there was no guarantee that I would have another opportunity to perform his music under his direction. The same combination of circumstances would likely never arise.

Second, the official channels I needed to navigate in order to see that justice was done would not remain patient for long. If I did not offer some tangible proof, or at least convince Captain Bauer that I was in earnest about what I had seen the previous night, those channels could well be closed to me for good. It all sounded so utterly logical. I couldn't figure out why my decision left me with a sour feeling in the depths of my stomach.

Greta—bless her—had left me a bowl of soup and some bread with a hunk of cheese. We might clash about nearly everything, but Greta took it as her personal responsibility to ensure that we were all fed.

I had not realized how hungry I was until I removed the lid from the bowl and smelled the rich broth. I took the tray into my room and set it on the table. Soon I had gobbled down what was there and could no longer delay confronting the sheet of paper before me. I struggled to find the right words to send to Sophie. I would have to lie to her, and it pained me. I also knew that, had they not been a Jewish family, I would never get away with breaking my engagement with them without severe censure. I invented an ailment for my mother, knowing full well they would not believe me. The letter was brief. I signed, folded and sealed it, and laid it in the center of the table to send in the morning.

Figuring out what to do about Frau Bachmann was harder. She had given me no way to contact her. She would be there tomorrow by the gate, and I would have to snub her. My only hope would be to arrive early and intercept her before the captain appeared. I thought she would understand, and I hoped, in so doing, not blame me.

The letter I had written to Frau von Eskeles and her daughter kept drawing my eye as it lay accusingly on my desk. Even after I had extinguished my bedside candle its whiteness somehow glowed and expanded despite the dark in my room. At that time of year, the moon reached a position in the sky where it was visible through my window if I looked straight up, between our house and the next. That night it was full, and I put it down to its fullness that my room appeared to grow brighter as I lay there. I was exhausted from my strange day, but my eyes would not close. I kept thinking about the letter, imagining how Sophie would react, having been so excited earlier that we would all go together to hear Mozart. Worse was the way I imagined Herr von Eskeles would greet the news that I had broken my engagement with them. The lie in my letter, concerning my mother's health, was surely believable. She had not been entirely strong ever since Anna was born. The trouble was that I was not in the habit of changing my plans around the ups and downs of her health, and would never do so unless I believed she were on the brink of death.

I felt my stomach clench as I thought about my mother. We had shared such a deep sorrow, and she had been in a very weak state when it all happened. I could not imagine being in her situation, heavily pregnant and waiting for her husband to come home, only to be presented with the sight of his murdered body. She collapsed. Who would not? And yet I don't think I will ever be able to forgive her completely for that, even though I knew in my heart it was natural and excusable. Little Anna had been born ten days later. Mama regained most of her strength afterwards, but we had to get a wet nurse, and she still tended to retire to her room with the curtains drawn complaining of headaches. Greta and I took care of Anna between us—mostly Greta, because I had been left to support the family.

I suppose that was the thing I could not forgive her. I was not angry that I had to work—I loved music, I loved to teach violin and perform when I could—but I was deeply hurt that she never mentioned it, as if my laboring to provide for us was a shameful secret. I once overheard her saying to a neighbor who asked where I was one evening that I had been invited to a party in a prince's palace, that our connections with her brother had at last been recognized and that I was going into society and would no doubt soon make an honorable match. I wondered that none of her friends chose to set her straight about Uncle Theobald, whose conspiring to send forced child labor to the Hungarian nobles had been punished with banishment. I never told her at the time. If I told her now, she would not believe me.

And now, here was this pianoforte, which I had bruised myself on when I entered in the dark that evening, and which I knew meant more than it seemed. Mama was up to something.

She lay asleep in the other room. What did she dream of? Did she still imagine my Papa's arms around her? Or did her schemes about me creep into her night visions, and did she still believe I should marry a prince—or at least a baron. For all her social sensibility, I did not think of asking her advice about what to do concerning the Arnstein's soirée. I didn't have to. I knew she would forbid me to enter the house of Jews, and that she would tell me I was foolish to have accepted such an invitation in the first place—but of course, she did not know some of my pupils were also Jewish. She did not care to know that I could purchase my own gowns and give Greta money for special delicacies I knew Mama liked because those Jews paid me fairly and were very appreciative of the lessons I gave their daughters.

I rolled onto my side so that my back was turned away from my desk and the letter, and watched a tiny beetle skitter up the wall next to my nose. It was the time of year when bugs found ways to get in out of the increasingly cold nights, and during the day Greta always kept a broom handy so that she could swat anything she saw. I grew accustomed to the thwacking sound and Greta's grunt of satisfaction as she murdered each tiny invader.

I realized I must have fallen asleep eventually when I awoke in a start from a terrible dream. I was on the road from the Augarten again, and the murdered man had sat up from where he lay and tried to speak to me, his mouth forming the words but no sound coming out. He gestured wildly in the air with his hands. As I watched, streams of light shot from his fingertips and it looked as if he were drawing figures in the air. Just before I awoke, I realized that he was trying to draw the symbols I had copied from the trunk of the tree.

In contrast with the beautiful day before, the sky that morning was heavy and glowering. It put everyone in the apartment in a petulant mood. At breakfast, Anna pushed her bowl of gruel off the table in front of her and Greta picked her up and spanked her behind with a wooden spoon.

"How dare you!" I shrieked. I don't know quite why. Greta's beatings were never particularly painful—I had suffered enough of them as a young child myself to know.

My outburst had the result of silencing Anna completely and bringing my mother out of her room. She had thrown on her dressing gown, but I could tell from the pinched look around her eyes that she would spend the day in bed with a headache. A feeling of intense pity welled up in me.

"Theresa Maria Schurman, I forbid you to treat Greta like that!" she yelled.

Any sympathy I felt for my mother's suffering vanished in that instant. She lashed out at me without even knowing exactly what had happened, or why I had yelled at Greta. The assumption was always there. If anything went amiss, it must be because of me.

I wanted to start fighting back with her, as we had on only one previous occasion. I had come perilously close then to informing her of her brother's evil deeds, but on that occasion she had crumbled in front of me, sobbing and pulling on her hair, accusing me of not caring for her and not understanding her suffering. After that, she locked herself in her room and I was not allowed to enter. She had avoided seeing me for three complete days.

No, arguing with my mother would not accomplish anything. I simply looked away, went to my room, gathered up the letter I had written the night before along with my violin, put on my cloak and left. I missed Toby then, more than I had since he went to live at Herr Goldschmidt's workshop for his apprenticeship. I decided that I would pay him a visit later that day, or at least send word to him that we needed to talk.

The heavy grey clouds threatened overhead as I strode quickly through the city streets. I stopped a young boy and gave him a Groschen to deliver my letter to the von Eskeles. The deed done, I immediately regretted it and turned to call after the messenger, but he had disappeared around a corner. Nothing I could do about it now, I thought, and did my best to turn my thoughts to what I faced ahead: how to warn Frau Bachmann that a captain of the Hussars had also come to meet me, and that I must go with him and would have to postpone taking her to the place where I had witnessed the murder. In any case, I told myself, there was nothing to connect the event of the night before last with her husband. The fact that Herr Bachmann the flutist was missing could be entirely coincidental.

I reached the gate early, despite my detour to leave the Amati in my room at the Palais Esterhazy. Tradesmen and artisans, flower sellers and vegetable sellers were still streaming through to go to their daily work in the city. A few set up their stalls right by the gate to take advantage of passing traffic. Amid all this busy-ness it would not do to appear idle, and so I climbed the stairs to the Bastei as if I intended to promenade there. It would afford me a view over the lanes below and I could watch for Frau Bachmann, perhaps intercept her before she arrived so that I could explain to her about Captain von Bauer.

The weather was not propitious for taking a leisurely walk atop the broad wall that ringed Vienna, and I found myself alone but for an old man leaning on a cane and a woman who might have been his nurse. The two of them walked slowly up and back, tracing a short path on the side of the Bastei that looked out toward the Danube and the Augarten. I could see in the distance a rain shower approaching, and wondered if they were watching for it so they could depart before it struck.

I hoped my own drama would be concluded long before that slow-moving shower reached the Bastei. I leaned on the wall and watched, scanning the lanes in all directions since I did not know where Frau Bachmann would come from.

As if the heavens had conspired to create the exact circumstance that would most interfere with my project, I saw Captain Bauer and Frau Bachmann approaching rapidly at precisely the same moment from opposite directions, and both of them had been hidden by buildings and people until they were too near for me to run back down the stairs and intercept one of them before they were within each other's sight.

I took a deep breath and steeled myself for having to insult Frau Bachmann by pretending not to know her, and was about to go down to the streets again when I saw something that froze me to my spot. The captain and the Jewish lady stood face-to-face, not as if they were strangers who just happened to pass by each other, but as though they knew one another quite well and were only surprised to find themselves in that place at that time.

I was too far away to hear what they were saying, but first Frau Bachmann pulled herself up short and drew a little away from Captain Bauer. He reached out his hand to her without touching her, but clearly beseeching her to listen to something he had to say. I could tell by his abrupt gestures that he spoke hurriedly, and her shoulders gradually drooped and she caved in on herself a little as though she were weeping quietly. He reached out to her, touching her arm in a way that even from where I stood appeared tender. He leaned toward her and bent down to her, but she looked up quickly and shook him off. She had turned away from me so I could not see her expression, but she pulled her cloak around her tightly and hurried off toward the eastern part of the city.

Captain Bauer stood with his arms hanging by his side, staring at the space where Frau Bachmann had been only moments before.

Well, I thought, *at least I don't have to disappoint Frau Bachmann.* But what an odd thing, that they could know each other—and apparently quite well. If I was not mistaken, they had a relationship of affection at the least, if not more. Yet the captain was a count, and she was a Jew.

I felt I had gained an advantage over Captain von Bauer by having witnessed such an intimate scene. Now I knew something secret about him, and better yet, he did not know I knew it. I descended from the Bastei and went to meet the captain, now more confident of myself, and also forewarned. If there was one hidden aspect of this man, clearly there were others. I decided I had better tread more cautiously where he was concerned, and as I made my way through the crowds to meet him, I prepared myself for more surprises.

CHAPTER TEN

I approached Captain Bauer quietly, hiding myself from his view as much as possible so that I could judge his expression before I made myself known to him. What I saw of his face when I was near enough to him frightened me. He looked not only stern, but angry. I wished I could have heard the exchange between him and Frau Bachmann. What had she said or done to anger him? He let her go. In fact, it seemed that she had some power over him. Might it not be unwise, I thought, to put myself in the power of this man of whom I knew very little, other than his name and appearance? I had been taken in by his enchanting smile and commanding manner. How, I suddenly wondered, had he come to know of my report to the police, when he apparently did not serve in their ranks? Why would a noble captain of the Hussars care about an attack that had been witnessed by a girl dressed as a young man, when the victim might well be only a humble musician—a Jewish one at that—and married to someone of whom he was apparently fond?

I feared there was something more behind his actions, but I did not know how to discover what it was. I found myself wondering what Mirela would do in my circumstances. She trusted no one—not even me. If she were facing my choices now, she would no doubt flirt shamelessly with the captain, draw him in, and keep him completely ignorant of the real truth. I had never mastered this ability and doubted I ever could. However handsome he patently was, the thought of trying to ingratiate myself to him sickened me.

I held back when I reached the place where I would have to be exposed to the captain's view if I were to approach any nearer. He cast his eyes around, looking for me. Did I want to spend an hour with him, first in a closed Fiaker, then in an isolated place where few people would pass at that time of day on a morning that threatened rain?

No, I did not. That meant my only choice was to depart before he noticed me. I could easily say that I had been unable to get away from home to meet him if I chanced to encounter the captain another time. Whatever my excuse, I determined that I must find out more about him before I trusted him any further.

Instead of meeting the captain, I decided I would seek out Mirela. It was time for me to get some help. She, at least, believed me, and knew enough of what had happened to give me advice. She had come to my assistance often, and I had once saved her life. She owed me honesty. I hoped she realized this as well as I.

I slipped unnoticed through the market crowds along to the eastern city gate, which I passed through without difficulty. The delay had, unfortunately, allowed the rain shower that had seemed so distant before to catch up with me, and by the time I was halfway between the walls of Vienna and the Roma encampment, I was soaked through. Fortunately the day was mild, more like late summer than early autumn, and I did not get chilled.

The camp was deserted—at least, most of the inhabitants had chosen to shelter themselves from the rain inside their huts and covered wagons and were therefore not wandering about—but I found Mirela tending a pot over the communal fire, protecting it and herself from the wet with a large, silk umbrella. This magnificent contraption looked new, and I wondered how she had come by such a thing. Only the finest shops sold them—at least, sold the ones that were well waxed and did not become drenched in a heavy rain and let the water soak through to the unsuspecting person who carried it. The sight of such a marvel in its pristine blackness above her threadbare, patchwork shawl and skirt whose lace trim was coming off here and there was so odd that I nearly exploded with laughter. She heard my approach, which I took no pains to disguise.

"Ah, Rezia! Have you found your murderer yet?"

The way she said it knocked me a little off balance, as it sounded almost as if she thought I was searching for someone who had killed me—either that, or as if I sought nothing more important than a lost glove. "Not only have I not found the murderer," I said, "but now even the dead body has disappeared."

She stopped stirring the fragrant liquid, pulled a towel from around her neck and in a deft, one-handed movement wrapped it around her hand so that it would be protected from the hot handle of the pot. She lifted the pot and jerked her head in the direction of her hut. "You're very wet. Come dry yourself and tell me everything."

Mirela's hut was always in a state of disarray, but somehow it never looked messy or dirty. I followed her through the door into the dim interior. A red silk scarf was draped half on the pallet that served as her bed, and half on the floor. The trunk that held her clothes stood open and indeed had little hope of ever being able to close. It was so full of bright-colored skirts and shawls that they spilled out over it. Two wooden chairs were pulled up to the table in the middle of the room where Mirela occasionally brought unsuspecting thrill-seekers to have their fortunes told. Today the table was covered with clay pots, some of which held the remains of her breakfast while the others were full of colorful glass beads and trinkets. Mirela had started making jewelry to sell at the market, too. Olaf would pierce the holes in the stones and bits of glass she found and she would string them together in a haphazard way that actually ended up looking quite pretty.

"Take off your clothes. I won't look. Then you can wrap up in this—and try my new scent." Mirela tossed me a soft, knitted blanket. I did as she said and she laid my wet cloak and dress out over two stools near the small stove in the corner. I watched fascinated as she soaked a cloth in the liquid she had been brewing over the fire and gave it to me. "First, pat this on your neck, then speak."

The smell of the herbs and essences she had been combining was very pleasant and soothing. I breathed them in and stilled my pounding heart before spilling out everything I knew. The entire recital didn't take long because I knew so little. Mirela listened in that absent way she had, picking at loose threads on her skirt, examining her fingernails and digging some dirt out from under them, tossing her voluminous, black curls about occasionally as if she knew they looked best when they caught the half-light of the one oil lamp she allowed to burn on this dismal day. If I didn't know her better, I'd have assumed she hadn't heard a word I said. I wondered at what point it was that Mirela, who was a year younger than I was at least and therefore not quite sixteen, had become the wiser one, the one whose worldly ways frightened me a little. I thought perhaps her change in temperament dated to the time she first allowed Olaf free access to her hut at all hours of the day or night. I knew the Roma ways were different, but Mirela's casual attitude toward the kind of intimacy that most girls waited until after marriage to enjoy made me uncomfortable.

"So," Mirela said, standing and strolling around the tiny space of her hut as if she were in one of the grand receiving rooms at the Hofburg, "You would have no reason to lie about this murder, but there is no body. You found some scribbles on a tree trunk that might mean something or absolutely nothing, but they have provoked odd reactions in the people you shared them with. You have met a handsome captain who is really a count and despite his offer to help you, you do not trust him. And it seems likely your musician might have been a Jew, the husband of this Frau Bach-something you met near the police headquarters, and that she is intimately acquainted with the unlikely captain."

"Yes, sort of," I said. It sounded absurd when Mirela spouted it all back to me like that.

"Just how handsome is this captain?" she said, affecting nonchalance, but I could see the wicked sparkle in her eye.

"Mirela you wouldn't!" I said, but a part of me indeed hoped she would. The captain clearly thought very highly of his ability to charm women, and it would give me some satisfaction to have him confused and tormented by Mirela.

"I shall require some fine clothes—yours no longer fit me I am afraid. Perhaps Alida can be of help. You say you are busy this evening?"

I told her about the coming concert at the Arnstein's apartment in the Graben. I left out the part about Sophie von Eskeles.

"So you consort with Jews now," she said, her tone full of scorn.

"What do you mean, 'consort?' They are good people who have talent and spirit. And without them, I would not earn half so much money from teaching." I think my guilty feelings about Sophie made me defend them as a group more vehemently than I might have done.

Mirela sniffed. "Well, nonetheless, your Captain also appears to have a weakness for the company of Jews. And so therefore if I am to help you I must also become acquainted with these people. My, you do mix yourself with such odd folks—Jews and Gypsies and the like."

Mirela was maddeningly able to keep her expression closed and make you think she was serious when all the time she was joking. I felt stupid for being taken in by her, but also a little relieved that she did not really disdain the Jews. As a Gypsy, she existed even more on the fringes of society. Yet still she gave all these assorted, mysterious characters to "me," not letting me forget that the players in my little drama were now inextricably interwoven with my life, not hers.

We concocted a plan where she would seek out the captain-count to deliver a note saying that I regretted not being able to meet him as planned due to the illness of my mother, but that my cousin—Mirela— would take him out to the Linden trees. It gave me a combination of satisfaction and shame to have a use for my mother's incessant head-aches. "After that, what will you do?" I asked.

"Leave that to me. I shall find out about him. I shall discover why he is interested in your case, why it matters to him that a mere Jew-ish musician has disappeared. I will also try to discover who are his *mouches*."

"His mouches?" And then I remembered these undercover agents who dug up dirt for money. "If the poor fellow whose body has disappeared actually is Herr Bachmann. We don't know. And if the captain actually makes use of mouches to spy for him in his in-vestigations rather than relying on the legitimate police." Mirela was all too apt to make the leap from conjecture to fact in the blink of an eye. I would have to watch for this tendency, or we could land in real difficulties.

"Trust me, he will have his spies. The police always do. Oh," she said as she turned away to see if my dress and cloak had dried, "did you know that Zoltán is coming to visit Alida and Danior? They say he will stay through Alida's confinement."

Zoltán! Why did I not know, I wondered. Perhaps he did not want me to know. I could feel the blood rushing into my cheeks. Mirela no doubt noticed it and would start to tease me at any moment.

"I expect you will have received the invitation to the dinner to-morrow night. They sent them this morning."

My clothes were now dry, and the rain shower had passed by. Mirela opened the shutters that covered her window and we could see a patch of blue sky struggling to grow into fair weather through the clouds. I dressed quickly—I wanted some time to practice before the rehearsal at the Arnstein's later, and I also wanted to stop by Herr Goldschmidt's workshop and find out if Toby was going to be able to come home on Sunday. So many musicians passed through the luthier's workshop that Toby often heard things before I did.

I had a sudden thrill of pleasurable panic that I would perform under the direction of Mozart himself that evening. The thrill was short-lived, however. Soon the image of Sophie's shining face and the promise I had broken made me feel a little sick.

"Perhaps you will see Danior and Alida this evening?" Mirela said as I turned to wave at her.

I shrugged. It had never occurred to me to wonder who would attend the private concert in the home of the wealthy Jew and his children who had converted to the Catholic faith.

CHAPTER ELEVEN

I'm not sure why I trusted Mirela, since in many situations with me she had shown herself to be rather capricious when it came to other people. Nonetheless I had in this instance, and I must therefore let her do as she wished. I did my best to put her out of my mind, judging that she could take better care of herself than almost anyone.

I arrived back at the Palais Esterhazy to find another note tacked to my door. I opened it, expecting it to be more details concerning the evening's performance, and it was—in a sense. The letter simply asked that I attend an additional rehearsal in a building where a number of Jews lived. This seemed not unreasonable, as there were still only a handful of houses they were permitted occupy—although rumors abounded that our emperor would soon lift the residence restrictions on Jews, and in any case once they converted they could live wherever they chose. Sophie and her family had not converted, and were forced to live in a place that was much less grand than the kind of accommodations they could actually afford. They were from a family of bankers from Berlin, and upon whom apparently even the emperor himself was dependent. I wondered why they didn't confess to the Catholic Church, and indeed Sophie had once complained bitterly that her father would not consider it. She wanted to be able to attend the private parties she had heard about, to show off the beautiful silk dresses she owned.

Without undue haste I changed my clothing and hid my hair under my wig with its convenient bag at the back. I was a little hungry. If I left early, I could buy a hot roll at the bakery on my way.

Funny the things you remember. I recall how I waved at the porter, slumped in his chair taking a midday nap, and that I noticed how he lifted his chin and hand in one movement, rather slowly, as though something were pressing him down into his spot. I remember the puddles between the cobbles, thinking that at least the rain would have quelled the dust, and being glad I wore practical, black boots in my guise as a young man. I recalled the freshness in the air, all washed clean yet smelling of leaves just starting to decay.

The address on the note took me to a part of the city I rarely entered. Although we were not wealthy, we lived in a tolerably comfortable manner in a neighborhood where most of the inhabitants were more affluent than we were. The houses I performed in were usually very grand, and the families whose girls I taught had to be well enough off to afford the price of music lessons for daughters who could count the ability to play the violin as little more than an accomplishment rather than a trade—even if they had settled on the violin because all the clavier teachers were too busy to come to them, or because their daughters had no voice for singing. That's why I enjoyed teaching Sophie so much. For all her impatience, she had talent and interest.

With some difficulty I located the building. The ground floor was not given over to shops as in most of the city, but all boarded up and quiet. A dingy towel hung off a sill out an open window on the second floor, but otherwise there was no sign of any activity. A few thin children played a game of tossing stones on the cobbled street in front of the building. They glanced up at me with their eyes only, not fixing me with frank stares such as children often do with strangers. I smiled at one, a boy, who averted his gaze quickly in response.

I still wasn't certain I had the right house. Even straining hard, I could hear no music coming from it. In fact, that entire neighborhood was quiet to the point of eeriness at this time of day. Perhaps I was early. The big doors to the house were shut tight—there didn't even appear to be a handle I could grasp and turn, and the wood was so heavy and thick I had the impression that knocking would produce no sound within at all. They were that sort of doors that came to a pointed arch at the top but that were broad and tall enough to admit a carriage. Perhaps it was a disused stable, I thought. It wouldn't be unusual, here where no one could afford to keep horses let alone a private carriage.

I walked a short way down to where the house ended and saw a narrow alleyway separating it from the next building. The alley did not lead straight through to the street behind, so it was probably some kind of tradesman's access. The note hadn't said which door I should come to, and with the main one so utterly closed, I decided to walk down the alley and see if there was another door. The passage was very narrow. I had to hold my fiddle case in front of me to avoid knocking it against the damp, dirty stone.

To my relief I did find a door, about halfway down. It was unmistakable, even in the midday twilight created by the structures around me. The wood it was fashioned of had darkened with age, and the handle had rusted. What an odd place for a rehearsal, I thought. I tried the handle. It did not give. It was rusted solid.

I tried a tentative knock. I don't know why I didn't want to rap loudly. Perhaps something about the quiet of the place had begun to make me uneasy already, as if I realized I had stumbled on the abode of a slumbering giant who would eat me if I disturbed him. Then, when nothing happened, I gathered my courage and knocked louder. The noise sent a crow that had been nesting on a ledge above cawing away into the air, which started my heart pounding in earnest.

I had almost given up hope that anyone at all was in the building when I heard something on the other side of the door. I was so relieved when the rusted latch lifted at some pressure from the inside that I almost started laughing. The door opened a crack and an old lady's lace-framed face peeked around it. She knitted her brow and peered at me, not opening the door wide enough for me to get through.

"I'm here for the rehearsal," I said, and took a step forward.

"The rehearsal?" she asked, then tapped one gnarled finger on her pursed lips.

"I received this." I handed her the note with the address on it.

She looked at it, turning it front and back as if she didn't understand the words written on it. "Extraordinary," she muttered, then looked up at me. "You may as well come in. He'll know."

I stepped through that unassuming door and entered the most bizarre place I had ever seen in my life. The interior of the building had clearly been completely refashioned. All vestige of its former purpose had been eradicated, and it was a warren of narrow corridors with doors leading into what were evidently small chambers. The walls were covered in expensive, red and gold silk. Old-fashioned sconces held oil lamps that appeared to cast as much shadow as light. I followed the old woman's black, swishing skirts through this maze. An odd scent permeated the place. I thought perhaps my guess that it had once been a stable was correct.

My guide moved very quickly, her small-footed, rapid steps reminding me of a mouse, and she turned corners without waiting for me as though she could see around them. I found it difficult to keep up with her.

She had taken a turn out of sight when I heard her open a door, and the sound of a man's voice flooded out before it stopped abruptly. "The lodge must remain—What is it now? Oh."

I hadn't heard very much, but I thought I recognized the voice. Either it was the captain's, or he was so fixed in my imagination that any man's voice sounded like his. Since it was so unlikely that he would be in such a place, I decided I was mistaken, and continued toward where the old lady stood. By the time I drew close enough to see through the door, she had closed it, standing with her back to it and gesturing on along the corridor. "You're to wait in the next room."

The next room was some way down. This time she followed me, herding me as if I were an unruly goose. I thought perhaps she didn't want me to go back and open that other door, although I still could not imagine why. Was the man in the room another of the musicians?

I found myself in a space that was bare aside from a chair in its midst. I sat, not knowing what else to do. The old lady left me alone, and I heard the jangling of keys on the other side of the closed door. Immediately I rose and tried the door. It was locked. Why would she lock me in here? I was beginning to wonder if I had simply not awakened from my dream last night. Certainly all that had happened so far that day was peculiar and wrong, from Captain Bauer apparently being well acquainted with Frau Bachmann, to this sudden change in the plan for the rehearsal.

I realized that it would be futile to panic, and so set myself to the task of remaining calm. Perhaps there was some good reason why I must not be allowed to roam through this building. Perhaps any moment the man whose voice I had heard would come to take me to the rehearsal.

I did not own a pocket watch, and I was too deep within the house to hear the bells from St. Stephen's ringing the hour, so I had no clear idea of how much time passed as I sat there. I began to grow afraid that I would not make it to the other rehearsal, the one at four-of-the-clock at the Arnstein's apartment that had been settled with the original invitation to play. It had just chimed one when I arrived where

I now was. I suspected that, alone with nothing to do, the time passed more slowly than I thought, though, and hoped that whatever else happened, I would not be late. But still, if there was supposed to be a rehearsal, where were the other musicians?

I don't think I dozed off, but I must have fallen into a dreamlike state when a loud noise, as of a door nearby slamming shut, startled me so that I nearly fell out of my chair. The noise was followed by footsteps approaching. At last, I thought. We are to rehearse. I stood up and picked my violin case up off the floor.

The footsteps paused in front of my door. I knew it wasn't the old lady—these steps were slower and heavier, I thought probably belonging to a man. I heard fumbling with the lock, then a scrabbling toward the bottom of the door. A folded piece of paper poked under it. The door did not open, but the footsteps hurried off, continuing away down the corridor.

I immediately tried to open the door, and succeeded. I was no longer a prisoner, for whatever reason. I stooped down to retrieve the folded note, opened it and read:

> *The Grand Master sees all, and knows what you want. You would be well advised to give up your inquiries, or the next time you may find yourself truly lost to the world.*

The note was not signed. So, I had been given a warning, taught a lesson. But a warning against what? And what was I to learn? I was more mystified than frightened. It all seemed so unreal. I tucked the note in my pocket and hurried down the corridor, attempting to retrace my steps. I soon realized, however, that I had come by so many twists and turns that I could not remember the way. I paused to listen for sounds of the outside world, hoping I would be guided to the door. In most houses in Vienna, it would have been impossible to escape the calling of the street merchants, or the squeaking of carriages and clattering of horses' hooves over the cobbles.

But here, there was complete silence. Nothing at all to guide me.

Except, after a time I did hear something. It was a kind of breathing, with something deep and guttural in it. I walked on. The breathing continued. It came from behind me. Someone was following me.

I tried to still my heart, but it refused to cooperate. I hastened my pace, at the same time trying to make the heels of my boots strike the wooden floor more quietly. At least the many corners might befuddle my pursuer and help me evade him.

Instead of concentrating on finding a door to lead me out, all I could think of now was not being caught. Yet the breathing drew closer, no matter how quickly I moved and how many corners I turned. I clutched my violin case in front of me and wondered why I did not hear footsteps, which should have been louder than the sound of someone breathing in that odd way, almost as if he had a cold, with a deep rumble in every inhalation and exhalation. But I did not hear footsteps, only a soft padding, like well-worn slippers.

Before long I was running, desperate to escape. Every door I passed I would grab hold of the handle and rattle, but all of them were locked. I no longer cared if I made noise: speed was the thing. I felt hopeless panic rising in me, ready to choke me and make me unable to breathe, when after running to the ends of my strength I found myself in a corridor with no way out—unless the door at its end would prove the exception and be the only one yet that would open.

I reached it and doubled over, my eyes watering and my breath rasping in my chest, too weak even to reach out. I heard the padding and the breathing approach the last corner I had turned, knowing that the chase was over. I watched, fascinated, to see what manner of person could track me so relentlessly through this maze.

What I saw surprised me so greatly that I don't know whether wonder or fear was a stronger force in me at that moment. An enormous, black cat, like a lion or a leopard but without spots and completely black, stood staring me down with its round, green eyes. Its mouth was slightly opened and ears flattened back against its head, and I could see its chest expanding and contracting with each growling breath.

I did not know what else to do but stand utterly still, as Mirela had cautioned me once when we came upon a lone wolf in the woods near the Gypsy camp. "If you run, they will know they should chase you," she had said. In any case, I had nowhere to go.

Just as the cat had lowered its head, pulled its lips back to reveal rows of pointed teeth, and started to lift one paw to take a step in my direction, I heard a door around the corner behind it open, and a man's voice—I thought the same one I had heard the last time a door opened—called out, "Midnight! Come."

I thought I saw a look of disappointment flash through those feline eyes before they turned away from me and obediently followed the command of its master.

The imminent danger had passed, but I still did not know how to escape the labyrinthine building. I turned and tried the door that had stopped my flight, not holding out much hope for success. But to my surprise, it opened easily, and I found myself in the alley again, free to run away from that place forever.

CHAPTER TWELVE

I paused a moment to collect myself, mopping my perspiring face with my *Handtaschen*. In the distance I heard the bells of St. Stephen's strike four times. I was late.

I hardly thought my legs could support me, let alone get me quickly to the opposite side of the city to the Graben, where the Arnsteins lived. I received many curious stares as I hurried along. I think my face was probably a picture of horror still. I shuddered every now and then thinking how narrowly I missed being mauled by that vicious beast, whatever it was. How could there be such a thing in Vienna?

As I entered familiar surroundings, the busy streets with the carts and vendors all crying their wares to fashionable ladies strolling by, the uniformed porters standing importantly beside their doors as though they had some real business other than collecting bribes, I felt an almost irresistible urge to grab hold of someone's hand and kiss it. My world had never appeared quite so lovely to me, even with a chilly wind and a sky that had clouded over again and threatened rain once more, with the dirty streets and general disorder that had always disturbed me before.

When I reached the Arnstein's house—which I had once heard someone explain they didn't officially own because Jews weren't allowed to own property—I could hear musicians above tuning their instruments. I ran in and the porter directed me to the grand apartment they inhabited, where I knocked and was admitted by a smartly dressed maid. "They'll be starting soon. You're late!" she hissed at me. But her expression was kind. I slipped in, hoping no one would notice me, and hoping no one I knew would be there.

Yet who should I see sitting in the second desk, but Danior himself. And seated in one of the chairs in the almost empty rows that would later be occupied by a wealthy and discerning crowd was Zoltán.

Danior was well aware of my double life. He had been the source of most of my performing engagements, as well as several of my teaching positions. But I had never had any reason to tell Zoltán how I lived since I had hardly seen him in the last two years. I didn't know whether Danior or Alida would have said anything to him in a letter. Right then I was too overwhelmed with everything else to look at this man who had featured so prominently in my dreams, so I quickly settled myself in the remaining seat available in the violin section of the small ensemble, which numbered about a dozen in all: four violins, two violas, two cellos, a flute, a French horn, a clarinet, and a drum and cymbals—these last an unusual instrument to find in a chamber orchestra. As I tightened the strings on my bow I could hear Monsieur Mozart's light, energetic voice from the other room, talking animatedly to someone and approaching us.

"It's only the beginning of it, but I've completed most of the music, and I think it's coming together quite nicely. Monsieur Stephanie vows he will accomplish the remaining changes to the libretto I have requested in time for the opera to be considered for the coming season."

Two liveried servants grasped the handles of a pair of double doors and pulled them open simultaneously to admit Mozart, his arms full of sheets of music, accompanied by a dapper young man I assumed to be Monsieur Nathan Arnstein, the son of the old man who was head of the family.

"It's a pity we could not persuade Thorwart to come," young Arnstein said, "But you know how he is."

"All too well, I'm afraid. I cannot even get him to give me an interview. That lump of flesh stands in the way of more than my career, I tell you!"

"That's because you aren't pretty enough!" Arnstein said, and the two of them laughed. "But enough of that. Here, Amadé," said Arnstein, sweeping his hand toward all of us, who had stopped talking and sat tall and ready to play, "is your orchestra."

I tried to take in the sight as Mozart must have. We were an ill-assorted bunch. Since I didn't know most of the musicians there aside from Danior, I assumed they were Jews. They no longer had to wear their yellow patches, but I could account for no other way for not being acquainted with so many players.

"Gentlemen," Mozart said, bowing graciously, "I shall distribute the parts—it's an overture from my new opera, The Abduction from the Seraglio. As I give you yours, do me the kindness of telling me your names, as I am afraid only one or two of you are known to me—although my friend Monsieur Arnstein here assures me that he has assembled the finest in Vienna."

I could not tell if he was being facetious. Of course, the musicians whom most people considered the finest in Vienna would never deign to set foot in that apartment, even if only the old man was still a real Jew, let alone willingly take part in a concert sitting among Jewish musicians. Yet there did not seem to be anything but genuine enthusiasm in Mozart's words.

One by one the members of the little orchestra stood to receive the parts and bow to Mozart. He reached across people and even walked around the back to shake hands, and repeated each person's name. I was afraid my voice shook when I told him mine. I could not look into his eyes. I still didn't know whether I would rather he met me as Thomas Weissbrot, violinist, or Theresa Maria Schurman, violin teacher and eligible young lady.

How can I describe Mozart? Now he is famous—his operas have had great success—but then, he seemed to embody a peculiar mixture of arrogance and humility. He knew, I could tell, that his music was far superior to anything that had yet been heard in the elegant reception rooms and concert halls of Vienna, and yet he was still an outsider, with all the nervous uncertainty of a débutante. Adding to my impression was the fact that he was quite a small man—several inches shorter than I was—and his hands were very delicate.

I expected that we would tune up and start right away, but instead Mozart sat at the pianoforte, and in an excited rush played excerpts of his opera and sang bits of the arias from it, from beginning to end that we might know the story that was to unfold after the overture we had come there to rehearse. He became so deeply engrossed in what he was doing that I thought he would leap off the chair during the exciting moments, and shed real tears during the sad ones.

I had seen several operas at Esterhaza when I was younger, and Danior had taken me to an opera in Vienna a few months ago when Alida was too ill to go with him, so I was familiar with the forms and style. But the music Mozart played for us that afternoon caught at something deep inside me. Perhaps I was feeling exposed and fragile after my strange adventure just before, but at the very end, which was happy and satisfying and in no way bittersweet—except for poor Pasha Selim, who had to forgo his love for the beautiful Constanze and forgive the young hero Belmonte his treachery toward him—I could not stifle the tears that flowed down my cheeks. I hoped no one noticed. I bent forward to get a lump of resin from my fiddle case, surreptitiously wiping away the evidence of my girlish emotions before sitting up and preparing to play.

When I did, I saw Mozart looking directly at me, with such an expression of sorrow in his face that I did not know what to think.

"Gentlemen, let's start from the beginning and read straight through, then we'll go back and tidy it all up."

CHAPTER THIRTEEN

Normally, a second-violin part is relatively easy to play. It wasn't that this one was particularly difficult, but Mozart set a tempo that had us all scrambling and I was surprised that almost from the first notes, the cymbals crashed together, and not once, but over and over again. Usually they would be reserved for a grand finale, but Mozart had explained that the music was meant to evoke the Janissaries, the Turkish infantry troops that marched to very shrill music with bells and drums.

I was soon swept up in the thrilling mood of the overture. The frantic beginning was followed by a slower section that brought to mind one of the arias Mozart had sung, full of yearning sadness. I felt a little guilty for being able to lose myself so completely in the music, when there were such vital concerns that needed my attention, but if I hadn't concentrated hard I would never have been able to keep up.

Our first run-through wasn't very good, and I could tell that Mozart was a little frustrated. He took Danior's fiddle and demonstrated the bowing and expression he wanted, and explained a few things that were not very clear in the score—including one mistake. I thought the copyist's work was rather sloppy, that I could have done a much better job myself. How would that be, to act as Mozart's copyist? More interesting than the work I was doing for Herr von Gluck, certainly.

Once the rough edges were polished off the overture, we rehearsed a charming Divertimento. It wasn't new—I'd played one of the movements at one or two of the Viennese balls, a March—but it was something, to have Mozart himself directing us and setting the tempo, telling us that here the winds should be more prominent, while there the strings were the romantic hero, like the *primo uomo* in an opera.

The ensemble had only been engaged to perform two works, I found: the Overture and the Divertimento. Not much effort for the six *Thaler* we were each to be paid. Apparently Mozart and Danior would play a sonata for violin and pianoforte, and Mozart would also perform some variations on the piano to make up the rest of the program.

After the rehearsal, which lasted a little over an hour, we were invited to eat some dinner in the servant's hall on the floor below. Mozart stayed with Nathan Arnstein, though.

We were led down a back stairway, which wasn't unusual for hired musicians, and wouldn't have been in the slightest bit noteworthy but for something that caught my eye and nearly made me stumble. We passed an open door that led into a sort of shrine, but instead of a crucifix or a picture of the Virgin and saints, it simply held a large book draped with ornate silks embroidered with odd characters and pictures. This was not what startled me though. It was the design above the shrine, carved into a wooden panel and gilded. It was a more elaborate, finished version of the marks I had copied from the base of the Linden tree.

I slipped through the crowd of hungry musicians and found Danior. "I have to talk to you," I whispered as we waited respectfully to get our plates of food and sit at the long table that had already been set with tankards of ale and loaves of bread.

"What's the matter Rez—Thomas?" he said, correcting himself quickly.

"Did you see the symbols? Above the shrine we passed coming down the stairs?"

He couldn't answer right away. The flutist, a young man who looked a bit frightened to be there, approached Danior. "Monsieur Varga, I am honored to play in the same ensemble with you. I am only sorry that Herr Bachmann could not be here—I am certain the divertimento would be better with two flutes instead of one."

Herr Bachmann! I looked quickly at Danior to see if the name meant anything to him. He reacted as though he knew the man, but not as if he had any special concern about him. After all, I thought, I had only been able to associate the name of Bachmann with the victim near the Augarten that morning. I would have to find some excuse to speak to the flutist before the end of the evening. He might tell me where I could find Frau Bachmann. But before then, I simply had to have a private moment with Danior.

This private moment proved difficult to arrange. Danior, as one of the best violinists in Vienna, was well known and revered in the community of musicians. Every member of that odd assortment of players came up to him as we sat at the table eating to express gratitude for his being there. They looked, I thought, as though they had been wandering in a desert and Danior had been responsible for bringing them fresh water to drink. Could it be that everyone there, except Danior and myself, was a Jew? And he was a Gypsy—despite his marriage into the Varga family—and I was a counterfeit man.

The food was very good, but plain. And I noticed that there was no pork—sausages or bacon would have been the easiest and least expensive repast for a horde of ravenous artisans. Instead we had potatoes and turnips with chicken stew and dumplings, and the ale was plentiful. I had not realized how hungry I was until then. I tried not to drink much of the ale though. It was hard enough to play my part—both in the music and in life—without being befuddled by drink.

"What did you want to say?" Danior asked me at last when almost everyone had gone off to the water closet.

"It's complicated. Did you notice the shrine we passed on the way down here?"

"I glanced at it, but didn't remark anything much."

I reached into my pocket to pull out the by now tattered scrap of paper where I had committed the marks on the Linden tree so I would not forget them.

Danior turned the paper around and around, finally settling on the direction that made sense to him, then shook his head. "It means nothing to me."

"But it is precisely the same design I saw above the shrine. Here! Look when we go by again."

I had no opportunity to mention the added coincidence that the flutist referred to Herr Bachmann before we were all called upstairs to take our places for the performance. I would have to depend on being able to talk to Danior afterwards.

The afternoon's events had driven the morning's anxieties out of my mind, so that I was completely taken aback when I saw not Mirela seated in the audience, attired in a magnificent silk gown that must have been Alida's, quickly altered to fit Mirela's voluptuous figure and petite stature. We exchanged a knowing glance—I knew I could count on her to keep my secret. I wondered, though, why she had chosen to come to this concert, to hear music that she normally disdained. Perhaps it was Danior's artistry she had desired to hear—she admired him well enough.

A few moments later, the Eskeles's entered the room. Sophie looked lovely in a pale gray silk dress that reached to just above her ankles, and showed a pair of dainty silk slippers with embroidered flowers on them. Herr and Frau von Eskeles were also elegantly attired in velvets and silks of richer colors. Perhaps it was my own guilty conscience, but I thought I saw anger in the eyes of Herr von Eskeles, and sadness in Sophie's. I could not bear to look at them, and focused on the music instead, humming my part to myself and trying to drive all other thoughts out of my mind. I wished more than anything at that moment that I could explain it all to Sophie. I knew she would understand.

I nearly succeeded in putting all the unpleasant thoughts out of my mind, until just before Mozart himself came out and took his bow in front of the eager audience. In that moment, I understood what must have transpired unknown to me while I was imprisoned in the labyrinth of that strange house on the other side of the city. Mirela had been successful beyond imagining. Captain von Bauer himself walked in and took his place in the chair next to Mirela, who gave him a smoldering look before lowering her eyelids. I could hardly believe she could not only have found the captain-count, but bewitched him to the point where she would have an assignation with him at a concert.

Even more important, though, was the disturbing fact that he was here at all. He could not be Jewish—he had a title—and so he must have some personal connection with the Arnsteins. Perhaps it had been he who originally made the connection for Herr Bachmann to play the flute there. Whatever it was, I was vexed that he was there. I wanted to shrink away to nothing. He knew of my disguise, and if he wished to could embarrass me in front of everyone. It would have been better, so much better, if I had simply kept to the original plan and come as Sophie's guest.

Everything had now spiraled out of my control. I did not know what to expect next. I prayed fervently that I could just perform my role as musician and slink away after the concert.

CHAPTER FOURTEEN

We played the Divertimento first, then Mozart and Danior performed a Sonata for violin and pianoforte. Because it was a private party the musicians all remained seated for it, becoming an audience in our own right, surrounding Mozart and my friend in an embrace of appreciation. It was exquisite. Danior brought his Gypsy fire to the elegant music, and it was easy to see that Mozart admired his ability deeply. I hoped that he was enthralled enough to ensure that Danior led the orchestra for his opera premier—if it ever came to pass—despite being one of the Romany.

After the Sonata, Mozart remained at the keyboard to perform a set of variations. I had heard some of them before, but others were new to me, and so inventive and full of difficult passages that he amazed everyone.

When Mozart finished he stood up and after taking his bow said, "I have been challenged to a duel." He deliberately let that shocking fact hover over the heads of his appreciative audience, enjoying the sensation he had caused for a while before continuing. "I have been challenged to a musical duel, *mano a mano* at the pianoforte. In December, at the request of His Imperial Majesty, to determine who is the greater artist: my humble self . . ." This provoked polite laughter from most and a loud guffaw from Nathan Arnstein. " . . . or Signore Muzio Clementi.

"As an expression of my gratitude to my kind hosts, I shall ensure that, if for some reason the distinguished company here are not permitted to attend, the contest—between me and Signore Clementi—shall be repeated in this very room."

A scattering of applause ensued, as well as a good deal of embarrassed silence. How could he ensure that an Italian musician would consent to perform at this elegant home that just happened to be occupied by an extremely wealthy Jewish family?

Without seeming to notice the effect of his unnecessary bravado, Mozart turned back to the orchestra, let the oboe give the A, and then his lively eyes and the slight movements of his tightly strung body indicated to us the mood and the tempo of his remarkable overture. Once we were all poised and with him, he gave the downbeat.

Perhaps I was simply swept up in the general feeling, but I felt as if I played like a genius that night. The notes flew out of my fiddle and into the air, blending effortlessly with all the other notes that my fellow musicians produced. I felt buoyed up by the brilliant first-violin part that ran up and down atop my steady repeated notes, and stirred by the cymbals crashing on the downbeats. I didn't want the overture to end. I felt safe there, enveloped in the music. I was no different from all the other players—the men, so many of them Jewish. We were united in one glorious wash of sound. This was what my mother would never understand, the part of being a musician that had been so important in my father's life and now was so in mine. Not only did she not understand, but if she ever had an inkling of what I really did when I left our home for hours at a time, she would put a stop to it immediately and either marry me off to some old merchant or send me to a convent.

All too soon the music ended and the guests stood and began to chat and wander about, and I was plunged back into my difficulties. I had to figure out what to do next, how to escape Captain Bauer's notice, and how to make Danior understand about the symbols in the shrine I had seen. Out of the corner of my eye as I loosened the hairs on my bow and nestled the Amati securely in its case, I saw my pupil Sophie being presented to Mozart. He shook her hand warmly. I strained to hear what he said to her, knowing that I should have been next to her to tell him what a dedicated, enthusiastic student of music she was.

But Sophie was bold enough on her own and didn't really need my help. "I play the violin, Monsieur Mozart," she said.

"I have a sister who also plays the violin, and very well, and the pianoforte too, but not so much any more," he replied, patting her on the head.

"Where is your sister now?" Sophie asked. I saw Frau von Eskeles take hold of her and try to pull her away so that she wouldn't question him further.

"She is at home with my papa in Salzburg," he answered.

I had gotten so involved in trying to witness the encounter between my eager young pupil and Amadé Mozart that I failed to notice the presence of Captain Bauer—the one person I most wanted to avoid—at my side.

"I waited for you this morning, Herr Weissbrot." He addressed me as a man, but in such a way to make me understand that if he could he would expose me then and there. He reminded me in a subtle way that my immediate destiny was in his control, that a simple word from him would unravel my deception embarrassingly at a very sensitive moment.

"My mother was ill and I had to attend her," I said, willing the blushes away from my cheeks.

"I went without you to the interesting place you suggested," he continued, following me as I made my way toward the door where the other musicians were filtering out very slowly, stopping to receive their fees from old Herr Arnstein, who bowed to them one by one and thanked them. Some he greeted as if they were acquaintances of many years, and carried on a conversation as if there were not several others waiting. I dared not pass through this courteous gamut as long as the captain stuck to me. I wanted to tell him to go back and flirt with Mirela, but I didn't want him to know how close we were. I would let him believe that I had simply used her as a messenger.

"Yes," he continued, "I went to the place we had gone together and searched all over the Linden trees. I did not find anything at all. Do you realize, Monsieur," he said with sarcastic emphasis then lowering his voice, "that I could have you brought before the magistrates for leading me on this merry chase?"

"You wouldn't!" I hissed. "Besides, I know yet more, about the symbols and about you, but if you do not care to continue your investigation, then I shall pursue the solution to this mystery on my own. I don't need you!"

He had taken hold of my elbow in a way that was meant to appear companionable, no doubt, but I could feel the imprint of his fingers on the soft flesh just above the joint. Fortunately, almost everyone else was clustered around Mozart listening to him talk about his new opera, and my fellow musicians had by now nearly finished receiving their fees and departing. I was confident our *sotto voce* interactions had not been observed—at least, I thought they hadn't at that time. I jerked my arm away from the captain and quickly stepped into the midst of the last few musicians.

"Ah, there you are Captain!"

I heard Mirela claim him and draw him away. Disaster narrowly averted, I thought, thanking Mirela with a look.

But the awkward moments had not ended for the evening just yet. No sooner had I turned to go than I felt another hand on my shoulder. I hoped it was Danior and turned, ready to tell him quickly where the shrine was and that he must find a way to go there himself, or at least discover what it meant.

"Thomas?" The name sounded peculiar coming from Zoltán's lips and referring to me. I truly wanted to evaporate in the air like a puddle after a hot summer rainstorm. I never wanted Zoltán to see me as anything other than Rezia Schurman. "You looked so at home there in the orchestra, I hardly recognized you as the . . . boy I used to know."

I assumed Danior had told him. I couldn't think what to say, only smiling weakly. Besides, I didn't trust my voice not to sound utterly shrill and girlish.

"I'm going in your direction. I must leave now, as it happens. Could I walk with you?" Zoltán asked as though he knew I would accept his offer. And how could I refuse? Doubtless my face was bright red. All I wanted to do was leave—immediately.

The delay first with Captain Bauer and now with Zoltán had made me the last of the musicians to greet the Arnstein patriarch. I reached out my hand to him, but to my surprise, instead of clasping it in his and smiling, thanking me in his slightly accented German, he stood tall and handed me my bag of coins, clearly going out of his way not to touch me. "*Danke sehr*, Herr Weissbrot," he said. I cast a quick glance around to see if anyone else noticed this discourteous treatment. He knew. He had seen through my disguise.

I met Sophie's wide, astonished eyes just before Zoltán ushered me out the door of the apartment ahead of him.

"Now that we are outside, can we drop this pretense?" Zoltán said.

I wanted to weep. What had ever possessed me to accept this engagement to play? I saw the entire fragile construction of my double life crumbling before my eyes. The captain, Sophie, Zoltán, and clearly old Herr Arnstein now knew that I was not a young man, and three of the four also knew which particular young woman I was. But I did not have time to wallow in self-pity over it. There were much more important matters to attend to.

"Zoltán," I said, "I need your help. Never mind about this." I swept my hand across my body. "It's of no moment. What is much more important is that someone, and I'm beginning to suspect who, has been murdered."

"Danior told me something of this. But Rezia, how do you know for certain?"

I stopped. Could it be that Zoltán did not believe me either? "I know because I saw it!" I felt my voice pinch closed with suppressed tears.

Zoltán put his arm through mine and instead of taking the direct route back towards the Palais Esterhazy, where I would return to change before going home, we headed toward the Bastei. "Suppose you start from the beginning and tell me everything," he said.

We walked for a long time that evening. I hadn't had the opportunity to speak to Zoltán, to really talk to him, since right after my uncle was banished. He had been busy on his family's estates in Hungary, and according to Danior and Alida, had rehabilitated them to the point where they were starting to produce a handsome income. No doubt with his baronial title and new wealth he was the object of scheming on the part of plenty of eligible young heiresses. And he was still as handsome as ever—no, more handsome. His face had matured. Its lines were sharper, and his eyes held an even deeper expression. I found this very attractive, but I also felt, as we walked and I talked and he listened, that he had taken a position as a father to me. Or at least, an older brother. I supposed that would be better than nothing, but my heart ached. The difference in our ages was not so very great. Zoltán was twenty-three. If he had remained nothing more than a musician in Prince Esterhazy's orchestra—but it was no use going down that path.

Once I had given him the entire tale with all its mysterious twists and turns, and told him about my terrifying encounter with the big cat, we descended the stairs from the Bastei and returned to the city streets. He took me over to the light of a street lamp and turned me so that he could see my face clearly. I thought I saw tenderness there, and it stabbed me through.

"Tell me honestly, Rezia. This is all so fantastical, and even the police and this Captain von Bauer you met have not been able to find any evidence or corroborate anything. You would not invent such a tale? I know you have had a hard life since that horrible night two years ago, that you have been the one who has taken care of your family, and not even Toby there to help. You could be forgiven for being carried away by your imagination."

I knew what he said was difficult for him. I also felt that he really wanted to wrap his arms around me and comfort me. But his words sent me into a state of turmoil. I had seen what I had seen. Or had I? Could I truly have imagined it all? "I swear, upon my honor and upon the Holy Virgin and Saint Cecilia, that I did not invent this. How could I? Why would I?"

He touched my cheek. I leaned my head on his hand and closed my eyes.

All at once the curfew bell rang so loudly that it sounded as though we were standing in the belfry. Zoltán took his hand away from my cheek as if it was a hot coal, and I jumped backwards. We were right by the Michaelerkirche, I realized. We looked at each other and laughed. "But truly," I said, "I begin to doubt my sanity. And there is one thing more."

We turned and I slung my violin case over my shoulder. Zoltán gently took it from me and pulled my arm through his. The streets were almost deserted. No one would notice the odd spectacle of two young men walking arm-in-arm like sweethearts. "What is the one thing more?" Zoltán asked.

I still hadn't been able to bring myself to tell anyone what the murdered musician had said with his last breath. It was time, perhaps, to do so. And if I could not trust Zoltán who could I trust?

"The man who was killed, when I bent down next to him, he whispered a name to me."

"Why did you not say before?"

I took a deep breath. "Because the name was Mozart."

Chapter Fifteen

Zoltán's expression registered both shock and fear. "You are certain that is what he said?"

"I wish I were not." We had reached the Palais Esterhazy. "I have tried to imagine any other possibility, but his words were quite distinct."

"Why Mozart? He is not—" Zoltán stopped speaking abruptly.

"He is not what?" I asked.

Zoltán hesitated almost imperceptibly before answering. "Well, so far circumstances would indicate that there is some connection to the Jews in all this. Didn't you say that Frau Bachmann is Jewish, and that her missing husband may be this musician you saw killed?"

Something made me think Zoltán hadn't been about to say that Mozart wasn't Jewish. Why would he have stopped himself from speaking if that were all? There was something more. I realized that I had not yet put the pieces together, that there was a fact that was obvious to Zoltán, Captain Bauer—even Herr von Gluck—that I did not understand. At the moment I doubted Zoltán would tell me what it was. I would have to figure it out for myself, or remain hampered in my search for the truth. "I must go and change before I go home," I said, preparing to take leave of my friend.

"You will be locked out," he said, turning me toward him. "And anyway, your clothing suits you."

His face was in shadow, so I could not see whether he was teasing me or not. I reached for my violin, but before I knew it he had threaded his arms around my waist. The feeling of him holding me was so familiar, and yet so strange. I thought perhaps it was because I was taller. My head used to reach only to the middle of his chest. Now, with very little trouble I could rest it on his shoulder, and I found myself doing just that. Somewhere in my past I remembered that feeling, the strong, muscular arms reaching around me to comfort me, but I didn't remember it having such a disturbing effect on me. Zoltán patted my head, which was shielded by the woolly mat of the bag wig. I wished I had my hair down. I longed to feel the touch of his fingers entangled in it.

"I really must go," I said, pushing myself away from him. The contact was confusing me, making me forget why I needed his help.

"Promise me you will not do anything more concerning this murder you witnessed," he said, taking my chin in his hand and tilting my face up to him. His eyes searched mine.

"You do believe me then? I wouldn't lie to you. I couldn't."

"I believe you. But I'm afraid. So promise me? I know people. I can make some inquiries."

"But you will keep me informed?"

"Of course. Now promise."

I looked away before I said, "I promise," not wanting to displease him, but also knowing that I had no intention of letting the matter drop, even if a person I trusted now knew all the facts and had said he would make inquiries. I was beginning to believe that I had stumbled upon something that was even more significant than one hapless stranger being set upon and robbed, and that involved some secret network—perhaps even a conspiracy—stretching across the world of both humble musicians and powerful officials in Vienna. Was my imagination running off on its own? Had I let the horrible, hidden facts surrounding my own father's murder make me see conspiracy everywhere?

No. I imagined nothing. And I would find a way to prove it. On my own.

I bid Zoltán an awkward goodbye, changed quickly into my dress and transferred the violin to its old case, then hurried home. It was so late by the time I got there that I had to awaken old Joseph from a sound sleep to let me in and pressed double the normal tip into his palm.

I could barely lift my feet to climb the stairs. Everyone in the apartment was asleep. Greta—thank heavens—had left me a tray of bread and cold meat. I carried it into my cubby room and started to undress as I nibbled on the bread. I don't know why it took me so long to notice it, but tucked just under the plate was a folded letter with my name on it.

I put the bread down and slid the blade of the knife under the wax seal. It popped cleanly away from the paper, which was very heavy and smooth—the finest paper I had ever held in my hands, in fact. Deeply imprinted on the top of the sheet was an ornate crest, consisting of a six-pointed star with interwoven arabesques. I could just make out the initial "E." The letter started immediately below the crest and was scrawled wastefully across the entire surface. I would not be able to salvage a scrap to use for myself.

Sehr geehrte Mademoiselle Schurman,

Please forgive the sudden notice, but we find that we are no longer in the position to retain your services as a violin teacher to our daughter, Sophie.

Abraham von Eskeles

Not teach Sophie? How could that be? They were wealthy. Yet I knew in my heart that this dismissal had nothing to do with money. They had seen through me completely, and were deeply wounded. And I deserved to be treated like this. I had thrown away their friendship for my own selfish reasons.

My stomach sank to the floor. This was a blow. For the first time since my Papa died, I felt that he would not be looking down upon me kindly. I had violated one of his principles, of treating everyone—no matter their station in life or relationship to me—with courteous dignity.

"I'm so sorry Papa. I'm so sorry Sophie," I said, my words muffled by my pillow and flooded with the tears I shed that night.

In the morning I awoke with a heavy feeling, wishing I could simply pull the covers over my head and shut out the world. I had had dreams in which everyone I knew—my mother, Zoltán, Danior, Alida, Mirela, Greta, Toby, even little Anna—turned their backs on me whenever I approached them, and the streets of Vienna emptied as I walked through, everyone shunning my presence as though I had the plague. And the dream was utterly silent. Usually I heard music in my sleep.

I forced myself to get out of bed and join the morning bustle of breakfast, with Anna's cheery nonsense prattle reaching into my room and reminding me that I had no time to wallow in self-pity. I entered the dining room to be greeted not only by the usual sight of Greta trying to get Anna to sit still in her high chair while she fed her gruel that dribbled down the towel tied around her neck, but by the sight of my mother looking much better, seated at the table with a paper knife opening letters. Mama rarely emerged from her room before Anna had finished her messy morning meal and been tidied up by Greta, so I was quite shocked, and stood in the entryway staring at her for a moment.

Mama had only three letters, but she took each one up languidly, gazing at it down her upturned nose, turning it this way and that—I could hear her thoughts running on, *is this one worth bothering about?* like the grand lady she thought she was. And once she decided it was—as of course she would since any contact that made its way into our enclosed world that had nothing to do with me was always welcome to her—she slipped the knife under the seal and opened her letter without so much as the tiniest tear to the paper. This was quite an accomplishment. Hers were not on the heavy, smooth linen sheets that barely crinkled like Herr von Eskeles's paper, but mostly tissuey stuff that was thin enough to see through. The first two were tradesmen's bills, which she laid aside carelessly. The third, though, was a long letter in a fine, round hand, on slightly better quality paper. As she scanned the lines, that delicate flush I had noticed when the pianoforte arrived a few days ago spread up from her shoulders to her neck, and from there into her face.

When I pulled out my chair to sit down at the breakfast table she looked up quickly and folded her letter, tucking it into the pocket of her dressing gown.

"You had a letter yesterday," she said, at the same time acknowledging that I must have seen hers and acting as if she were accusing me of theft. I said nothing in response. "An extraordinary gentleman delivered it. He asked to see me, but Greta quite rightly told him that I was indisposed and not receiving visitors."

"He was a Jew." Greta flung her words across the table.

"I don't know what sort of people you are associating with," Mama said, "but it's time we put a stop to your wanderings. I have been far too lenient with you. Things will change, and soon." Her eyes softened on her last words, and the blush crept back into her cheeks.

"What are you saying Mama?" I asked.

She turned her wide eyes upon me. They shone with triumph. "I am going to marry again."

I'm not sure quite why I was so shocked. There had been plenty of hints in recent weeks, the largest and most obvious of which was the extravagant gift of a pianoforte from Herr van Swieten. The librarian was a well-to-do man. I couldn't begin to imagine what changes would occur. "Marry?" I managed to squeak out. "Who could ever . . ."

"Is it so surprising someone would want to marry me?" Her eyes registered hurt. I didn't mean what I said to sound as it had, but it was too late to take back the words. "It is Herr van Swieten, of course. He is very important in musical circles. He wants to meet you, and has asked you to visit him today."

"I'm sorry Mama, I didn't mean . . . only Papa . . . So soon . . ." I couldn't get my thoughts to form into proper words.

"Gottfried said you would be upset, and I knew it too. But you must see that it is the best thing for us all. You will no longer have to work to support us." She did not look up from her plate, as if the half-eaten bread and nibbled cheese were the most interesting things she had ever seen and demanded all her attention.

"Does Toby know?" I asked.

"I was hoping you would tell him," Mama replied.

I had lost all my appetite for breakfast. "Where shall I go? At what time." I had no engagements that day, only a vague plan to see Mirela and find out what had happened with the captain.

"He expects you at two," she said. She lifted her eyes again and attempted a weak smile. "Why are you so critical of me? Remarrying is the right thing to do. A widow without resources must remarry, if her children are not of an age to take care of her. That, or take the veil."

She said it as if she were repeating lines from an etiquette manual. And indeed, Mama was young. She had been only sixteen when I was born. I hoped she didn't see it simply as a duty, but actually had a desire to marry. Yet I could not blame her for feeling she must justify her actions to me.

In the course of our conversation Anna had finished her breakfast and Greta had changed her into her little brown frock and white apron. "I'll take Anna out," I said. "I've been so busy lately I've hardly seen her." I crouched down and opened my arms. Anna ran into them, her warm child's body filling the empty space. "I'll bring her back in time for dinner."

Soon Anna and I were out on the Vienna streets, I in my blue dimity dress with white lace under-blouse and short cape, Anna in her black coat. People smiled as we passed. She was a joy to behold with her golden curls and round, pink cheeks. I had to keep a tight hold on the straps of my little sister's harness to prevent her running off after every pigeon or horse she saw. Normally I would talk to her and play games as we went, swinging her up into my arms to make her laugh and shriek with delight. But I had too much to think about. I wondered first if Toby would be able to talk at all. He was almost a prisoner in Herr Goldschmidt's workshop. The luthier kept a close watch on his apprentices, letting them go home only once every other week. My visit was out of the ordinary, but times were desperate. I hoped that Herr Goldschmidt would give us a moment alone.

Anna and I walked in through the shop, where Frau Goldschmidt greeted us.

"*Ach*! The little one!" she exclaimed, bending in half and putting her face in front of Anna's. She was a large-boned, loose-limbed woman who was almost as familiar with the process of making a fiddle as her husband was, and a great deal more canny about the process of selling one. Her watery eyes were the color of aged wood, and her skin had the sallow tone of newly sawn ash. But she had been kind to us, and I knew it was only due to her efforts that the apprentices had decent food to eat and were not worked beyond endurance.

"*Guten Tag,* Frau Goldschmidt," I said, "I wondered if I might have a word with my brother."

"You are not here to trade in your old fiddle for something new?" she said, winking as she did so. The Goldschmidts had been trying to persuade me to part with the Amati ever since my father died, had offered me a great deal of money for it, in fact. The question was more a matter of form now, though. They knew that the violin would never leave our family, except in the direst of circumstances. "I'll look after little Anna here while you go into the workshop," she said. "It's no place for a nosy child!" She hoisted Anna up and sat her on one protruding, shelf-like hip. "Now, let's see if I can find some sweets here for the sweet."

I knew that Anna, who looked a little worried at first, would brighten up as soon as a bit of boiled sugar was given to her, and so I quickly passed through the door at the back of the shop to the atelier.

I had forgotten how much I enjoyed the smell and sounds of the workshop. The raw wood, newly cut to size; the aromatic varnishes; the squeaky, hollow sound of the planes; faint odors of human sweat mixed with everything. It was all permeated with an air of deep concentration and care. The life of an apprentice to any trade was grueling. Here, though, I sensed that the apprentices felt themselves fortunate to be overworked, underfed, and treated almost like slaves.

"Well! If it isn't the lady violinist!" Herr Goldschmidt laid down the nearly completed fiddle he had been examining, took off his spectacles and advanced toward me with his hand outstretched. I took it and curtsied, at the same time glancing around to see Toby, who stood at his workbench towards the back, a huge smile on his face. He didn't dare say anything or leave his bench without permission from Herr Goldschmidt.

"Herr Goldschmidt, I was wondering if I might have a private word with my brother. I have important family news to give him."

"News that could not wait a few days until Sunday? It must be important indeed!" He turned and spoke to my brother. "Tobias! Leave that aside. I have an errand for you. Take this bow to Herr Kimmelwort." He scribbled an address on a scrap of paper with a bit of charcoal that served as a pencil.

I knew that the luthier's jocular tone hid a criticism, and that Toby might be punished by being made to work extra hard until his Sunday off in two days, or kept late before being allowed to go home so that he missed dinner. But Herr Goldschmidt, said Toby, did not beat his apprentices as some masters did. That was something at least.

Toby kissed me and took the package from his master. "Is Mama well?" he asked.

"Yes, she is well. And Greta. Anna is in the shop. We can all walk together," I said.

Once we had collected our sticky-fingered little sister from Frau Goldschmidt's care and stepped out into the bustling morning streets, I gave Toby the news of Mama's coming remarriage.

"To Herr van Swieten? You are certain?" he said. His reaction surprised me. I had expected him to be shocked at the idea of our mother marrying at all rather than at the identity of the person she had chosen to marry. "But of course, she should marry," he said, surprising me still more.

"Why?" I asked. "Why should our mother marry?"

Toby stopped where he was and looked deeply into my eyes. How tall he has grown, I thought, remembering the diminutive, eight-year-old boy I had delivered to the luthier to begin his apprenticeship nearly two years ago. Now, although his build was still slight, we could look each other straight in the eye.

"She should marry because she is young, and because she needs a man to take care of her." Toby stood even straighter as he said these words, lifting his chin and trying to make his voice sound commanding and older.

"I don't see why," I said, "We are doing quite well. I bring home enough money from my teaching and copying and playing for us to live almost as well as we lived when Papa was alive."

"Come now *Schwester*! Even I know why, and I'm much younger than you." Toby asked.

"I *do* know why," I said, the anger I had suppressed while I was in my mother's presence welling up and creeping into my voice, "I see it all too clearly. You're just like everyone else. What have they done to you in that workshop? You used to be my friend." Having Toby take my mother's side was just the same as Zoltán making me promise him I would not continue my investigations. What was everyone hiding from me? I felt as if all the people around me knew something I did not, that they had a huge secret among them, a whole hidden castle of knowledge that they barred me from entering because I was a girl. Toby had always depended on me, looked to me to lead him and teach him. Now here he was acting like all the others.

Tall or not, he was just a boy! I pulled Anna toward me and scooped her up so I could walk faster. She wriggled like an eel, pushing against me to get down, but I held onto her with all my strength and marched off I knew not where.

"Wait!" Toby called, hurrying to keep up, although once he had overtaken my sudden burst of speed, his long strides more than matched my own and he was hardly out of breath. "What's the matter with you? Don't you think Mama deserves to be happy again?"

"Happy? Do you really think marrying that old man will make her happy?" My voice was shrill and I knew it. People turned and stared at us.

"Mama's not like you," he said, trying to drag my tone of voice down with his own by speaking quietly and slowly.

"Tell me something else I don't know," I said. Now Anna was crying with frustration. "Hush!" I said to her, losing patience. Toby handed me the wrapped violin bow, took Anna from my arms and swung her up to sit on his shoulder. She quieted instantly. "Besides, it will ruin everything, and I've just started to figure out about this murder, and—"

"What?" Toby said, reaching his free hand out to take hold of my arm and stop me. "What did you say?"

He sounded as angry as he ever did, which wasn't very. But I decided that—contrary to what I'd thought that morning—I would not talk to Toby about everything and see if he had heard any rumors that might be helpful to me, I would not make the mistake of telling him the story and being disbelieved and discourage by my own younger brother. "Never mind. It doesn't concern you."

"I think you'd better say, now that you've mentioned it."

"No, I need tell you nothing at all. Your attitude surprises me. I'll take Anna home. Besides, your errand is in the other direction."

I handed him the parcel and held my arms out for Anna, putting her on her own feet again but keeping the straps of the harness short so she wouldn't stray.

"Don't let's quarrel," Toby said, a look of genuine sadness in his eyes. "Why do you think I'm against you?"

Why indeed? I realized I had reacted out of all proportion to what he had actually said. Toby was entitled to his own opinion, and surrounded by men in the workshop, how could he avoid coming to think as they did? Of course a woman on her own must desire the care of a man. It was natural. Toby was not part of some devilish conspiracy to prevent me finding out what had happened on the road from the Augarten that night. He was just my little brother, who was trying hard to act as though he were the head of the family, even though he spent weeks away from us tied to an apprentice's bench. I decided I ought to give him a chance to redeem himself in my eyes. I fished the tattered paper from my pocket and handed it to him. "If you can tell me what these marks mean, I shall then confide everything to you."

"And if I can't?"

"Then it won't matter anyway," I said, all at once exhausted with the effort of disagreeing and being angry.

Toby kissed Anna and then me, and I watched his lanky, rhythmic walk as he continued down the street to complete his errand.

CHAPTER SIXTEEN

I delivered a tired and cross Anna back into Greta's hands in time for her morning nap, and immediately got my fiddle and left the apartment again.

"Don't forget! Gottfried expects you at two!" my mother's voice called after me from within her bedroom.

Gottfried. God's Joy. Not mine, however. If we went to live with this old man in his palace apartments, it would put an end to my ability to come and go as I pleased. I would be subjected to eternal visiting, and have to sit at home while suitors were trotted out in front of me one by one to look me over. I hoped he would not give me a dowry. The last thing I wanted was for material gain to be the lure that drew a continuous stream of young men to my door.

I had a few hours to pass as I wished before the appointed hour. My intention was to use some of that time to practice in my cabinet room at the Palais Esterhazy. I went directly there, freed the Amati from its case, and began my warm-up exercises.

But the kind of concentration required for serious practice was beyond my ability just then. Too many disturbing thoughts swirled in my head. Most of all, I kept returning to the concert at the Arnstein's apartment, to Mirela and the captain, and to Sophie—seeing me and recognizing me, I was certain. And then, there was Zoltán. The memory of his arms around me gave me alternate feelings of deep pleasure and faint sickness. How could he think well of me? I was dressed as a young man and leading a scandalous double life. I was meddling where I had no business meddling.

And I was not an honorable person. My treatment of Sophie had been despicable. I wanted to run to them and beg their forgiveness, but I knew the door would be closed to me. I had to do something, though. I could not concentrate.

With regret I gave up on my practicing for the time being and put away my violin. The noon bells had just rung out over the city. If I hurried, I could seek out Mirela. At least I thought I could depend upon her not to judge me harshly, and I was desperate to know how she had managed to convince Captain Bauer to take her to the Arnsteins' party—and how Captain Bauer himself happened to be among the invited guests.

It was a fine day, and I arrived at Mirela's hut without dirtying my dress—it was essential to remain decent if I was to present myself to my future stepfather in a little over an hour. Mirela made a fragrant, herbal tea that we sipped while sitting on a rug outside her door. The Roma children ran about playing games while the women did their washing in the brown river—I did not know how they managed to avoid making their clothes look dirtier after such an exercise.

"So, tell me what happened. I have to know everything."

"Your Captain Bauer was not so easy to find. First I borrowed some clothing from Alida. Then I went to the Hussars' stable—I have a friend there who knows everyone—and he was not acquainted with this fellow, but suggested I go to the officers' mess and inquire. The wealthier officers often send their servants to the stable, and they are better known than the officers themselves.

"So I went to the mess and inquired there. The porter was very rude, but a fine looking fellow who happened to be passing stopped and told me he knew where to find Captain von Bauer, and that he would take me there himself.

"I said, 'Oh, no need kind sir. I am his cousin and I have a letter for him.' Then he said, 'I did not know my friend had such a beautiful cousin,' and he tried to persuade me to stay with him, but I told him 'No,' and begged him simply for the address, which he gave me eventually."

Mirela paused in her narration, and I was afraid to ask what transpired before he "eventually" gave her the address. "So, where did you go?"

"It was the oddest thing. Your Captain-Count does not inhabit very elegant quarters. The address was in the poorest part of the city. Right next to a Jewish house."

A Jewish house? Could this be how Captain Bauer knew Frau Bachmann? But why would someone who was a captain of the Hussars and a noble choose to live in such an unfashionable neighborhood? "And?" I asked, impatient for her to continue.

"I decided not to seek him out in his lodgings. Something told me he would not take kindly to it. So I waited until I saw him emerge and I followed him. Then it was simple—a stumble, a turned ankle—you know what gentlemen are like."

"And so you threw yourself at him! But how did you come to be at the Arnsteins?"

"I told him I was a singer from Italy, and that I had been hoping to gain an introduction to Signore Mozart so that I might sing for him."

Mirela's brazen lies went so far beyond anything I could ever fathom saying that sometimes she took my breath away. And yet, even when she lied she was more wholly herself than I was myself every day, pretending to be a boy so that I could fulfill my secret dreams. I had no right to judge her. "And how did the captain know about the Arnsteins' party?" I asked, just beginning to tie up a few dangling threads, to make some connections that started to make sense.

"Well, it seems a neighbor of his is a flutist, and is acquainted with the Arnsteins. He got him an invitation." The smile of triumph that spread across her face reminded me of my little sister Anna's expression when she discovered a store of sweets that Greta had hidden.

"A flutist. Did he mention a name?"

"I did not like to ask. It seemed clear from the way he told me that he didn't want to say."

"If only you had pressed him!"

"I said I did not ask, but I did not say I remained ignorant."

Mirela infuriated me when she teased me. I refused to give her the satisfaction of pleading with her to tell me.

"I simply said that I had heard of a wonderful flutist by the name of Bachmann, and asked if he would be there too. Your captain went quite completely white, like *Spaetzle*. I know he wanted to ask me how I had heard of Bachmann but he did not. And the rest you know."

I didn't, in fact, know the rest. But I did know not to inquire too closely concerning what happened between Captain Bauer and Mirela after I left the party. "I suspect the Bachmanns live quite near the captain, from your description. Can you give me his address?"

"You have not asked if I discovered where the captain gets his information."

Now she really was making me impatient. "All right, tell me and be quick about it," I said, not very graciously.

Mirela lifted her impossible nose in the air and said, "You may think such a thing is unimportant, but I have found that it is best to be as informed as possible. I never know when I will need certain facts and names at my fingertips."

"I'm sorry, of course. What can you tell me?" I struggled to keep the edge out of my voice.

"Only that he intimated strongly that he had someone with the very closest connections to the police working for him. Someone no one would ever expect. When I asked him why, he replied, 'Because my spy is about as threatening as a Titmouse.' Then I could not think of a way to get anything else out of him without showing too much interest."

I wasn't certain why she thought this information was so important. Of course Captain Bauer would have contacts with the police. I had met him at the police headquarters after all.

Once Mirela was satisfied that she had delivered the intelligence I needed, I convinced her to describe the location of the building where Captain Bauer lived. I assumed once I was there that a few inquiries would lead me to the Bachmann's residence. The trick would be to avoid the captain. In the meantime, I had to go and visit Herr van Swieten at the Imperial Library. What would I say to him? What would he say to me? I could not pretend that I was happy about the impending change to our lives. I had not chosen it.

I'm afraid I was not in the most gracious mood by the time I reached the Hofburg and gave my name to the porter at the door leading to the library, in the wing where Herr van Swieten had his apartment. He walked away at a measured pace, making hardly a sound with his highly polished boots. What seemed ages later the old man returned to me and said with a deep voice and precise pronunciation, "The Prefect will see you now."

For some reason Herr van Swieten elected to receive me in the grand reading room of the library. Perhaps it was because he knew it would make me feel small. The enormous chamber was lined to a height of three floors with glass-encased shelves of books. A system of staircases and ladders led to narrow galleries that would allow a person who was not afraid to climb them access to the enormous collection. A magnificent painting decorated the ceiling, and I found myself craning my neck to look at it as I walked in.

"You must be Theresa."

I quickly adjusted my view to straight ahead of me and saw a man well advanced in years, but still trim and well-groomed walking toward me with his hand outstretched. He had clearly never been handsome, yet he had open, friendly brown eyes that smiled along with his mouth.

"Your Mama has told me such a great deal about you. She says you are very musical, and that you play the violin extremely well."

I had to admit, I was surprised that my mother had said even that much. I always assumed she tried to hide those things about me. I was unaccountably vexed that he knew even these few facts and reacted rather uncharitably, I'm afraid. "Yes," I said, "and did she tell you that I earn our living teaching and copying music?" I thought that would be shocking enough, without telling him that I also performed incognito in some of the finest orchestras in Vienna.

"She mentioned something of the kind. As a music copyist, perhaps you would be interested in seeing some manuscripts I have here, by a very famous musician?"

He was generous to ignore the provocation in my remark, and continued speaking as he started toward a large, ornate chest with long, flat drawers. As he reached it he tugged on a chain that was attached to his belt. On its other end was a tiny key and some sort of charm I could not see from where I stood. Curiosity overcame my reticence and I moved toward him. At least, I thought, he did not ply me with platitudes about how much he cared for my mother and what a happy family we would be. That would have been unbearable.

"Would you kindly help me, Mademoiselle Schurman?" he asked, easing out one of the drawers and then taking hold of a stack of fragile looking music manuscripts. To my surprise he turned and handed them to me. "If you would take these and lay them gently on the table over there, I shall lock up again."

I did as he said, but could not resist gazing at what I held in my hands and in the process nearly bumping into a chair that was in the way. My cargo was safe, though—which was a very good thing. I had managed to read the elaborate *Fraktur* script and made out the words: it was a cantata, by Johann Sebastian Bach, in the Name of God.

I hardly noticed that Herr van Swieten had come up to stand next to me, and when he spoke his voice startled me. "Yes, it is by the hand of the great Bach himself. The supreme master of the art of counterpoint. I have learned at his feet, although I never met the man."

"You are a composer?" I asked, surprised that my mother hadn't mentioned this fact.

"A very humble one. I do not have the same gifts as your godfather Haydn, say, or young Herr Mozart."

We spent about half an hour perusing the manuscript. It thrilled me to see how Bach had worked things out, trying this and that, then scratching out what he didn't like and settling on something that was ultimately perfect.

Once we leafed through the entire cantata, Herr van Swieten pulled on another chain in his pocket, one that terminated in a handsome gold pocket watch, and after peering at it said, "Shall we have a drink of chocolate?"

Again without waiting for me to reply he tucked the watch away, took up the manuscript and walked over to the drawers.

"How foolish of me. I forgot to unlock. Would you . . ." He nodded toward the chain dangling from his waistcoat, the one that held the key. I pulled it out of his pocket and fitted the key into the keyhole in the drawer.

Then I noticed the charm. I had been too far away to recognize it before, but now I saw that it was identical to the design I had copied from the trunk of the Linden tree—at least, the part that had the open eye enclosed in a triangle. I tried to cover up my surprise in a cough, and did not have time to examine it closely as he tucked the key and the charm away in the tiny pocket in his waistcoat immediately after he replaced the manuscripts in their drawer.

"Now, our chocolate. Follow me."

At first I thought Herr van Swieten had taken leave of his senses and was leading me directly into one of the bookcases in the wall. But soon it became obvious that the one we were headed for had a false front, and he pressed a little spring that opened a door into a cozy office furnished with a desk, a table and two chairs. The table had already been laid with a steaming pot of chocolate and two delicate porcelain cups. The cabinet had two windows that looked out over the busy street, and another door that obviously led to other offices in the building.

I don't even remember everything we talked about, but I found myself liking this man much more than I expected I would. He had been to so many places, done so many things. He was Dutch, and had begun as our late empress's medical advisor, so perhaps for that reason he was not so deferential and self-contained as the Viennese, nor so set in his expectations of young women. He looked me straight in the eye when he spoke to me and answered my questions eagerly. Perhaps that was why I let down my guard and pushed my inquiries in a direction that surprised even me with its frankness.

"Why do you want to marry my mother?" was the first ill-advised query that leapt out of my mouth before I had the good sense to stop myself.

He did not answer right away, but thought for a moment before responding with the same directness as if I had asked him about how he had come by one of the rare volumes in the library. "I believe we can help and comfort each other. It's a lonely business, growing older. And it's a lonely business being a widow, and a frightening one unless one is of vast independent means."

"But she has us!" I protested, "Not that you are not a perfectly respectable gentleman whose acquaintance I am very pleased to make, but . . ." I didn't know what to say. This thing that seemed so obvious to me was clearly only obvious to me. "How came you to know her?" I then asked, realizing suddenly that this question was part of what disturbed me so about the whole matter. My mother had been determinedly reclusive since Anna's birth. She mainly stayed in her room—at least, when I was at home she did.

"We met at tea with the Lady Alida Varga."

"You wha—" I decided it wouldn't do to admit that I had no idea my mother had ever even been to tea with Alida. "I mean, when?"

"Some months ago. Elisabeth—your mother—was returning a visit, I recall. I thought she was beautiful. There is much of her in you."

Of course, I had done all I could to ensure that I spent as little time as possible at home. My mother could be entertaining half of Vienna in my absence and I might not know it. I was caught off balance by these revelations, and before I considered the consequences carefully, found myself asking the other question that had been burning on my lips since I had unlocked the case to return the rare music manuscripts to their protective enclosure. "What does the symbol on your key chain mean?"

He appeared startled by my question. He must not have expected such a sudden turn in my thoughts. He shook his head as if to clear it of something then pulled the key and its charm out of his pocket and held it out to me. "You mean, this one?" I nodded. "It's the all-seeing eye of justice over all men. A symbol that is very important to a certain brotherhood of philosophical men, and by which we all know one another."

He answered so simply and without evasion that I didn't dare push my line of questioning further by asking, *Which brotherhood? Who belongs to it? What does it mean? Why would I have found those symbols on the tree near where a man was murdered, as well as in the Arnstein's house?*

I was saved from having to decide what to say next by the bells of St. Stephen's tolling the hour of four. "I must go," I said and stood. I extended my hand to the prefect, but instead of taking it, he took hold of my shoulders and kissed me on both cheeks.

"I hope we shall be good friends," he said, and I felt that he meant it. "I should like to hear you play the violin sometime."

A footman showed me out into the crisp, autumn afternoon. I did not know what to do and stood for a moment on the street, watching the people rushing back and forth attending to their daily business. I had so wanted to detest this man who was trying to step into my father's place in the family, and he had completely disarmed me with his courtesy and sincerity. I walked slowly back to the Palais Esterhazy, armed now with at least a little knowledge, and very, very confused.

Chapter Seventeen

Meeting Herr van Swieten had an odd, calming effect on me. I found that I could concentrate on my violin practice more fully than I had for days. I wasn't certain exactly why my feeling of oppression had lifted. Perhaps it was that I realized that the man who had chosen to marry my mother might actually let me continue as I was, that he would not try to force his will upon our household. Perhaps it was that he had told me something concrete and real about one tiny aspect of this investigation I appeared to be making without the help of police, guards, or anyone with any official influence.

Whatever the reason, it was vital that I make the most of my private time to work before the prince's court returned to Vienna at the beginning of November, when not only would my performance schedule become very busy, but my convenient little cabinet room would be taken over for other uses as necessary. The prince and his household generally remained in Vienna through the winter months and departed for Esterhaza after Easter, although my Godfather had written that his princely employer was considering extending his stays in the country. Who could blame him? Now that the emperor did not keep much of a court in Vienna, the nobles who lived there ended up putting on all the lavish entertainments and parties at their own expense, with the emperor himself more often than not guest of honor. I had overheard people talking on several occasions about the complaints of the Auerspergs, the Khevenhullers, the Lobkowitzes and many others that this compulsory entertaining drained their resources. I myself thought it rather clever of Joseph II, who was a widower and himself not much given to pomp and show. Besides, I had a fondness for the emperor because of his intervention in Danior's trial and my uncle's banishment.

Hunger eventually forced me to lay down my fiddle and release the tension on the hairs of my bow. I would have to return home to eat. Although I had enough money in my purse to purchase a meal at a coffee shop, I didn't dare enter one alone dressed as myself. Young ladies did not do so. I sometimes went with Mirela, if she were not all got up in her Gypsy togs, but Mirela was at home. Or so I thought.

In any case, I decided that I was not so hungry that I couldn't take a circuitous route back to our apartment, a route that would take me through the neighborhood of the address Mirela had given me earlier, where Captain Bauer and Frau Bachmann lived.

Burdened with my fiddle case and reams of unanswered questions, I set out through the twilit streets, skirting the lamplighters with their long tapers and dodging carriages full of gaily dressed people going to the theater or to private assemblies and parties. Although the fashionable set in the city appeared to be engaged in a flurry of activity, the principal noble households were still enjoying the hunting at their country estates and the demand for musicians was not enough to keep me employed every evening at that time of year. During the Christmas season and all the way through Carnival it would be a different matter. Then I would sometimes have to decline work so that my mother would not become too suspicious.

I'm not certain why I hadn't made the connection before—perhaps it was because the name of the street was not familiar to me—but in going to look for Frau Bachmann, I found myself once again in the neighborhood where I had been summoned to a mysterious rehearsal that never took place, and where a huge, ferocious cat had stalked me through endless, twisting corridors. There were fewer street lamps in this poor neighborhood, I noticed, and the shadows deepened more quickly here. The narrow alleyways between houses—like the one I had ventured down that led me into that odd house—made deep gashes in the taut skin of the city. I half expected to see the dark ooze out like congealed blood onto the cobbles. I thought about giving up my project and returning home. But something made me press on.

The address Mirela had given me took me to a small house squeezed between two much larger structures. Its narrow, street-level door had at one time been painted some dark color, but was now peeling to reveal time-blackened wood beneath. There were two barred half-moon windows close to the ground, which gave the effect that the building was an emaciated lady peeking up from below the level of the street, the floors above like a crumbling headdress.

Yet the house was most certainly not deserted. I could see a glow from around the shutters that covered two windows on the second floor, and the door stood slightly ajar to reveal welcoming candle glow in the vestibule.

Something drew me to that door. A day ago I might not have dared to proceed, but armed now with a morsel of knowledge about one item that connected several threads of this bizarre mystery, I felt more secure. Herr von Gluck, the captain, the Arnsteins, Herr van Swieten and apparently even Zoltán knew what the symbols I had found meant, and now I knew too. Yet all but one of them was unwilling to tell me. What could be the great mystery in a brotherhood of like-minded men?

I was about to enter the vestibule of the dilapidated building when something stopped me where I stood, fixing me to my spot like a lightning bolt sent from the heavens. The mournful, sweet sound of a flute being played with consummate artistry sailed out from the windows above me and filled the evening air.

There was no time to waste. I gathered my skirts in one hand, tucked my violin under my other arm and flew through the door and up two flights of narrow wooden steps, the sound of the flute drawing me forward and growing louder and more immediately present as I neared the door that led to an apartment at the front of the house.

I hardly paused to collect myself before knocking. "Hello, I want to speak with you. I am a friend—we met the other day!" I called in breathless gasps, knocking all the while. The flute playing had stopped with my first tap, and I was sorry to interrupt such music, but other matters were far more pressing. I heard voices behind the door, sounds of shushing, and then the light step of a lady coming toward me. The door opened a few inches and I recognized the eyes of Frau Bachmann peering out, a crease of worry between them.

"Frau Bachmann, I beg you. I must apologize for my unforgivable behavior the other day, but I had reasons, and I need to talk to you."

"Mademoiselle!" she exclaimed in a surprised whisper. "How did you—" She cast a glance over her shoulder as if looking to see if someone were there, then turned back. "You may as well come in. I'm afraid I can offer you no refreshments."

She opened the door and led me into an apartment I would have taken for unfurnished if I did not know she inhabited it. All the parlor contained was a bare wooden table and two straight-backed chairs, a tiny stove in the corner that would never produce enough heat to prevent freezing in the winter time, a small clavier and a wooden stand with music upon it. A flute lay across the table. It looked so incongruous there, not for being a musical instrument in an otherwise empty room, but for being as beautiful and fine a flute as I had ever seen. The keys were burnished gold, and the wood of the barrel dark and smooth. I thought perhaps it was made of ebony.

I glanced around the room, expecting to see someone else there who must have been playing when I arrived. There was no one, of course, only a door leading to what was likely a small room next to the stairwell. I imagined whoever else I had heard could be hiding in there now. "You were not alone just now. I heard music. Beautiful playing," I said.

Frau Bachmann crossed her arms over her thin chest. "You of all people, Mademoiselle, should know that musicians do not all look alike."

So, it had been Frau Bachmann herself who played the flute with such artistry. I was so ashamed of my assumption that it must have been a man, that I wished I had never entered the room. "Of course, how foolish of me. You are a wonderful musician." For a moment, my discomfort overshadowed the fact that in addition to music I had heard two voices. When I recalled that fact it occurred to me to wonder if she was telling me the truth. She had the lips of a flutist, full and well shaped. And they were rosy, and there was a red mark on her chin as if she had just been playing. But who had been with her in that room only moments before?

"You have questions. As well you might," Frau Bachmann said, gesturing toward one of the chairs. I sat, laying my violin case down on the ground.

I had achieved a measure of success already that day by being direct with Herr van Swieten, so I decided I should try the same approach again. "My first question is—I mean—whether or not it was you playing, you were not alone just now. I heard voices."

"I guessed you were observant. Yes, there was someone else here."

She made no move to call anyone, nor did she suggest that she intended to tell me who her guest had been. I thought I saw the light of amusement in her eyes. This troubled me, in a woman who only a day or two ago had been distraught about her husband's unexplained disappearance. "And your husband, Frau Bachmann. Has he returned home?"

A shadow passed across her eyes. It was no more than a momentary darkening in the very depths of her pupils. "My husband is well. I beg you not to trouble yourself about him any longer."

I thought I saw the tiniest shift of her gaze toward the door. A moment later I heard quick footsteps and another door opening and closing, then more footsteps in the hallway. I knew I should be polite, that I should simply bow to Frau Bachmann and leave. Clearly she did not want my interference. But after her distress the other day, after I had become so worked up and convinced that her husband and the dead man near the Augarten were one and the same person, I felt I had a right to some assurances, that I was entitled to be inquisitive for a brief while longer at least. Especially if her husband were indeed safely returned to her, and had not been the man who was attacked. The footsteps outside now approached her door and stopped.

Before she could go there herself, I stood, took three strides to the door and flung it open.

"Herr Mozart!" I said, so astonished that a single breath could have pushed me over.

The young composer stood there in a rose satin evening coat and powdered bob wig, a portfolio of music under his arm, clearly on his way to a performance. He smiled at me. "I don't believe I have had the pleasure."

Of course, he had met me as Thomas Weissbrot, and would not recognize me now as Theresa Schurman. In an instant Frau Bachmann was at my side. "Amadé, this is the young lady who has been so kind and concerned about Abraham. I have told her she need worry no longer, that he is out of danger."

Frau Bachmann and Herr Mozart exchanged a glance that meant something, and I felt she had chosen her words very carefully when she introduced me, as if she meant to prevent him giving anything away and at the same time wanted to convey a great deal of informa-

tion quickly. She had been very clever. Without being extremely im-
polite, I could not do anything but smile and say my goodbyes. "I am
pleased to meet you at last, Herr Mozart. I am Theresa Schurmann.
My father was a violinist under Haydn's direction. I hear that you are
hoping to present an opera at the Burgtheater." I tried to keep my
voice from sounding as nervous as I felt. "I hope I shall be fortunate
enough to be present for that great occasion."

"God—and Herr Thorwart—willing, Mademoiselle," he replied
with a bow.

Thorwart. His name again. I had not realized that one person
could have such control over the fate of the musicians in Vienna,
especially since he was only the finance director of the theater, and
there were others who had a say in the programs.

"Surely he will recognize your ability," I said, "as all the really
musical people in Vienna have already done."

"If it were only ability that he had to recognize, I would not fear
for an instant," Mozart said. "But he has set himself against me, for
other reasons. However, we are doing our best with the man."

Frau Bachmann shot Mozart another warning glance, but made
no move to invite me to stay, rather hinting by standing next to me
near the door that I should depart. I fetched my violin and prepared to
go, more questions in my mind than I when I arrived.

"You are a violinist?" Herr Mozart said, surprise in his voice.

"Yes," I answered.

"My sister plays the violin and the pianoforte, but she rarely
plays the violin any more. Papa objects. I am surprised that you are
permitted."

"My papa did not object, and in fact he taught me," I said. "My
mother would rather I stayed at home, but since we need the income I
earn from my music, she keeps her opinions to herself."

"You are very fortunate." He turned to Frau Bachmann. "I have some time before my engagement this evening. Perhaps we could make some music together? All three of us? I can play the clavier."

His face was so eager. Could it have been Mozart who had been there, listening to Frau Bachmann before, and who had left by a back door and reappeared as if for the first time? He obviously knew how supremely talented she was. I looked at Frau Bachmann. She seemed doubtful, as if she wished she could say something right out but was afraid.

My initial reaction of sheer pleasure at the thought of an intimate musical interlude with these two superior musicians was soon superseded by panic. Mozart had played my Amati. He would be certain to recognize it if I took it from its case. I did not want to have to explain any more than was necessary at that moment. I would have to let the opportunity slip by. "Unfortunately I am expected at home," I said. *And besides,* I thought, *you would no doubt be frustrated and disappointed at my abilities.* It was all right to hide in an orchestra, to be swept along with everyone else. I was not ready to expose my many shortcomings to Herr Mozart, even in such a secluded setting.

Gottverdammt, I muttered to myself as I left Frau Bachmann's apartment.

CHAPTER EIGHTEEN

I had not walked ten paces in the direction of home before I saw something that stopped me cold. Just turning the corner onto the street where Frau Bachmann lived were Captain Bauer and Mirela, walking arm in arm. I was certain they hadn't yet seen me. They were clearly deeply engrossed in one another. I stepped quickly back into the shadows and watched them approach.

If it had been in any other neighborhood, hiding like that would have been impossible. But here, where the shadows were deep and plentiful and the population hidden away and not spilling onto the street as they headed out to evening entertainments, I felt as if I could have remained concealed until the next morning if I chose to.

The couple approached. I began to hear a few words, peppered with Mirela's bewitching laughter.

"Captain, you tease me!" she said. I was astounded that she could so disguise her accent, which, when she allowed it to be—for instance, whenever she told fortunes for curious tourists in her hut in the Gypsy camp—could be very strong. Now she sounded like a Viennese aristocrat. She had a good ear. If she had been taught, she might have been an exceptional musician.

"Tease you!" Captain Bauer exclaimed. "You as much as told me that you are bored with the usual entertainments and wish for a new sensation. You virtually accused me of being always on safe ground. You challenged me to show you something that will at once thrill and terrify you, and hinted that there is some great reward in your gift if I succeed—if that is not teasing, then I do not understand the meaning of the word."

He stopped her and pulled her to him, lacing his arms around her and embracing her so that he practically lifted her off her feet. He lowered his face to hers. She turned aside in a mock coy gesture at the last moment.

"Captain! You take advantage of our solitude." She pushed him away, but in a manner that didn't say *no* so much as *not now*.

This little scene had been enacted nearly opposite to where I was hiding. Mirela and the Captain continued their stroll and rounded the next corner, heading in the direction of the house I had been lured to for the mysterious rehearsal the day before. My stomach growled. I was hungry for the dinner I knew awaited me at home. But I was desperate to know what Mirela was up to. When I had seen her earlier she had not told me that she meant to meet the captain later. She was keeping secrets from me. I would be more than justified in sneaking around after her.

Although there weren't very many people about, I was uncomfortably aware that the few there were all noticed me. It cannot have been the usual thing to see a decently dressed young lady by herself with a violin case in her hands. I had to pretend I knew where I was going, and at the same time stay far enough behind Mirela and the captain so that they would not realize they were being followed. I was confident that the captain wouldn't notice. Mirela, though, had an uncanny ability to sense everything around her. It was what made her such a successful fortune teller. She would pick up clues from details of dress and modes of expression and make guesses that were convincingly near the truth to amaze her duped customers.

I followed discreetly as they wound all around the dingy quarter until I was quite disoriented. I had the feeling I had passed the same buildings several times, but certain details made them appear just different enough that I doubted myself.

After what seemed a very long time, Mirela and the captain stopped in front of what had once clearly been a grand structure, perhaps even a church from some distant time past, but was now dilapidated. It had enormous double doors that came to a point where they met at the top, exactly like those of the house I had been to the day before. The doors were so huge, in fact, that there was a smaller door cut out of one of them, tall enough for the captain to pass through without stooping, and yet it could have been duplicated one and a half more times before the height of the main door was exhausted. Such doors must lead—or have led—into a massive chamber. How could a space so large exist in Vienna and I not know about it, even if it had been carved up into smaller ones by now?

I had taken refuge in the shadows again down a way and opposite the building. I was too distant to hear anything, but I saw Captain Bauer raise the bronze knocker on the small door and tap in a deliberate pattern: two quick knocks followed by three slower ones, spaced out at regular intervals. They waited in silence. I could feel Mirela's calculations from where I stood. I knew she would be debating whether she dared enter a place she did not know, and put all her trust in a man I had told her had some hidden motivation for his actions. When the door opened quickly to let them inside, the captain cast a glance over his shoulder to ensure that no one saw them, then took hold of Mirela's arm, and although he didn't precisely push her in, made it impossible for her not to precede him through.

I left my sheltered spot and walked along until I was opposite the door. The street was completely deserted. I could hear a horse clopping on the other side of the houses behind me, and at the end of the street, trudging along with his gaze focused on the ground, a laborer with a spade resting on his shoulder passed on his way home for the evening.

I considered presenting myself at the door, using the same knock I had witnessed Captain Bauer use to gain admittance. But as soon as the door opened, they would see I was someone unknown to them.

As so often was the case, a narrow alleyway separated the building with the huge doors from the one next to it, which I noted was in a state of disrepair so great that it appeared uninhabited, with gaping holes where the windows had been and roof beams exposed to the sky—extremely unusual for Vienna, where space was coveted and all available living quarters patched together and occupied as soon as they fell vacant. I had wandered down another such alleyway the day before and found myself a prisoner, however briefly. Yet here at least I knew that Mirela was inside. She would not be one to be tricked into captivity. I hoped.

I decided that exploring could do no harm. I would take more care this time than I had the last. I first looked around to make sure I was still alone, then darted across the street into the obscurity of the alleyway.

At that time of day, the sun had set but its light was not quite extinguished. Yet instead of shedding illumination on the world, this pallid glow blurred the edges of things and created deceptive shapes and contours. And in the space between these buildings, none of the feeble twilight penetrated. I advanced only a short way before I realized that I was virtually in premature darkness, and had no way of telling what lay between me and the exit at the other end. As if to prove how foolish an enterprise I had embarked upon, a mangy, black cat slunk past me, hissing as it went, rounding the corner of the building with liquid movements and disappearing as if it had been nothing more than a phantom.

The alley was so narrow that two people could not have walked next to each other in it, and I felt the awkward bulk of my violin case as a hindrance and knew that my dress could easily be torn and spoiled by catching on a nail or a splinter of wood. That should have been enough to make me give up the project. But I had an uneasy feeling about Mirela. She was canny, but sometimes she relied too heavily on her own cleverness, placing herself in situations that contained more danger than she realized because she assumed she would be able to talk or connive her way out of them.

I paused to get my bearings and let my eyes become accustomed to the dark. After a few moments, I saw the outline of a shutter against the wall of the building I wanted to enter, or at the very least see into. I picked my way toward it, my violin clutched to me. I wished I could have had the new case with the strap that Toby had fashioned, but that was the case for my professional life, and it stayed at the Palais Ester-hazy to be used on occasions when I was dressed as a young man.

The shutter was fastened closed from the inside, but the hinge that held it to the window frame was rusty and the wood its screws clung to rotting. I could easily lift one corner of it away and peer in. What I saw was so unexpected I nearly let the shutter fall back with a clatter.

A blinding light shone from within the building. Having adjusted my eyes to the dark only recently, it took some time before my eyes could gaze upon what was inside without pain.

The room was as huge and grand as the doors suggested it would be, and its walls were leafed in gold and splashed with brilliant colors, of which the most prominent was blue. Although my line of vision was only a foot or so above floor level on the inside, I had a comprehensive view of the interior. Every surface shone with glowing images, like a church, except the images were not familiar to me. No Stations of the Cross or Lives of the Saints. The cast of characters in the pictures was dressed in a bizarre combination of modern fashions and ancient robes. A figure of an old man with a long beard, who might have been God in a church but who looked far too human to be a divinity, stretched out his arms to embrace all the men around him.

Men. I had thought there was something odd about these pictures. Even in church, many of the saints and certainly the Virgin was a woman.

I didn't have much time to ponder this oddity. In the distance I heard singing. It wasn't so much singing as chanting, like the monks who once a year paraded through the streets with the Host. Perhaps this was the chapel of a monastery. But which one?

As I watched, a door on the opposite side of the grand room opened, and a procession did indeed enter. But the men were definitely not monks. They wore splendid embroidered robes shot through with gold thread. Their garments dazzled my eyes almost as much as the walls around them. I had the feeling I was witnessing something very private and secret despite its pomp, but I could not force myself to look away. I watched as the file of about twenty men of different ages, shapes and sizes entered. I only knew they were men because of their shoes, though, because their faces were all covered with masks.

These robed men took up positions by the walls, blending in with their splendor, and continued to chant. I thought the procession had finished, but the door opened again, and this time admitted an even more splendidly arrayed figure with a towering headdress, carrying a gilded hammer in one hand and some other sort of tool in the other. But what astounded me and nearly made me drop the shutter with a bang against the window frame was the embroidery on his robe. It was there: the eye inside the triangle, only now I could see that the triangle had substance. It was a pyramid.

Van Swieten had said this was the symbol of a brotherhood of men. Here, then, must be that brotherhood having some kind of meeting. I don't quite know why, but I shivered.

The leader walked forward to the center of the room and turned so that he was flanked on both sides by the ranks of the men who had preceded him into the space. He lifted his hand and the chanting ceased.

"We are gathered today to welcome an apprentice unto our midst. Bring the entering apprentice forth." The man's speech was booming and hollow, as if it came not from his body but from a cavern deep below him. The way he phrased his words was very elaborate and quaint, old-fashioned, yet they were words I had never heard before. They were solemn and formulaic, liturgical almost, but containing a strange mixture of references to biblical passages—mostly having to do with King Solomon's temple—and tools for building. I found it difficult to attend to the precise words. The sonority of the leader's voice—who the others called Master—beguiled my attention away from the meaning of what he said.

I was unprepared, therefore, when the doors opened again to admit more men, but these had on their shoulders a platform, or bier, atop which lay a man. I could not see if he was awake or asleep until they turned and bore their burden solemnly forward to where the master stood. What I saw then made me draw my breath in sharply.

It was the man I had seen killed in the Augarten. I was absolutely certain. He was pale as death, and yet I thought I saw him breathe. Perhaps the man was dead, but why were they welcoming him as an apprentice, and not chanting the Requiem?

Before this extraordinary turn of events I had been preparing to creep away, to go home and forget all about Mirela, assuming she could take care of herself. But now I could no more depart than forget everything that had happened in the past two years.

Where had Mirela and the captain gone? And why would he bring her to this place that was evidently a sacred space where men performed a mysterious ritual?

If I went to fetch help, told Alida, Danior, or even Zoltán, what would I say? Doubtless by the time I brought them back this strange pantomime would have ended.

No, I had only one choice. I would have to enter alone, find Mirela, and discover the meaning of all this.

I slowly replaced the corner of the shutter, allowed myself a moment to adjust again to the inky blackness of the alleyway, and started walking deeper into it, looking for an open door that would lead me God knew where.

CHAPTER NINETEEN

I didn't really expect to find an easy way into the building. There was no door, as there had been the last time. No obvious door, that is. I walked frantically, quietly, up and down the alley three times before I discovered the way in. It wasn't so much a door as a hatch low to the ground that led into the space below the floor, which, as often was the case with Viennese houses, was raised above ground level. How I longed for my man's clothing then! I had dressed more elegantly than usual that day as well, for my tea with Herr van Swieten, and tearing or staining my gown would mean the destruction of my best afternoon dress. And there was the matter of the violin.

I decided in a moment that if I was captured in my quest, my appearance would make little difference, but if I succeeded and was able to creep away as silently as I came I would regret the damage to my dress—and find it difficult to explain. I unhooked my skirt from my bodice and untied my pocket hoops, turned them inside out and folded them as best I was able. I placed my clothing and the violin where I would be able to reach them once I had crawled inside, then headed feet first into the obscurity of an unknown cellar, dressed only in my chemise and under petticoat.

As I suspected, the cellar was not very deep. The beams that held the floor above me grazed the top of my head and the bottom of the hatch was at waist level. I quickly pulled my bundle of clothing and the violin after me, and rested them against the wall by my planned escape route. I kissed my fingertips and touched the violin case. "Please God let it come to no harm," I whispered.

At first, I thought I had landed in a place that was darker than the innermost coils of a French horn. Hearing was the only sense I could depend on, and my ears fed me muffled sounds above my head, and the creaking of boards as the men walked slowly here and there in their ritual. I hoped that they would continue long enough for me to make some sense of this subterranean cavity, find Mirela, and figure out why she was here with the captain.

I don't know how much time it took for my eyes to readjust to the dark, but they did eventually. As is the way with such things, what would hardly count as light under normal circumstances gradually became so obvious I might have been outdoors looking at the patterns in the stars on a moonless night. I perceived a faint glow that filtered from around squares cut in the floor above me, spaced evenly throughout the entire huge area in a rough crescent. The squares were about large enough for a man to fit through, although not too big a man, and hinged so that they would fall down into the cellar rather than lift up into the space above. I pictured the robed chanters disappearing one by one, dropping through the floor to vanish for all eternity. I had to stifle nervous laughter.

Every so often, the minuscule gap around one of the doors would be covered in a space about the width of a foot as someone walked unknowing or uncaring over the juncture. I supposed that even if one of the hatches suddenly opened and someone from above descended to join me I would be invisible, hidden away in the surrounding obscurity. But the possibility of it made me nervous nonetheless, and I hastened my efforts to find some other way into the rest of the building. I had determined that, cavernous as the room above me was, it did not extend all the way through to the street behind. Besides, I had not seen Mirela when I peeked through the broken shutter. With a vague sense of direction to guide me, I inched toward the farthest edge of the cellar space, wondering if I would encounter a wall to stop me.

The floor beneath my feet was rough, slippery stone, and I stumbled and slid more than once. After landing hard on one knee and tearing my petticoat I decided to rely on the wooden joists that held the floor above me for balance.

Soon I had passed well beyond the boundary of the large, ceremonial room. I knew this because the voices and intermittent chanting faded, and the dim outlines of light from the hatches in the floor were barely visible. By the time I reached a damp, stone wall, I knew that I had measured the depth of the structure, and so far had not found a door or a way to reach the upper floors, aside from the hatches. Yet there must be one. Unless I was the first person ever to enter this place in hundreds of years. But it did not have the feeling of complete abandonment I would have expected if that were the case.

I could feel the sticky tendrils of spider webs brushing my face and was glad I could not see the black creatures lurking in them, or see the size of the other creatures I heard scrabbling in corners. I could not help thinking of that time two years ago when I found myself navigating the sewers to escape captivity. At least I was on dry ground now. But so far I had utterly failed to progress toward my goal of finding Mirela and discovering why she was here.

Having not encountered a door or a stairway, I turned my attention to the ceiling again. Perhaps the hatches in the grand hall were not the only ones. Perhaps there were others above me in that other part of the building that led into darkened spaces and therefore had no tell-tale thread of light outlining them.

Much as I didn't want to reach my hands up and feel around between the beams above me, I realized that would probably be my only means of finding a way out without simply returning to where I had entered and admitting defeat in my enterprise. I pretended that I was running my hands over the form of an enormous musical instrument, and that anything living I encountered was simply a sound that had escaped into a silent realm beyond my hearing. I wasn't certain why, but my self-deception worked, and I was able to scrabble with my fingers all around the dark spaces above me.

As I hoped, my diligence was soon rewarded. I felt the unmistakable edges of a square hatch, large enough so that one of the joists had been cut to accommodate it. A simple latch held it closed from the underside. Why, I wondered, would that be the case? If it was latched shut from down here, no one above would be able to open it. Still, I did not spend too much time examining my good fortune, but found the lever that would trip the latch.

I assumed it would be rusted and unyielding, and so I hooked my finger around it and pulled with a great deal of force. To my surprise, the latch was instead well oiled and gave easily, and the door flap fell open and banged my head. It was fortunate, really, that it did so. The initial blow dazed me momentarily and caused me to duck out of the way of a wooden ladder that slid down to the ground, creating a stairway out of the subterranean chamber.

I held my breath. The mechanism of the ladder had made quite a noise. I crept cautiously around so that I could peer up into the room it led to.

I saw and heard nothing coming from the room directly above me. Only muffled chanting and voices from the other end of the building.

Before I had a chance to debate the wisdom of what I was about to do, I gathered my petticoat up and pulled it through my legs, tucking it into the tie in front. Then I grasped the sides of the ladder and climbed up into a small chamber that I could see from the dim light filtering in through a high window covered with iron grating was stuffed with wood and iron implements and contraptions—clearly a storage room. I could just discern a narrow passage through the clutter to a door that led back toward the gaudy chamber where the ceremony was taking place.

Obviously, I couldn't just remain where I was, no closer to Mirela and a good deal farther away from safety. I stepped carefully, afraid of a creaking floorboard or of bumping into one of the tools. They appeared to have been flung about without any care or organization, some precariously balanced so that the slightest alteration in the overall arrangement might bring a mighty crash.

As I picked my way through I noted that it was the oddest assortment of implements. I nearly tripped over an anvil, but mostly I could not recognize what purpose these tools might be—or have been—put to. There were large pincers with flat ends studded with needle-like points. A wooden chair with a dome suspended over it on a lever. A frame with two iron cones, one pointed up from the ground, the other looming overhead. A large wheel, with iron chains and leather straps—

And then, all at once, I knew. My mouth flooded with bitter saliva. These were instruments of torture—thankfully in a disused state. The emperor had outlawed such cruel punishments no matter the crime. Perhaps this was simply the place all those horrible machines had been deposited now that they were no longer needed. Why had they not been destroyed?

I quelled the urge to vomit, to quell my vivid recollection of the time when my father had taken me to witness a public chastisement. I had had nightmares for years afterwards. The nightmares started again after Danior's near miss, when without the emperor's intervention he would have been hanged, and then worse.

I had been distracted by the horrors around me and nearly failed to notice the sound of voices. Not the distant chanting of the robed participants and dark baritone of the one they called the Master, but much nearer and more distinct. A man's first, and then a woman's: quiet, conspiring. *Mirela.*

Taking even more care not to make a sound I continued toward the door, certain that Mirela and the captain were just beyond it. Their voices became louder as I approached, and I could hear what they were saying.

"You must be quiet as a cockroach, my sweet!" the captain said.

"You compare me to such a vile creature? This is not very gallant, Captain!" Mirela's whisper had a liquid challenge in it.

"A spider, then, who has wrapped me in her dangerous web?"

"It seems that I am the one who is caught in fine threads of bondage."

The captain's answering laugh came from deep in his throat, as if it responded to something other than Mirela's words, which were, on the surface of it, not at all humorous.

Next I heard a muffled squeal, I couldn't tell whether it was of pleasure or pain. I crept noiselessly to the door and put my ear against it.

"Are you certain no one will find us here?" Mirela asked. "There seems to be something rather important going on out in the front. Will they not hear us?"

"They are busy with their ceremony. Once they get chanting and exclaiming my brothers are so lost in their own world they hear nothing." His last word was strained, as if he were yanking on something, or lifting something heavy.

"Ouch! You're hurting me," Mirela said. I could tell she was trying to keep a light tone to her voice, but I recognized a slight edge in it nonetheless. "Your brothers, as you call them. One of them seemed rather dead to the world, I must say!" I presumed she must have seen the fellow on the bier.

"Never you mind about that. Just a bit of drama they like for their ceremonies."

"Poor man didn't seem to be enjoying it much, though."

"As I said, it's no concern of ours." The captain had lowered his voice. "We have our own ceremony to perform. I promise you, you will never forget it."

They stopped talking for a moment, but I thought I heard a little moan of pleasure from Mirela. It turned my stomach, to think that she was dallying with this captain when she had already given herself in all important ways to Olaf, even if her actions now were a ruse to get information from the captain.

I did not have much time to indulge in righteous indignation, however.

"I'd like to get down now, please," Mirela said.

"I thought you wanted to be my captive," said the captain, chuckling.

"I cannot use my hands as I would like to," she said, the sound of struggle in her voice.

"No, I think it would be safer to leave you there while I attend to some business. I'm beginning to think you are a dangerous creature."

"Let me go!" she yelled.

Without pausing to think what the consequences might be, I opened the door, flinging myself into the room in the belief that only surprise could aid me in extricating Mirela from her bizarre tryst with the captain.

"What the—"

I looked to the right, and what I saw there stunned me into immobility. There was Mirela, strapped to a contraption with leather belts holding her wrists and ankles spread apart. Her face was red and her eyes flashed with anger. Her bodice had been unlaced part way, and her full breasts were near to tumbling out.

The captain was still tidily attired in his uniform. He stood a little apart, his arms crossed over his chest, an amused smirk on his face.

"Well, it seems I that we have company, my Gypsy queen!" he said, clearly amused.

I ran to Mirela and started working at the straps, trying to set her free. I could not untie the knots that held her fast. The captain sauntered over. "Allow me," he said, sarcasm dripping from his words. I stood back and watched him work quickly at the knots, and soon Mirela was standing on the ground again, rubbing her wrists, but looking otherwise unhurt—except perhaps in her pride for having been tricked into putting herself in such a vulnerable position.

I wanted to slap the captain for his insolent expression. All I could do, though, was pour my anger into my words. "How dare you hold my friend captive!"

"Ah, so, as I guessed, the beguiling Mirela is not just a message bearer. You forget, Mademoiselle Schurman, that I know something of your history, and your relations with the Romany people."

I realized suddenly how I must appear, half dressed with my petticoats secured out of the way, and in a building where I had no business and to which I had gained access by sneaking in through the cellars. "It's not what you think!" I said, "I was worried. So many strange things are happening. We'll leave now. Thank you, Captain Bauer."

"I'm afraid I can't allow that, ladies," the captain said, placing himself between us and the door.

Mirela and I linked arms and walked forward until we were inches away from him. He did not move.

"Please, Adelbert," Mirela said, tossing her curls and looking up at him from beneath her dark lashes. "We won't say anything. We'll be as quiet as—well, not cockroaches."

He sighed, only settling himself more securely in our path. "I truly had hoped it would not come to this. For all your fortunate guesswork, you are very far from figuring out the details of what is going on, and it is my intention to prevent you getting any closer to the truth."

"You cannot conceal the truth," I said, standing as straight and tall as I could and still feeling a little dwarfed by the captain. "It will come out sooner or later. Sooner, if I have anything to do with it."

"Very well," he said. "I shall tell you a story that may help you understand why you must go home and pretend none of this ever happened, that you did not witness an attack, Mademoiselle Schurman, and that neither you nor your young friend has ever been within these walls."

"How can I, when I saw Herr Bachmann—or at least, I saw the man whose attack I witnessed—elsewhere in this building. Whether he is alive or dead I cannot be certain. And I know you have some close connection with the Bachmanns, as well as something to do with Herr Mozart, the Arnsteins, and even my stepfather-to-be, Herr van Swieten. You are all part of some brotherhood. At least I persuaded one person to explain to me what it was, if nothing more."

"Very good, Mademoiselle! But as I said, it is not enough. I cannot tell you more about our brotherhood, as I have vowed never to reveal certain things. But I can give you some insight into my own past. Perhaps that will suffice to quell your curiosity."

He pointed to a rough bench over to the side. "You may as well sit. This will take a while."

I pulled Mirela toward the bench and we sat as instructed. All the while I could feel her heart beating hard. Was it fear? Or something else? I could not tell. But she never took her eyes off Captain Bauer, who began to speak as if we were not there, as if he were reciting a story as old as time itself. We said nothing, only listening with all our attention.

CHAPTER TWENTY
THE CAPTAIN'S TALE

I was always an adventurous child, going where I shouldn't, riding the wildest horses, jumping from the tallest trees and getting into trouble with the peasant children on the estate. I suffered beatings at the hands of the monk who was my tutor, and later, when my mischievous nature turned to gambling and drinking, my father and I often quarreled. He used to hold my inheritance over my head to prevent me doing things he disapproved of. He did not want me to become a soldier. He refused to allow me to marry where my heart dictated. And he insisted that I must stay home and care for the estate, and for him and my mother as they became old.

I was an only child, and therefore it was my duty to carry on the family traditions, but my father's way with me rankled. I grew to detest the man who put so many obstacles in the way of what I thought was happiness, and dreamed of escaping. Secretly, I studied the arts of war, becoming adept with a sword and a firearm, perfecting my skills as a horseman. I did it all without letting my father know, so that he would not suspect that I was making myself ready to act, as soon as I was confident of being able to support myself with a career in the emperor's guards. I had friends who encouraged me, who promised their support when I eventually made the break. At least, I thought I had friends.

My mother and I were very close. She understood my need to get out from under my father's thumb. Until her dying breath, she was always my ally.

So when she became very ill, I was distraught. She suffered from a wasting disease that none of the doctors could cure. She had been bled and examined and given vile medicines, but she became thinner and weaker by the day. I took to lurking near her bedroom—they would not let me in, afraid I would upset or tire her, but I had to know how she was doing. Whenever the doctors left shaking their heads I wanted to run after them and say, "You must be able to do something! Cure her, or I shall run you through with my sword!" But of course, I did no such thing.

Our house was ancient and constructed for a now extinct family of heretics, who were driven from it centuries ago. They had created hiding places and secret passages so that they could escape in the event of a surprise attack. I had discovered them all, even places my own father did not know about.

My mother had taken a turn for the worse and my father summoned three doctors to examine her and consult. I hid myself in a passage that led from their bedchamber through a door concealed behind an armoire. By pressing my ear against it, I could hear every word that was spoken in the chamber. This is what I heard:

"The countess is gravely ill and may not last the night, let alone a week. There is but one doctor I know who has knowledge that could help her. I can send for him and he will arrive in a few hours."

"Who is this doctor? I thought I knew them all," my father said.

"He is a very erudite physician, schooled in all the latest techniques, but he is a Jew."

Silence greeted this pronouncement. I could not understand why my father hesitated! What did it matter what the fellow believed?

All I cared about was what he knew. And what he knew might save my mother.

You cannot imagine my horror when I heard my father say, "I am sorry, no Jew will ever come near my wife. I shall call for the priest."

If there had not been a heavy piece of furniture to prevent the door from opening, I would have burst through and plunged my sword in my father's breast, then told the doctors to fetch this fellow immediately. As it was, I could do nothing but bury my sorrow in drink at the local tavern. I could not bear to return home. Once my mother died, I knew nothing would restrain my father from exercising his control over me.

That night, I took only what small amount of money I possessed and my favorite horse and rode to Vienna, to present myself at the guards' barracks as a common soldier. I wanted to be anonymous, but there were too many fellows who knew my family, and before I knew it, I had become an officer in the Hussars.

I heard about my mother's death through a friend. I did not return for her funeral. I did not trust myself. I was afraid I would call my own father out in a duel and accuse him of negligent murder. Although I did not know for certain whether my mother would have been saved by the Jewish doctor, I believed that my father owed it to her to give her every opportunity to live, and that only his fear and prejudice had denied her this.

And I had taken on a project. In Vienna, I discovered the means by which men achieved lucrative positions and influence. It was not always through merit and ability. Not even family ties were enough. I discovered that there was a growing, surreptitious movement towards a kind of club, an association of men who told themselves they had high principles and that all are equal in the eyes of God, that whether one had a title or not was an accident that should not determine personal worth. The group was open to all, and men of all classes and stations could mingle in it. Merit was the key, and a desire to do good anonymously. I felt perhaps I had at last found something worthy of loyalty. This association was the brotherhood of the Freemasons.

My imagination was fired with the good I could do as one of them, and a friend of mine was kind enough to put me forward as an apprentice—they have fictitious titles, lowering the high-born to the level of tradesmen so that all will be on an equal footing. Quite absurd, really. Because I discovered that this noble enterprise, while it enabled those of lower social standing—artists, musicians, poets—to be introduced among those who could help them thrive, it but continued most of the bitter prejudices that existed outside of it, and was yet another means of exclusion for certain people. I mean primarily the Jews.

I remained, for a while, in the lodge I had joined. But I kept my ears open for something—anything—that might indicate a change of heart, or a new way. This came about when I met Nathan Arnstein.

I believe you are acquainted with him? You were fortunate enough to perform in that intimate gathering at his father's house. I know you hoped I would not recognize you, my dear Theresa. But no one who has seen you once and known you for who you are would mistake you. I am certain there was not a person there who did not recognize you and choose to let that recognition slide. You have an unforgettable face, no matter what you are wearing.

But that is beside the point. Nathan Arnstein and I became fast friends. Of course, he is not a Jew any more, but his father is, and there are many men of great ability and often wealth in Vienna who are prevented from ascending to their true positions of influence because they are descended from the race of Levi. I shared some of my views with Nathan, and told him—although I had vowed never to say a word about it outside the small circle of brethren—about the lodge.

His response was typical of him. Full of confidence. "Why can't we start our own lodge? Surely there must be others who think as you do, and who would not deny such as myself entrance among their numbers? The principle's good, and we could do so much."

And so we began to create what you have stumbled upon, Theresa. The men you saw performing the ceremony in the grand room next door are Christians, Jews, rich, and poor. The only difficulty is that we are as yet quite illegal. Our activities must remain secret because such mixed organizations were forbidden under the empress's reign and have not so far been permitted by the emperor. We could all be heavily fined or even banished, if Joseph II were called upon to act. And while he himself might wish to turn the other way, there are those in every established field of government and the arts who would not permit him. We can certainly not yet be accepted among the international brotherhood, which extends throughout Europe—even into Russia.

Your missing "corpse"—as you may already have guessed—was indeed Herr Bachmann. And he is here now, being prayed over and healed by his brethren. The "accident" he met with had to do with all I tell you. The other lodge in Vienna does not want us to exist, and is trying to put the taint of crime upon us and associate us with certain radical, anti-monarchy movements, which they claim are led by powerful Jews.

The flutist, poor fellow, was simply in the wrong place at the wrong time. We believe he may have overheard something that could incriminate our most powerful enemy, and so was set upon and clings to life by a thread now. The finest doctors—of whatever religious stripe—have consulted over his case. We will do all we can to ensure his recovery, not only because he is a friend and an artist, but also because we wish to gain the information he might have taken with him to his grave.

If he does not recover, we shall have to resort to more extreme measures. Those, I am afraid, are nothing I would dream of sharing with you.

Now you have heard my tale. What are we to do with you? Will you promise to stay out of the way so I can accomplish my mission? Or will I have to find some other way to keep you safely out of harm's way?

CHAPTER TWENTY-ONE

By the time the captain had finished his narrative, my mouth felt dry. The flutist had imparted his knowledge to me, and I had shared it with no one—except for Zoltán. I wasn't yet ready to give the same information to the captain, in case he had just told us an elaborate lie. After all, he knew I had probably been the last person to see Herr Bachmann alive—or conscious, anyway. But I did not want to incriminate Mozart without exhausting every other possibility first.

"Who are some of these powerful men you believe are trying to thwart your enterprise, Captain?" I asked. If he told me, perhaps it would give me some direction of my own to follow.

"There are many. Prince Lobkowitz is said to be unfriendly to a rival lodge that permits Jews among its ranks. The artist Maulbertsch is unwilling to let some of his talented brethren into the ranks of the successful. And then there's Thorwart, who wants to keep the Burgtheater untainted by Jewish blood."

Again, Thorwart! "But surely he is not powerful enough to prevent it?"

"Thorwart can keep anyone he wants off the stage of the Burgtheater. Mozart, for instance. Without Thorwart's blessing, he will never present *The Abduction from the Seraglio.*

"The fact is that your nosiness is not welcome. Whatever you think you know, you will do more harm than good by becoming involved. I tried to warn you before, but still you persist. Therefore I regret to tell you that you and your delightful—if devious—friend here must remain the guests of the lodge until such time as it is safe for you to depart."

What the captain had said certainly cleared up many of the mysteries I had encountered in past days. But here Mirela and I were, in captivity, and still no closer to any kind of understanding. At the very least, whoever had attacked Herr Bachmann should be punished, even if the flutist lived to perform again. It seemed to me that the captain was, despite his lofty motives, not to be trusted.

I still didn't understand one detail of his recent behavior. "Why had you tied up Mirela just now?" I asked.

The captain surprised me by laughing out loud. "Are you really so innocent?" he said, a spark of something in his eye. "Why don't you answer your friend's question, Mademoiselle Mirela?"

I turned my attention to Mirela, but she had adopted her characteristic detached look, nose up in the air. She looked rather less shocked and offended than I thought she might have been. I realized that, if I knew about all her actions, I might be quite surprised to uncover her motivations. I felt myself blushing, and that made me angry.

This noble captain had seen through so much, had toyed with me and Mirela both. And his confidence now that he could keep us under lock and key for the indefinite future positively infuriated me. However much I realized that sharp words and angry retribution would not serve me now, that patience was called for, I longed to fling myself at him and pummel him with my fists. Yet I knew that would be foolish. Even the two of us would be no match for him, and by Mirela's look I wasn't certain she would join in the fighting at all. Our only hope was to lull him into thinking that we would stay docilely where he left us while he went away to do whatever he needed to, and then make our escape.

From deep in the center of the building came the sound of an immense gong, struck three times.

"Ah, I am needed," the captain said, "I'm afraid I must leave you here. Don't think of using your extraordinary ingenuity to get out. We have a guard animal, a little pet one of our members picked up on his travels, and that is under our care temporarily. I will ensure that he is roaming to bar your escape route after I leave you. There's water in that bucket, there. No food, I'm afraid. We weren't exactly expecting guests this evening. But all will be resolved, one way or another, ere long."

He bowed to us both and then left the room. I heard the grating of a key in the lock.

As soon as he disappeared Mirela leapt from her seat. "He thinks he can keep us here! He is an arrogant fool." She walked up and down, pacing like the cat I suspected he had meant when he mentioned the guard animal. I had no doubt the creature was the very same one that had chased me through those other corridors—which, judging by the extent of the building, may have been within these very walls but approached from a different street. What else could this guard animal be? If it had been a dog, he would have said.

"How did you get in?" Mirela asked.

"From underground."

"We must go out the same way."

"I don't know if it will be possible. Surely he is aware of how I managed it. Do you not think this beast he speaks of will be down there?"

"An animal. I can charm an animal."

Although I knew Mirela had powers beyond those of an average woman, I doubted she would be able to distract the huge, black cat from its duties. "Not this one," I said. "It is a creature like no other you have ever seen," I said. "I have met it before."

"Where? How?"

"In another place near here. At least, I thought it was another place. I was lured to a rehearsal, I supposed, but then there was no rehearsal. I think whoever it was—perhaps the Captain—wanted to frighten me."

"What did the creature look like?"

"Like a cat, only enormous."

"A lion?"

"No. Completely black, and sleek, with yellow eyes."

"Is there only one?"

"I imagine so," I said.

"Then it cannot run in two directions at once. And we do not know if it is truly beneath us."

She was, strictly speaking, correct. But I remembered that in my blind groping through the cellar I had not noticed the presence of any rats, nor had mice run across my feet. I had heard scrabbling in the corners, but that could have been snakes. Perhaps the big cat was accustomed to having the run of the place, but had been shut away because of the ceremony above. I felt ice flow down my spine at the thought that I might have encountered that creature in the dark of the cellar, when I would have had no chance to escape from it.

"Well, I, for one, refuse simply to sit here and wait," said Mirela, like a coquette afraid of being overlooked at a ball.

"I should tuck your skirts out of the way if I were you."

She dutifully put herself in the same state as I: half-dressed with petticoats fastened to make it easier to run if necessary. I led her into the store room where the hatch to the cellar was located, realizing that I had left it open and half expecting the leopard—or whatever sort of creature it was—to have climbed up after me and be lurking among the disused instruments of torture. I paused at the top of the ladder, looking down into the blackness below. Perhaps it was because I expected to hear it I thought I could discern that same, audible breathing, a deep growl at either end of every inhale and exhale.

"Well, if we wait we will surely not succeed." Mirela nudged me out of the way and climbed down. On her way she called up to me, "Be careful, I don't think this ladder can take much weight. Good that you are slim." My heart started thumping and a light sweat broke out on my upper lip. "*Komm!*" she commanded once she had landed on the ground below.

Mirela's courage, founded though it was on ignorance as to what we might be facing, was infectious. I took a deep breath and made my own way down the ladder.

"Where are you?" I whispered when I found myself once again in that subterranean space. It was so dark I could not see at all, and Mirela had stepped away from the pool of wan light let in by the open hatch.

"Over here!" she answered.

I inched forward, my hands outstretched, toward the sound of her voice.

"Not that way, here!"

I felt as if someone had put a black hood over my face. How could it be that the cellar was even darker than before? In my blindness I tripped on the edge of a stone in the floor and fell forward, landing on my hands and knees and grazing all four points of contact. Doubtless, I remember thinking, I had torn holes in my petticoat.

To my relief, Mirela arrived at my side to help me up. "It takes a moment," she said, "but you will be able to see."

I had noticed before that Mirela's deep brown eyes had the ability to adjust remarkably quickly to changing light. She cultivated that talent when she told fortunes, dousing the lamp and plunging her customers in darkness so that she could rifle through their reticules and coat pockets unseen. I would not have believed her capable of it, but she once confessed to me that she did this, although claimed that she never stole from those who paid her, only those who tried to take advantage of her services without the customary fee. She made me swear not to give away her secret. And indeed, the entertainment was normally well worth the few Groschen it cost the wealthy for the thrill of a Gypsy prognostication.

"Now," Mirela whispered, "how did you get in?"

I still couldn't see very well. But as I waited, shapes began to emerge from the blackness. I saw the great posts that held up the building above us, like ranks of shadowy wooden soldiers fading away. But something was different about the space. All at once I realized what it was. "They've stopped," I said.

"Stopped what?"

"Ssshh!" I put my hand on Mirela's arm and the two of us stood without moving, hardly breathing, listening to nothing at all. "There was chanting before," I explained, "and speaking. And there were hatches cut in the floor in the shape of a crescent. I could see them before because there was a bit of light coming from around them. Now, I cannot get my bearings. Which way did we come from?"

Mirela did not answer. Instead, she gripped my arm so tightly that her fingernails dug into the soft flesh on the inside. I could feel the trembling of her body although she clearly tried to stay very still. She had seen or heard something as yet imperceptible to my less acute senses.

Yet only a moment later, I heard it too. I heard that growling, that wild, threatening, taking-its-time-to-track-down-its-prey rumble of the huge, black cat. I thought my heart would burst. Surely it could smell the fear pouring from every surface of my body. We could not go forward with that creature waiting for us. There was only one course of action open to us. "We have to go back and climb up the ladder," I breathed, at the same time backing very slowly away from the noise, which now appeared to be pacing across our path, some distance away.

At first Mirela resisted my tug. She was rooted like a Linden tree to her spot. But slowly, we inched backwards, bumping once into one of the floor supports, the growling getting nearer and nearer. The cat's luminous eyes came into my line of sight just as we reached the area of dim light from the open hatch into the room above. The ladder was in reach, and the cat had still not lunged for us.

We continued retracing our steps until I felt the structure of the ladder itself against my back. "You go first. Slowly," I whispered, un-clenching Mirela's hand from my arm and nudging her. I could not take my eyes off the source of the sound and the disembodied, dully glowing embers of cat eyes that caught what tiny amount of light there was and threw it at me like arrows. I felt my heart pierced through again and again as the creature's head swung across our view, at even intervals interrupted by the intervening support posts.

It had drawn close enough so that I could hear the padding of its huge, soft feet against the stones of the floor. "It is evil. Possessed!" Mirela hissed. "I dare not move."

"Don't be a stupid Gypsy!" I said through clenched teeth. I felt her stiffen, and immediately regretted my choice of words. But I would have said anything to make her take the step, to force her to turn and climb up the ladder while I kept staring at this menace that toyed with us, walking up and back, up and back, coming closer and closer. Why didn't the beast leap forward and attack us? I had no doubt we would be powerless to run away. Yet it stayed where it was and watched us, the growl in its throat now occasionally erupting into a suppressed snarl and a flash of teeth.

My anger did its trick in releasing Mirela from her terror enough to grasp the sides of the ladder and scamper up. I could hear the relief in her voice as she said, a little too loudly, "Now you!"

Her exclamation halted the creature's pacing. I could have sworn it fixed me with a cold, menacing stare, as if it recognized me from the last time and had only been waiting for the opportunity to settle an interrupted score. I didn't dare turn away from it.

Keeping my head to the side, thinking, what? That I could fool it into believing I had not climbed out of the way so long as my eyes were locked with its eyes? That seeing the threat meant that I could control it? Whatever perverse logic compelled me, I would not turn away from the cat. I reached around for the sides of the ladder and lifted my foot up to the bottom rung. Then slowly, I placed the other foot on the next rung up.

It was working. The creature growled, but it did not come closer. I couldn't understand why, but I didn't care. I was within reach of safety. I hurried.

That was my mistake. The fourth rung of the ladder snapped under the pressure of my foot, and the sudden impact of my fall to the rungs below made them each break in turn. I clung to the sides of the ladder, my feet dangling into the void, probably only inches above the floor but once I let go, I did not know if I would be able to climb up again.

To my horror, I saw a huge, black paw reach out swiftly, felt the graze of a claw against my right calf. I closed my eyes, thinking that I must surrender myself to being eaten by this horrible, oversized cat.

"Don't let go! I'll pull you up!" Mirela's voice called me to my senses. She gripped my arms and braced her feet against the floor, straining with every ounce of strength she possessed. I kept my attention focused on her face, feeling the breeze of the big cat's swiping. Why didn't the creature lunge? I kept thinking. Why was I not dragged down and torn to pieces?

Just as Mirela began to falter in her strength, I found myself high enough up to get my elbows on the floor. With one huge effort, I pushed up on my arms and wormed onto the floor of the room.

"Quickly! We must close the hatch before the cat leaps up at us." Mirela's terror was frozen on her features.

"No. Something is holding it back. Otherwise I would have been dead. It must be tethered down there." I could think of no other explanation. We closed the hatch anyway. Clearly we would not be able to escape that way.

"Rezia! You are hurt!"

My hands were scraped raw from the wood of the ladder, and although it had not been quite able to reach me and drag me to my death, the creature had managed to make a sizable gash in my leg with one claw, which now streamed blood. Mirela tore a strip from her petticoat and with swift, expert movements, tied it around the jagged cut securely. The pain made me feel faint, and nausea rose into my throat. How would I explain such a wound? What could I ever have been doing to injure myself in such a manner?

A fine thing to worry about now, I thought, when there was no assurance I would ever have to explain it to anyone! "We must get out of here, one way or another," I said, swallowing the bile that sat on the back of my tongue.

"Yes. And now, I am angry."

Mirela had lost her panicked look, as if the need for action had driven it away, and now set her features in an expression that was all too familiar. It told me that she would think of some outrageous way to extricate us from this situation, that nothing she might do ought to surprise me.

"What right has that impudent man to lock us in here? We are not criminals! He thinks he can win me over with his brooding eyes."

I decided it would do no good to remind her that I had broken into the building, and that she had used the basest deception to accomplish her entrance. "What do you suggest?" I swept my arm in a gesture around the crowded storeroom with its one high, barred window.

"Good of him to leave us so many useful implements," Mirela said, trailing her delicate fingers across a nasty looking piece of machinery with a jagged, circular blade, then reaching behind it and pulling out an iron bar with a sharp point at the end.

Of course, how stupid of me not to realize what Mirela apparently just had, that the lock on the door would be no match for any number of the tools that surrounded us.

We set to work. Within a surprisingly small amount of time, we had broken the lock and splintered it away from the door frame and then accomplished the same feat with the next door we encountered. Mirela quickly put her outer clothing back on. Now all that remained was to make our way through the huge building without being seen and find a door that would lead us out to freedom—and to the difficult decision about what to do with the bizarre, dangerous knowledge we now possessed.

CHAPTER TWENTY-TWO

Whatever ceremony was previously taking place had ended and the building appeared to be deserted by the time we had broken through to the corridors that surrounded the great chamber. We did not pause to question our good fortune, but slipped out through a side door whose lock was easily broken.

"Where are you going?" Mirela asked as I made my way down the dark alleyway that had led to my entrance to the cellar.

"I have to get my violin and my dress," I said. She knew enough not to question my need to collect my precious fiddle. I prayed that no one had found it and carried it off. That would be a tragedy rivaled only by losing my father.

Fortunately, I had hidden it well and it appeared none the worse for wear. Mirela helped me into my dress, which, other than being rather dirty, was undamaged. After that we made our way as quickly as we could despite my painful hobbling through the dark streets, dodging from shadow to shadow to avoid the night watchmen and porters.

By the time we reached the Roma camp, my calf throbbed, and the makeshift bandage had soaked through with blood.

"Wait here," Mirela commanded, leaving me lying on the pallet in her hut, which, after what we had been through only an hour ago, felt as safe and secure as a palace.

She returned with Maya, who carried a sewing basket and a basin of water scented with herbs. Maya knew the healing arts. I trusted her as much as I would trust any fine Viennese doctor.

"I must get a message to my mother, so that she does not worry about me," I said. I winced. Maya pressed hard on the wound in my leg, cleaning it out and mopping up the blood.

"Drink this," Mirela said, and she gave me a beaker of some very strong liquor. I had eaten nothing since the afternoon, and the alcohol went straight to my head. When I screamed at the intense pain in my leg after that, Mirela made me drink more. I craned my head around, wondering what Maya was doing to hurt me so. "Don't look," Mirela said.

I may have fainted for a while, because the next thing I remembered was awakening with only Mirela in the room. I looked down at my leg, but it was securely bandaged and I could see nothing.

"Maya stitched you up nicely. She said the wound was jagged, but clean. And you will have a scar, but it will be hidden by your skirts, so you won't need to worry about it until such time as you are married, and your hus—"

"That's enough!" I said, covering my ears. A scar. Now what would I do? It was true that I could probably hide it from my mother, but what if she accidentally saw it when I was in my nightclothes? How would I explain it?

"Olaf delivered a message to your apartment to say that you had stayed here with me last night," Mirela continued.

Last night? I glanced at the entrance to Mirela's hut. Bright sunlight outlined the door. We had made it through the night. Now it was day again, and now I must find some help, find someone who would return with me to locate Herr Bachmann and ensure that the captain was telling the truth, and that he was being given medical attention.

But who could I go to? Who would dare to intervene?

All at once it came to me. The solution was obvious. I would seek out Mozart himself. He was too well known to be attacked or imprisoned. I would have to tell him everything, though, and that would cause me pain. More pain, ultimately, than the big cat's scratch.

Fortunately, the gash was situated so that walking did not put too much strain on it, and with a little practice I was able to get around without much difficulty. Mirela loaned me her magnificent umbrella to use as a walking stick if I grew tired. Indeed, after a bright start, the sky had clouded and threatened rain.

I had no idea where I might find the maestro from Salzburg, and so I decided I had better call upon Danior and Alida. It was a Wednesday. Alida generally received visitors on Wednesday mornings. I wondered if she would still be receiving despite her advanced state of pregnancy, but felt sure she would see me even if she was not.

The porter barely lifted his head as I passed him nodding in his cubby by the door. Climbing the stairs was exquisitely painful. I found I had to use both the umbrella and the banister for support. By the time I reached the Varga's apartment door I had to pause to let a wave of faintness and nausea subside, and so I leaned my forehead against the door, closed my eyes and breathed deeply.

"I should like you to teach my daughter the violin."

I heard the voice on the other side of the door, one I knew only from the briefest of conversations, but its commanding roundness and slight foreign accent had impressed itself deeply on my ear. It was Herr von Eskeles.

"What is the difficulty? I thought Mademoiselle Schurman was getting along very well with Sophie," said Danior.

"It seems she does not care to continue the lessons. Apparently she has more important students."

"I–I find that . . . I mean, I cannot imagine . . ." Danior was clearly sputtering. "I'm sure there is some misunderstanding. Rezia would never . . ."

How I ached to burst through the door and run to Herr von Eskeles and explain everything to him! I wanted nothing more than to teach Sophie again. Her next lesson should have been the very day after that. But I saw now that I had behaved unforgivably. I also saw that, had they not been Jewish but Catholic and therefore more influential in society, I would never have made the choice I had, to lie to them when they had invited me so kindly. I deserved to be cut off from them.

"Well, of course I can teach her until you find someone more suited to the task. I am afraid my duties require me to be much occupied, and I would at best be able to come only once every few weeks."

"I thank you, and am grateful for your kindness. I shall pay double your customary fee."

"That will not be necessary," Danior said.

I heard the approach of their footsteps. One part of me longed to stay where I was and walk with Herr von Eskeles so that I could explain myself. But other matters were more important than my own sense of shame and embarrassment. I stepped quickly out of the way around a corner and waited until I was certain the older man had left the house and Danior had returned inside before knocking. I heard the strains of Danior's beautiful playing as I waited for the footman to come and open the door to me.

The fellow knew me and led me in directly. Danior came forward and embraced me heartily. He pulled me a little off balance, and I put more weight than I could bear on my injured leg. A yelp of pain escaped from me before I could suppress it.

"Rezia! What's wrong?"

"I cannot tell you now, there isn't time. I came only to find out from you where Mozart lives so that I might speak with him."

A puzzled, somewhat guarded and suspicious expression crossed Danior's face.

"I know what you're thinking, but it has nothing to do with gaining his favor to play in the orchestra for his opera—else I would not have dressed like this!" I tried to make light of the matter, but Danior knew me too well.

"What is it, Rezia? You have not been acting like yourself lately. I had the most extraordinary conversation with Sophie's father. Have you given up teaching her? And why, when I went to so much trouble to get you the lessons?"

"I can explain everything, but not now. I don't want to stop teaching Sophie. They asked me to stop coming—I did something unforgivable, but when all this is over I shall try to make it up to them. Just please don't ask me about it now."

Thankfully, Danior accepted my promise of later clarification and did not detain me, writing Mozart's address down on a scrap of paper. "Last I knew he was staying in the widow Weber's house. She's a bit of a nasty piece of work, but the daughters who are still there are kind, sweet girls. Ask for Constanze if Mozart is not in. She will help you find him, or give him a message on your behalf."

I kissed Danior's cheek. "How is Alida?"

"Staying in bed today. She says she doesn't feel equal to greeting the world."

"That's because she demands so much of herself when she does. I wonder if she'll ever stop being the lady-in-waiting and accept that she is simply a lady?" I suspected, too, that this baby she was going to have was nearer to arriving than anyone thought, but I did not want to alarm Danior by saying so.

I feared it was possible that the pain in my leg would eventually become so bad that I would have to give up my activities for the day and admit temporary defeat. But for the time being I gritted my teeth and made a supreme effort to walk briskly through the streets as if I were no different from anyone else on the way to shop for a new hat or visit a friend. Walking was a little easier because I had left my violin in Danior's solicitous care, knowing that he would probably take the opportunity to play it as soon as I was gone—which of course I did not mind.

Frau Weber's address was Am Peter 11, and the house in which her apartment was situated was called *Zum Augen Gottes*, To the Eye of God. I had not met the Webers, although I had certainly heard of them. One of the sisters was a well-respected singer in the opera. Another had gone to Berlin, I heard, to make her own way as a singer. Constanze, the one Danior told me to seek, was younger than they, and I believed there was a still younger daughter.

This belief was confirmed when I knocked on the door at the street and a girl around my age opened the door to me, wiping her floury hands on an apron and then streaking what was left of the flour across her face as she brushed her unruly hair out of the way.

"Forgive me, I'm looking for Herr Mozart. Danior Varga said that he has lodgings here." I curtsied, not wanting to put the girl in the awkward position of having to decide whether it would be rude not to take my hand and spare me becoming involved in the baking she had just left off.

"Please, come in, Mademoiselle . . ."

"Theresa Schurman. And I have the pleasure of meeting?"

"Sophie Weber." She tossed her name back over her shoulder, as we had already started through the vestibule, up the stairs and into the Weber apartment to a comfortable parlor with a pianoforte and a crackling blaze in the stove. "Herr Mozart is not here at present, but perhaps Constanze will know where he is and can help you find him."

I thanked her and gratefully took a seat on a settee, stretching my throbbing leg out as surreptitiously as I could. I wasn't certain what to expect, nor even how much of my purpose I should share with Constanze Weber. The rumor was that she was engaged to Mozart, but that his father did not approve and therefore the betrothal was meant to be secret. While I waited I noticed that the pianoforte, far from being a parlor ornament, was open both printed and manuscript music scattered across its desk and piled on the floor next to it. Two chairs stood at rakish angles to the keyboard, as if a companionable duet had been played there recently and the players just stepped away for a glass of punch.

By contrast, a portrait draped in the black crape of mourning hung above it, the very picture embodying its own contradiction in being of a jovial, apple-cheeked man with laughing eyes.

I sat up a little straighter when I heard footsteps approaching. I straightened my skirt and pinched some color into my cheeks, which I felt must still be pale after my recent ordeal.

But when the door did not open to admit anyone, and I realized that two pairs of feet had arrived and stopped at the door, and two voices—a man's and a woman's—were speaking in hushed tones, I held my breath to listen.

"You are certain that he will not consent to this condition?" whispered the woman's voice.

"You and I both know that all Mozart wants is to be able to have his opera performed. I think Constanze could be much more favorably matched given the right patronage."

"But supposing he gives it up for her!" The woman's whisper became loud and pinched.

"I know these types. They're all bluster, no courage. We'll send him packing from Vienna with his tail between his legs."

"Cousin Thorwart, how can I thank you enough. All my dreams . . ." The woman's voice became lost in quiet weeping. I wanted to leap out of my seat and throw the door open to see if it was indeed the infamous Herr Thorwart who was standing on the landing talking to Frau Weber. But I did not have time.

"Hush, Cecilia. Constanze is coming. Don't let her know I was here."

Thorwart hastened down the stairs, much lighter on his feet than I would have thought, having witnessed his ungainly performance on a dance floor.

"Ah, there you are, Stanzi!" said Frau Weber, her voice now calm. "Will you help your sister with the baking?"

"Presently, Mama. I have a visitor with whom I must speak first."

"Is it someone I know?"

"No, Mama. Only an inquiry about the pianoforte," Constanze answered. I wondered why she lied.

"Hmmph. Well, mind you get what it's worth."

Were they really contemplating selling their pianoforte? I didn't have time to think further on the matter, because the parlor door was at last opened to admit a pretty, dark-haired lady with eyes a little too widely set.

"I'm Constanze. My sister tells me you wish to speak with me?"

I had risen, and she motioned me to take a seat again.

I did not have much time to spare, really wishing to get to Mozart as quickly as possible, and so I launched directly into my intended line of questioning. Something told me that if anyone knew something secret about Mozart, it would be Constanze. "Forgive me for being so abrupt, but I come to you looking for Herr Mozart, as your kind sister has no doubt already told you."

"Yes, however I am afraid Wolferl—Herr Mozart—has given up his room here and moved to an apartment in the Graben." She blushed when she said it, confirming that his move was for propriety's sake. "I will of course give you the address, but you probably will not find him there at this hour. He has an appointment with Gottfried Stephanie, at the opera house."

Mozart might no longer have been living at Am Peter 11, but I gambled on the fact that his affairs were still very much a matter of everyday concern to Constanze. I decided that the desperate circumstances justified whatever impropriety I was about to commit. "Mademoiselle Weber," I said and had opened my mouth to continue when she interrupted me.

"Please, call me Constanze. We are not formal here."

"Very well, and I am known to my friends as Rezia. But forgive me for asking, are you acquainted with a flutist and his wife, Herr and Frau Bachmann?"

She wrinkled her brow and pursed her lips. "No, I have not heard of them. Does Herr Bachmann perform at the opera?"

"I'm afraid not, although I understand he is talented enough to do so. Frau Bachmann is also a flutist of some ability. Perhaps you have heard of her?"

"A woman who is a flutist? How very odd. I do not know of any, and Herr Mozart has never mentioned her. But then, my family has only been in Vienna for two years."

And, I thought, if you are not Jews, you would have no reason to be acquainted with such people as the Bachmanns. They are not wealthy like the Arnsteins or the Eskeles's. Just humble musicians such as my father used to be, only without the opportunity to perform in a princely household or at the opera so that they might support a family. "Well, I know Herr Mozart is acquainted with them. I am very concerned about the welfare of Herr Bachmann." I thought for a moment about what else I could say to her without giving everything away. "Has Amadé—Herr Mozart—ever spoken about a secret brotherhood? An association of men of all conditions?"

That puzzled look crossed her face again, but it appeared a bit artificial this time, as if she knew something but had been told not to let on. "Again, I fear I cannot help you. Herr Mozart knows so many people. He is much sought after to perform. And people in very high places are awaiting his opera with great anticipation."

I might have been imagining it in my exhausted and overwrought state, but I thought I detected a distinct chill in Constanze's response. I asked her a little more about Mozart and his music. Her answers were short, and she no longer looked directly into my eyes. And she made no mention of any difficulties facing Amadé in overcoming the objections of Herr Thorwart—to which I had been an unwitting witness only moments before.

I made one last attempt to regain her trust and inquired about what she did in Vienna, how they got on, and who the kind-looking gentleman was in the portrait over the piano.

"That is Papa," Constanze sighed. "He died only a month after we came to Vienna."

"Then he died around the same time as my father," I said. I could have said much more, but I did not want to get drawn into that conversation just then. Yet the sympathetic warmth that flowed into her eyes, the perception of a shared grief, nearly brought tears to my own.

"Stanzi! Finish your business quickly! I'll need your help with the beds!" Frau Weber's voice called from somewhere deep in the large apartment.

"I fear I am taking you away from important matters," I said, using the umbrella to hoist myself up from the settee. Constanze smiled gratefully, and I thought perhaps she would have answered my questions more fully if some kind of silence had not been imposed upon her. "I hope we may meet again sometime? I understand you play the piano. I play the violin, and am always looking for friends with whom I can share an hour of music."

Her eyes brightened immediately. "It would be a great pleasure. I shall ensure that Wolferl—Herr Mozart—invites you to our next musical evening. It is how we met him, you know, when he came to take part in a humble gathering of my father's in Mannheim." She blushed again.

"Or you must come to us! We have a pianoforte now. Once my mother remarries, I may not have the freedom to invite whom I like, and so . . ." I didn't know why I blurted out this unnecessary intelligence to Constanze, or even what possessed me to think of inviting anyone to our cramped apartment. But she reached over to me as I was leaving and squeezed my arm.

"If you have any trouble getting into the Burgtheater at this hour, ask for my sister Aloysia. Tell her I sent you."

I thanked her profusely. Despite her evasiveness following that one question, I was left with an impression that I liked Constanze Weber. This cheered me as I limped to the opera house in search of Mozart, wondering if he would remember meeting me the day before, and how he would react to the blunt questions I intended to ask him.

CHAPTER TWENTY-THREE

I had not been inside the Burgtheater since my father took me there three years before, to see the opera *Armida* by the great Salieri. Papa had been asked to but could not perform in the orchestra because of his duties for Prince Esterhazy, but Signore Salieri was kind enough to give him two tickets to attend the performance. It was a special night, a revival in honor of Herr von Gluck, and so there was just the one opportunity to see it. Mama predicted that she would have one of her headaches, although I later realized she had sacrificed her own pleasure for mine, since even without a deep appreciation for music, attending the opera would have provided her ample entertainment.

We sat in the center of the stalls, surrounded by wealthy people we did not know. I had a new dress for the occasion, and thought myself very grand, but compared to the jewels and silks of the Viennese society ladies I realized I looked plain and dull. At first I wanted to run home, perceiving that one or two cruel girls tittered behind their mirrored fans. But once the music started I was completely captivated. I had seen an opera before, of course, at Esterhaza. But not with so many people and with such brilliant effects. The singing was superb, and the orchestra played almost perfectly. The costumes were so ornate that the candlelight made them sparkle like sunlit snowflakes. The entire magical garden disappeared at the end, and although I knew that it was all done with fireworks and revolving platforms, by then I had so completely immersed myself in the story taking place on the stage that I felt as if it were I who was being dragged down to hell amid a shower of sparks and billows of smoke.

Now, they were showing Salieri's *Der Rauchfangkehrer, The Chimney Sweep.* It was a comic opera in German, not a grand opera in Italian, but it was enjoying a great success, so I had heard from all the musicians. It would succeed, since it was a pet project of the Emperor, who was determined to establish a German opera in Vienna instead of the imported Italian one that had been so popular until then. That's why Mozart's new opera was in German, I later discovered. He was hoping the Emperor would back him too.

Yet tickets for The Chimney Sweep were two Ducats each and beyond my reach. I longed to hear Caterina Cavalieri sing, though. German or not, they still couldn't get by without the Italian sopranos. Alida had gone to the premier in April. Danior led the orchestra. He had said he would get me in as soon as there were any tickets to spare, but so far there had been none.

It was a short walk down the Kohlmarkt to the theater built next to the Hofburg. To reach the back entrance where musicians and singers came and went for rehearsals I had to pass the police station. I hurried my steps as best I could, not wanting to encounter the captain accidentally. He must, by now, be aware that Mirela and I had managed to escape from the building where he last left us, and with my wounded leg I would not be able to run away from him.

I had nearly passed the point where someone looking out of the entrance would be able to see me and was about to turn down the alleyway that led to the back of the Burgtheater when a voice called out to me. I pretended first not to hear it and hastened my steps.

"You there! Young lady! Wait!"

The steps behind me were accompanied by the labored breathing of an old officer, and realized I could not ignore him. I turned, adopting the most placid, unconcerned expression I could manage, as if to say, *what could you want with me? As you see I am very busy.*

"Forgive me, Mademoiselle Schurman, is it not? You came to us with a wild tale of a murder you'd witnessed." He wheezed and bent forward, hands on his knees. He had not even donned his hat to come running after me, and I had to stifle a laugh at the strands of grey hair that had been combed over to cover a shiny bald patch on his head. When he recovered his breath, he stood up again and I recognized the fellow I'd seen in the station the first time I went there in the morning, to meet Captain Bauer. "I wanted to tell you that a lady came by the very next day to report her husband missing, a Jewish lady. We put the captain onto that as well—the one you were looking for, and I didn't know who you were talking about, but it was the Graf von Bauer, who isn't really a captain you see." He paused to catch his breath. "Not since he lost his commission for fighting an illegal duel over a lady—some say a Jewish lady—he wanted to marry."

By the time the fellow finished his breathless account, my head swam. The scraps of what he told me would explain so much about Captain Bauer! But could it be true? "What happened to the lady who came in to see you? Did she find her husband?" I wanted to keep him talking without letting on that I knew anything.

"Well, that's the odd part of it. She came back a day later and said that he had returned, and that we were not to bother ourselves about him any more. But you see, we'd made some inquiries, and his work-place—he was a stitcher at a tailor's shop—said he never came back at all and they'd given his job to someone else."

So poor Herr Bachmann had to earn his bread ruining his fingers with a needle, rather than by pressing the keys and stopping the holes of a flute. "Why are you telling me all this?" I asked.

"Because the count returned only yesterday with this. He said I was to give it to you in the event that you returned to the station." The fellow fished a crumpled note out of a small pocket in his waistcoat handed it to me. The note was not sealed, and I was certain that the guard had read it. There would be no need to tell him that it warned me to stay away from Frau Bachmann and a certain place in the poor quarter where I had lately been, that if I brought anyone there a search would prove futile.

"Thank you, Sir," I said, pressing a few *Groschen* into his willing hand. "You have been kinder than you know."

I turned away from him, intending to continue with my errand to find Mozart, but he placed his hand on my arm and stopped me. "It occurs to me, young Fräulein, that you have gotten yourself mixed up in something dangerous. My advice to you would be to do as the count says and forget all about it. Go home to your Mama and Papa."

His tone of voice was very different, and I looked more carefully at the fellow's face. The blundering stupidity he exuded when we'd spoken the first time in the guard's station had been replaced by a serious, warning expression. Here was a man, I thought, who saw many things, and spent his time perhaps weighing what he should be known to have seen, and what he should ignore. No doubt he feigned foolishness for his own protection. I wondered about the condition of his conscience. "Thank you. I shall consider your advice carefully."

This time he let me go. I don't know how long he stared after me, but I did not turn around to see.

At first, the porter who answered my insistent knocking did not want to let me into the theater, claiming that no one was there, although I could hear someone practicing scales in a light, flexible soprano voice.

"I have come to see Mademoiselle Aloysia Weber," I said, figuring that I might as well try the ammunition Constanze had given me. "Constanze sent me."

"Not another Weber!" he said, knocking his forehead with the heel of his hand.

"No, but a friend. Please, I must see Mademoiselle Weber." I wasn't certain why I did not simply ask for Mozart, but I was afraid the porter would claim he was not there. And there was something unseemly about coming alone to a public place to seek out a young, single gentleman. On the other hand, with the audible evidence of Aloysia's presence, the porter could hardly claim she was absent.

He sighed. "Wait here." He gestured me into a tiny vestibule hardly big enough for the two of us, then vanished through the one door that led into the building from it.

I wished there were a chair to sit in while I waited. The pain in my leg was beginning to distract me again. Perhaps that was why it took me a moment to register the fact that just on the other side of the wall from where I awaited the porter's return a conversation was taking place, and I recognized the voice of Mozart as one of the participants. The other was a deep, booming baritone, an actor, I thought.

"But you promised me you'd have the text of the second act completed by now!"

"I would have if you hadn't been such a stickler for certain details."

"My changes have only strengthened the drama. You know that. Don't be such a prima donna!"

"Careful young fellow. You need me. Without my words and my influence with Thorwart, your precious *Singspiel* will never be presented."

"Oh, a pox on this blasted city! Why can no one see how successful this will be? That it is a new kind of opera and it will make everyone's fortune. And as for Thorwart. . ."

I heard a chair creak, as if someone had either sat down or stood up.

"Patience, Amadé!" The man who had sounded a bit annoyed while he previously spoke to Mozart was now calm and comforting. "Yours is not the only voice of merit in Vienna. Herr von Gluck and Signore Salieri are fine artists with sterling reputations. The public loves them."

"Hah! *The Chimney Sweep* is as inconsequential a work as ever I heard—worse than the trash they put on in Munich before my *Idomeneo*."

"Shh! Mozart. That arrogance—and that tongue of yours will get you in trouble. And while we're on the subject, it is best not to get on the wrong side of Thorwart. He is an oaf, but a powerful oaf. You do not know what influence he wields."

"I know only too well. Especially his influence with Madame Weber. Oh, I know. I only say these things to you because you are my friend, and you understand me. I long to prove myself. Until I have an opera at the Burgtheater, no one will think of me as anything but an upstart from Salzburg. If only it were not Thorwart who held the key."

Their voices lowered and I could not hear anything for a while, until there was more creaking of chairs and then floorboards. It appeared that Mozart was leaving, and the porter had not yet returned, although I noticed that Mademoiselle Weber's singing had stopped.

"In any case, Stephanie, I have become acquainted with some very wealthy and influential people of late. The Countess Thun has invited me to her home to perform for a select group of friends. And there is money—and influence—among others in Vienna aside from the closed circle that rules the Burgtheater with an iron fist."

Any parting comments were drowned out by the squeaking and creaking of their footsteps across the room.

When the porter opened the door beside me, I let out a little shriek. I had been concentrating so hard on listening to Mozart and Stephanie that I'd forgotten I was waiting to be summoned inside.

"Mademoiselle Weber said to show you in," he said, his shoulders drooping as if navigating the corridors of the backstage area of the theater was going to be his most onerous task of the day.

I could hardly tell him I didn't really want to see Mademoiselle Weber, although I feared that in visiting her I would miss Mozart and lose my opportunity to talk to him. The porter walked so slowly I had to restrain myself from urging him to hurry. I followed him up a narrow staircase behind the stage, glimpsing rooms and alcoves full of coiled ropes and flat cutouts of scenery all jumbled together—pastoral scenes and castles, shop fronts and ballrooms.

By the time we arrived at Mademoiselle Weber's dressing room I was thoroughly confused as to where I was, having not passed a single window to the outside to give me any sense of direction.

"Here is the young lady, Madame," the porter said, bowing to a beautiful creature swathed in a crimson silk robe over her morning dress, standing in front of a long mirror so that there appeared to be two of her in the room. She had the dark eyes and hair of Constanze, but the resemblance stopped there. She not only outshone her modestly pretty sister, she knew she did, and I could see she was accustomed to dazzling everyone.

"Mademoiselle Weber," I said, curtsying, "forgive the intrusion."

"If this is a social call, I'm really Madame Lange, but I don't suppose anyone in The Eye of God told you that." She had the clear, careful speaking voice of an accomplished singer, and her gesture when she bade me take a seat filled the small chamber as if she wanted to be sure everyone in the gallery saw it. The porter bowed and closed the door. "Now, perhaps you can tell me what this is all about."

"I really must beg your forgiveness. I used your name to get in, when I really need to see Herr Mozart." Doubtless my admission would not ingratiate me to Madame Lange, whom I had already insulted by failing to address her correctly.

"I hope you don't intend to sing for him. I doubt his opera will ever come to pass in any case if our esteemed theater director has anything to say about it. You had much better audition for Signore Salieri."

"I don't wish to audition," I said. "This is another matter altogether, quite a serious one."

"Oh dear, has he jilted you too? What city have you come from? No, I can hear by your accent that you are Viennoise."

"Please, I fear Herr Mozart may soon be leaving, and I must, I simply must speak to him!" I had no more patience for prevarication. I was so fatigued that the room began to swim around me. If I lay down, I thought, I would instantly fall into a deep sleep.

"You are unwell!" Madame Lange said, with genuine concern in her voice. She rang a little bell on her dressing table. Within moments a maid appeared.

"Yes Madame?"

"Fetch Amadé," she commanded, "and bring some chocolate." She shifted her position so that she could see herself in the mirror and poked at her dark, glossy curls. When she finished she turned back to me. "I am sure you are unwell. Where do you live? You should return there at once. I'll have Hans call you a Fiaker."

I thanked her and was in the midst of protesting that I could not go home just yet when Mozart flung open the door, removed his tricorn hat and bent down on one knee in a low bow to Aloysia Lange. "Your servant. Your slave."

"Come Amadé, you don't have to flatter me to get me to perform in your opera—if it's ever finished. It's not my decision to make."

"But I know you could say a word in the right ear, and—" he stopped with his mouth open when he saw me. Blood tinted his cheeks and he stood, taking a short, awkward step toward me. "Mademoiselle Schurman, is it not? How strange that we should meet again so soon. And here."

I nodded. What could I say to him? I suddenly realized that Madame Lange could be thinking the worst; that I was perhaps trying to win Mozart away from Constanze. I wanted to reassure her as quickly as possible and so I started speaking without any hesitation. "I must ask you about Frau Bachmann, in the strictest confidence."

Madame Lange raised one eyebrow and pursed her lips in an amused pout, looking back and forth between us. I had blurted out my question awkwardly, and she probably thought I was just trying to cover up my real reason for being there. I had to dig myself out of the hole I had fallen into. I turned to Aloysia. "I cannot explain, but I shall give your sister a full account of my actions as soon as I am able. I know this seems odd, but it is nothing like what you are probably thinking."

"I assure you, I have no thoughts whatever."

There was no more time to waste trying to explain what I was doing, and so I turned my attention back to Mozart and said, "Now I must ask, Herr Mozart, if I may trouble you for a few minutes' private conference."

I gave the composer credit for seeing past the awkwardness of the moment to my serious intent. He kissed the soprano's hand and then opened the dressing room door, bowing as he made way for me to pass in front of him. I stood, without thinking putting my weight fully on my injured leg without the aid of the umbrella. "Argghh!" I exclaimed. Both Aloysia and Amadé took hold of my arm at the same time so that their hands touched. Madame Lange smiled at the look of confusion on Mozart's face.

"You suffer," Mozart said, gently helping me out.

"It is nothing, only a stiffness I sometimes forget to beware of." I would wait and see how he responded to my questions before thinking of telling him anything more. Once we were safely out of the Burgtheater I turned to him. "Would you do me the great favor of accompanying me in a Fiaker outside the city gates?" I asked. "I have something important to tell you and show you."

He drew out a pocket watch and frowned at it.

"I know it is a great presumption, and I have little to offer in return except an introduction to Baron van Swieten, who has many magnificent scores by Johann Bach in his care at the Imperial Library."

His eyes brightened unmistakably. "Very well. I am not expected anywhere until this evening."

We walked to the nearest Fiaker stand while I tried to think of how to question Mozart about a murder—or, as I had discovered of late, an attempted murder.

CHAPTER TWENTY-FOUR

I found it difficult to concentrate with every little jolt of the carriage over the uneven cobbles sending a piercing pain into my leg. Added to my discomfort was my increasingly gnawing hunger. We had passed the maid on her way down the corridor with the tray of chocolate, and the bewitching smell had awakened my appetite.

"You turn up in the strangest places, Mademoiselle Schurman," Mozart said to me. "I cannot imagine what you want of me."

"All I want, Herr Mozart, is the truth. First, I must ask you if you attended the concert at the Augarten these four evenings ago, and then I shall tell you what is my interest in Frau Bachmann."

"Well, yes I did attend the concert. I wore a mask, though, so that I would not be recognized. I wanted to get the measure of the competition before my own series of concerts, which I intend to give there next summer." A shrewd little light flickered in Mozart's eyes. I had never seen—or heard—anyone who was so single-minded in his purpose, always looking for ways to put his music before the public. His demeanor was almost desperate, as if someone had told him he had to succeed quickly or he would not succeed at all.

"And when you left the concert, did you go on foot or did you ride? And which road did you take?"

"I—I'm not entirely certain. I may have walked, or I may have taken a carriage."

"It was a beautiful evening. I walked."

"Well then, I expect that is what I did, and therefore I must have taken the shortest route, to the Kärntnertor."

That was precisely the road I took, and on which I had witnessed the attack. I wasn't yet ready to let on about that, though. By now we had passed through that very gate and were on the road to the Augarten. "Was it this way?"

He looked out the windows on both sides of the carriage. "Of course, it was night. But I suppose this is the way I came. Really, what is it you are trying to find out, Mademoiselle?" Mozart was beginning to sound a bit exasperated and had reached for his pocket watch again.

"Herr Mozart, I don't know how to say this, but is it possible that I saw you—that I witnessed you—could you have—"

"You're not one of the good Frau Weber's spies, or that snake Thorwart's? They'll do anything to turn Constanze against me!" He drew away from me and prepared to knock on the carriage hood with his cane, intending to get the driver to stop no doubt so he could leap out.

"No! Please sit, Monsieur. I simply want to know who attacked Herr Bachmann on this road." I blurted it out much more abruptly than I intended and it really all sounded so preposterous.

Mozart sat down abruptly and stared at me open-mouthed. "You think I—" He clamped his mouth shut, covered it with his white-gloved hand and started to shake with laughter. Soon he was positively convulsed. I did not understand what could be construed as funny about what I had said.

"Driver!" I yelled out the window. "Stop the carriage." I had seen that we were near where the road curved around the stand of Linden trees. If I could get Mozart to stop laughing I wanted him to see the scratchings in the tree trunk, which I had no doubt were there despite anything the captain had said. After recent events, I now knew for certain that the Count von Bauer could not be trusted. "Please, Herr Mozart, I beg you to stop laughing and come with me."

I climbed down from the carriage, again causing myself considerable pain, but this time I had Mirela's umbrella and used it without hesitation. Mozart followed me, his eyes still wet with tears of laughter. I felt my face full of heat and I ground my teeth with anger. How could he make light of such a thing?

"Please, please forgive me Mademoiselle. It was just too absurd a suggestion. The attack upon my dear friend Herr Bachmann is surely no laughing matter. Just that I might have perpetrated it." This thought brought on a fresh bout of hysteria.

"I would like to show you something." Although I did not believe Mozart was the culprit, he had unwittingly confirmed there had been an attack on Herr Bachmann. He had let that slip without even noticing it. I beckoned him over to where I knelt down by the base of the largest tree trunk.

Mozart again calmed his laughter and crouched down next to me. "How old are you?" he asked, incongruously I thought.

"Eighteen years," I said, for no particular reason exaggerating my age. Seventeen seemed so young and foolish. At eighteen I would truly be a woman. Although Mirela, at only sixteen, possessed more womanly characteristics than I ever would, I thought.

"*Achtzehn Jahre.* Are you certain you didn't say *Achtzig Jahre?*"

He smiled again. I was indeed hobbling around like an eighty-year old. "I know you mean to be humorous, but I would much rather you would tell me how these marks came to be here and what they might mean." I pulled the grass away from the very base of the trunk to reveal the pyramid and the eye, exactly where I expected they would be. I now saw how crudely drawn they were compared to the magnificent emblems in the great chamber where I had witnessed the bizarre ceremony, and the delicately fashioned charms on Herr van Swieten's key fob.

"Ah," he said, bending down quite close to examine the marks.

"D'you expect me to wait here all day?" the driver called from his box.

"Just a moment, please!" I called back, "We shall return to Vienna shortly." I turned my attention once more to Mozart. "You were saying?"

He sighed. "What is it you think has happened, Mademoiselle Schurman? I believe you have stumbled upon something that is no business of yours and concocted a fairy tale worthy of Monsieur Perrault."

"A fairy story! I hardly think so." I pulled my skirts up to reveal the bandage Maya had secured around my leg. Without thinking how I would put it back on as tightly and cleanly as she had, I untied the knot and began to unwind the cloth. As the layers were exposed, a stain appeared that became darker and darker, until the bandage was quite fused to the congealed blood of the wound. I could see the dark threads holding my skin together, and knew that if I yanked the cloth away I would no doubt provoke fresh, inconvenient and painful bleeding.

"*Gott im Himmel!*" Mozart exclaimed. "Please, hide it away." He turned, clearly distressed. Although I realized it was unkind of me to shock him so, I was at least satisfied that he would now pay attention to what I was saying and stop treating me like a foolish, capricious girl. I rewound the bandage as best I could.

"You may think Herr Bachmann's fate is no concern of mine, and perhaps at one time it wasn't. But as you see . . ."

"What happened?"

"First, you must tell me everything you know."

He stood from his crouching position and gave me his hand, pulling me upright. "Please, lean on my arm. You should not be walking about with such a terrible injury." Mozart led me back to the Fiaker and gave an address to the driver while I settled myself in my seat.

"I did indeed meet Herr Bachmann on that very night. But not until he had been carried back to Vienna, and lay awaiting the attendance of a doctor in his apartment."

"But how—"

"You must permit me to tell the story in my own way. I wish you to know the entirety of it, so that you may see for yourself that it is time you gave up this foolish inquiry and went back to your own concerns. I shall take you to someone who can satisfy your curiosity, and make an end of it. These are matters in which ladies should not meddle."

I leaned back in the Fiaker and closed my eyes. *Matters in which ladies should not meddle.* How often had I heard that in my life, and I was hardly yet a lady myself. Why must ladies not meddle in certain things? Why was it so shocking for me to do something as innocent and beautiful as play the violin? Why should I not try to discover the fate of a poor man who was attacked in my sight? I hoped in my heart that all the efforts our emperor was making to create more justice in the world might also do something for girls. But I had not heard of such a thing, and realized that I would probably have to continue hiding my true self if I wished to be allowed to lead the kind of life that men could so easily—without the slightest obstruction, and with every encouragement.

I was still exhausted from my adventures and must have fallen asleep in the carriage, because the next thing I remembered was being rocked awake as Mozart stepped down from it. He opened the door on my side and helped me out. I turned to pay the driver, but the fellow had already clucked to his horses and trotted off. Mozart must have paid him. "Please allow me to pay for the carriage at least, since it was I who forced this jaunt upon you," I said.

"Nonsense. Come."

I realized as soon as I looked around that we were at Frau Bachmann's dwelling. If I had been in any doubt at all, my ears would soon have discovered my location, because the sweet, piercing sound of a flute filled the air. The melody was familiar. "That's from your overture to *The Abduction!*" I exclaimed. Mozart smiled.

He helped me up the stairs, and when we knocked at Frau Bachmann's door, a light step hurried forward to open it, yet the flute playing did not cease.

To my complete amazement, Frau Bachmann stood in the doorway and inside, sitting on a cot that had been moved into the room, his face pale and drawn but appearing otherwise fully alive, was Herr Bachmann. He had just taken his flute from his lips. The music stand had been moved close to the bedside.

"Herr Bachmann!" "Mademoiselle Schurman!" "Herr Mozart!"

Three of us spoke at once. I'm not sure who was the most astonished. The only person in the room who was not surprised at all was Mozart, who stood to one side with a broad grin on his face. "And now, the second act finale should commence, with each of you singing in great confusion and all manner of chaos ensuing."

CHAPTER TWENTY-FIVE

Frau Bachmann brought in chocolate and buttered bread. No meal I had ever eaten had tasted so delicious. I felt the weight of my fatigue only after my belly was full, and struggled to stay awake to listen to the extraordinary account of what had happened that evening after the concert in the Augarten.

"I had finished playing—the concert had gone well and I was feeling very happy," Herr Bachmann said. "I do not often get the chance to perform at public concerts. Thanks to Amadé here, I was given the job when the original flutist became ill. Now that we are no longer required to wear our yellow patches, it is sometimes possible to remain unrecognized as a Jew in such situations. The conductor commended me on my playing afterwards and I believe wanted to offer me more work. I thought this would be the beginning of having all my dreams fulfilled. There were other influential people in the audience. I recognized even Thorwart, although I supposed he wasn't listening much, as he had a very pretty young thing with brown curls in tow.

"Something odd happened, as I remember it now . . ." Bachmann paused and closed his eyes, as if searching for something in his mind. "It had to do with Thorwart. He was speaking to someone, I don't really know who, but a man. And I thought I caught his eye looking in my direction. Well, since he can have no idea who I am, I cannot imagine that he truly was. But still, it seemed odd.

"Forgive me if I wander a bit. I am still weak, although healing well they tell me. What was I saying? Oh yes.

"That incident was a small one, and when I left I was hopeful that I would no longer be required to work long hours and ruin my fingers sewing, and only be able to play occasionally in the home of a wealthy Jew.

"My heart was so light as I walked home, not wanting to squander my fee on a Fiaker. I saw someone up ahead, a violinist, taking the same road as I, and I felt safe there. Then when I heard someone else following me, I thought everyone had decided to take advantage of the fine night, and that probably it was someone I knew, another musician perhaps.

"He was walking faster than I, and I could hear him gaining on me, and had already prepared a friendly greeting, a word about the weather, to share with him. The violinist in front of us had turned the corner and was hidden by the Linden trees. The steps behind me quickened, and I heard someone call my name out—not too loudly, as I remember. Just by the Linden trees the fellow caught me up. I turned to look at him when he tapped me on the shoulder, and thinking I recognized him from the concert, I greeted him as I had planned.

"At first I was only surprised that he embraced me, since I did not really know the fellow at all. Then when it became clear that far from embracing me in friendship he was attacking me with violent intent it was too late. As he did it, he muttered something in my ear, that I would never get away with it, that the Lodge could not protect me, and that I would never see the inside of the Burgtheater or any other concert hall in Vienna.

"Immediately after that I felt something hot in the center of my back and lost control of my legs. Even then, as the world was fading from my consciousness, I thought the man was confused, that this stranger with evil in his heart had mistaken me for someone else. Part of what he said made some sense to me, though: about the Lodge—"

Mozart made a movement to stop him talking and glanced in alarm at Frau Bachmann and myself.

Bachmann waved his hand as if shooing away a gnat. "It does not matter. My wife knows all. I was delirious and spoke in my fever. I had to tell her what I meant. And if you truly wish me to explain myself to this young lady, I must do so fully."

"I believe I have first-hand experience of this Lodge, as you call it," I said, "a Lodge that is protected by a rather fierce guardian."

Mozart pressed his lips shut, perhaps to force himself not to reveal anything more, yet he made no further attempt to silence Herr Bachmann.

"As I lost consciousness, I heard another voice, someone calling out, and then my attacker ran away. That other someone knelt down by me. I recall a court uniform, and that is all I remember—until I awakened in the Lodge, where I was being cared for by a fine doctor." He reached out for Frau Bachmann's hand and addressed her directly. "You see, my dear, once one is a part of such a brotherhood, one is taken care of when in dire need. We could never have afforded a doctor, and if Captain Bauer had not come along to take me from the deserted roadside I might easily have perished."

"Captain Bauer!" I leapt from my seat and began to limp around the room. "But you said—" I cast an accusing glance at Mozart and shed all feelings of drowsiness as if someone had jerked a warm blanket off me and left me naked in the freezing cold. "Why did you mislead me?" I asked Mozart, "And why did the captain not say? Why did he try to confuse and astound me?"

Frau Bachmann replied to her husband's puzzled look. "This is the young lady, the one who said she frightened away your attacker."

"But . . ." Herr Bachmann paused, as if searching his memory for something, "I am certain it was a young man who came to my aid."

I was not ready to confess my deception to Mozart, and I shot a warning glance at Frau Bachmann. Thankfully, she understood me. "Perhaps you are confusing the musician you saw walking ahead of you with your rescuer."

He nodded. "You were very brave, in any case, to intervene, Mademoiselle Schurman."

Now was the time to get the answer to the one question I most wanted to ask Herr Bachmann. I had the perfect opportunity, there in that dingy parlor. All I had to do was open my mouth and utter the words. But how could I, with Mozart himself in the room? Yet when I looked at the composer, I did not see a murderer, even one who had failed in his attempt.

Before I could lose courage, I said, "There is something I must ask you." I sat beside Herr Bachmann on his pallet and laid my hand on his arm. He looked into my eyes. His were a warm, brown shade, a little pink in the whites, as if some of the color from the irises had leaked out. "When I knelt down next to you on the road that night, you said something. Just before you—before I thought—well, I was certain, with all the blood, and you quite fainted away—"

"Of course you thought I was dead. It was dark, too."

"Yes. I did think you were dead. And you might have died! Which was why, perhaps, I attached so much significance to what you said, with what I thought was your last breath."

"And what did I say?" he asked.

I wondered if he truly did not remember, or whether he pretended not to for some reason of his own. "You said," I looked around at the composer, who leaned forward in his chair as if he had not already heard Herr Bachmann's story and was learning it all for the first time, and then I turned back to Bachmann. "You uttered a name. You said, *Mozart*."

In the silence that followed my revelation in which no one apparently even breathed, I became aware of the intimate chuckle of a pigeon under the eaves, followed by wings flapping into the distance as the bird flew away.

"More chocolate, Mademoiselle Schurman?" It was Frau Bachmann who finally broke the tense silence, bringing me a cup filled to the brim. I accepted it gratefully, drinking it down almost in one gulp.

I somehow found the courage to look up at Mozart. He appeared deeply shocked. "So, that's why you thought I . . .What can have made you imagine, other than . . . other than Abraham speaking my name?"

"That's exactly it," I said. "It seemed impossible to me. I was certain I hadn't really understood what he was trying to tell me. That's why I didn't say anything to the authorities when I reported the attack to them." I rose and walked to the window. That the world outside could have been going on in its normal, daily rounds while we discussed these strange matters seemed impossible to me. The sight of two children tossing pebbles back and forth with increasing violence until they were actually using them as missiles to fling at each other appeared more dreamlike than real.

"I seem to recall . . . something . . ."

At the sound of Herr Bachmann's voice I turned around to look at him, just in time to see Frau Bachmann put her finger to her lips to silence him. I pretended I did not see her.

"Have you told this to anyone else?" Frau Bachmann asked.

"No. No one," I answered, deciding that I did not need to bring Zoltán into the conversation at that moment.

"Well, now all is revealed, and you can let the matter lie and not bother yourself any more." Herr Bachmann laid the flute down and stretched out on his side on the cot, as if the few words we had exchanged had utterly exhausted him.

"I'm sorry, Herr Bachmann, but all has not been revealed, and I am far from satisfied concerning what happened to you—and to me."

I wanted to press them further, but all at once I felt extremely tired. Quite without warning I gave an enormous, open-mouthed yawn. At the same time, my legs suddenly felt as if they could not hold me upright any longer. I sat in the only empty chair, the one I had vacated to sit on the cot next to Herr Bachmann. A feeling of irresistible fatigue engulfed me, as if I were ready to sink into a down-filled mattress and be covered by a soft quilt, and the effort of holding my eyelids open became too great to sustain. Just before they closed, I saw both Frau Bachmann and Mozart bending at the waist and peering into my face. I thought I heard Frau Bachmann say, "I only used a drop. Her exhaustion has done the rest," and then Mozart add, "Nothing must interfere with tomorrow evening," before I let myself slide into the sweet oblivion of long-delayed sleep.

CHAPTER TWENTY-SIX

My head felt like a ball of lead when I tried to lift it off the soft pillow. The room I was in seemed very familiar, and yet completely strange. This effect was strengthened by the fact that over in the corner, at the foot of this familiar bed that was not mine, stood Herr van Swieten.

"What happened?" I asked, unable to think of a more coherent question at the time.

He stepped up to the bedside, drawing a chair over as he did so—and this chair was also familiar to me, almost as if I had dreamed of its existence rather than seen it in real life—sat down and took my hand. Or rather, didn't so much take my hand as my wrist, pressing on it quite hard with the fingers of one hand and taking out his pocket watch with the other. He stared in silence at the pocket watch for what seemed a long time in the stillness of the room, his air of concentration inhibiting any conversation.

At last, he dropped my wrist, looked into my eyes and smiled. But the look he gave me was not one of friendly inquiry, it was more calculated than that. He lifted first one of my lids then the other, peering into each eye as if he was looking for a lost jewel inside of it, or as if he was examining one of his precious manuscripts.

Sheer, lingering fatigue mixed with curiosity over what he might do next kept me silent. When at last he sat back in the chair and the look in his eyes changed to something more approachable and sincere, he said, "You have been ill. A fever. But now I see that you are recovering nicely. Your Mama has been very worried."

All at once I realized where I was. I was in my mother's bed. The reason I had not recognized the room was that I had never seen it from just that angle before. Although I had crawled into bed with my parents when I was a little child, Mama had rearranged her furniture in recent months. Since then, it would normally be I who would sit at the bedside, changing the compress on my mother's forehead during one of her headaches. But something else was different too. The walls had been painted a clean, fresh white. It was the second time in recent days that something had changed about our home. First the piano, now my mother had repainted her bedroom. "Where is Mozart? And the where are the Bachmanns?"

"I don't know who these Bachmanns are, but Mozart! Why, I expect he is in his lodgings, or perhaps rehearsing the singers for the coming audition of his opera, *The Abduction from the Seraglio* for Herr Thorwart and the other theater directors."

I pushed myself up on my elbows. Other than feeling as though I were looking through a film of haze at everything around me, I did not feel ill. I remembered once having a bad fever—I was quite small at the time—and when I was recovering my limbs felt very weak. It was more than I could do to lift a cup to my lips. Yet I felt perfectly strong at that moment. No, I was certain I had not been ill. "Why are you lying to me?" I asked him, hoping the question would catch him off guard.

"My dear Mademoiselle Schurman! What reason would I have to lie to you?"

"I thought you had begun to call me Theresa at tea the other day."

"At tea—really, my dear girl, you must understand that you have had very vivid dreams during the course of your fever. I assure you, much as I have heard about you from your mother, we have never had the pleasure of meeting before these moments."

"Where is Mama?"

"She is in the parlor, just waiting for me to proclaim you fit so that she can come in and welcome you back to the world."

"I should like to see her now." My tone was not polite. I had no idea why this eminent baron, librarian to His Imperial Majesty and former physician to the late empress, would want to lie to me so barbarously. If this was any indication of what life would be like in the future, then, I thought, perhaps I should go and live with Mirela among the Romany.

I had no further opportunity for reflection at that moment because my mother opened the door as if she were afraid of awakening a baby and tiptoed across the room. A light scent of lavender wafted toward me in the slight breeze she created, and her hair was whitened with more powder than she usually applied in the morning. I also noticed that she wore her best sprigged muslin day dress and had a black silk neck lace tied around her throat.

"Theresa my sweet! I was so worried about you." She bent down and kissed my forehead, then smoothed the covers over me and tucked in the side nearest her so that I felt as if I'd been swaddled—or strapped in so that I would not be able to escape.

"I'm sorry, Mama, I should not have been away for so long without sending word to you."

She glanced at van Swieten, then shook her finger at me. "What nonsense you speak! Unless by going away you mean that you should have taken care not to become ill with a fever for five days. I'm sure it's that teaching you do, going into strange houses where they don't wash properly."

"Mama! How can you?"

"How can I what, dear?"

My mother's expressions had always been as transparent as a pane of glass. Whatever was happening inside her heart and mind she clearly displayed in her wide, blue eyes, whether she wished to or not. I knew, therefore, that she was saying what she had been told to say by someone else. I could also tell that her desire to please that other person—doubtless the Baron van Swieten—outweighed any feeling that it was wrong to deceive me. "You may think, both of you, that you will convince me of this falsehood, but you will not. I am no more ill than you are. I am simply very fatigued, and I injured myself. I think the baron knows how." I cast an accusing glance at Herr van Swieten who once again gave me his patronizing smile. I thought I detected a note of warning in his eyes.

Clearly, protesting would get me nowhere. I lay back into the pillows and closed my eyes.

"Perhaps you should rest now," Mama said. I didn't answer her.

"I'll give you this in a little water," the baron said, putting two drops of something sticky and brown into the glass of water by my bedside and handing it to me. "It will make your head feel better." I lifted the glass to my lips. As soon as he saw me do so he turned away. "I'll check on the patient again this afternoon," he said to Mama in a gentle, reassuring tone.

"You are too kind. However can I repay you?" Mama's voice held a promise that, if she'd ever used such a manner with my father, I must have been too young to understand. Van Swieten lifted her hand to his lips. His attention was focused entirely on my mother, and so I quietly put the glass back down on the table, having not taken a single sip.

The door closed behind them and their voices became muffled, but were still distinct enough for me to hear the baron reply, "You will soon enough be repaying me beyond all measure by bestowing your presence upon me so generously." After that came a pause in the conversation and I took it to indicate that they had embraced, perhaps even kissed.

I rolled on my side to face the wall, away from the idea that my mother would soon be married to and share intimate hours with a man who was not my father. I could have reconciled myself to this drastic change in our lives. I liked the baron, and he was extremely well connected. Mama had certainly made the most of her remaining beauty and caught herself quite a respectable man to end her widowhood. I did not have to hear her say the words to understand that she assumed part of the benefit would be in placing me in the sights of a wealthier class of young man.

But all wasn't over yet. I knew I had to get away from Mama and the baron's watchful eyes and go back to the Lodge, this time with the police. At the very least, that dangerous cat should be destroyed. What if an unsuspecting child crawled into the cellar and became its dinner?

I heard the door to our apartment open and close, and Herr van Swieten's steps decrescendo away. For the next hour or two I remained on my side with my eyes shut, pretending to be asleep whenever my mother entered the room. It wasn't long before I heard Greta return with Anna, whose noisy babbling was quickly hushed up by my mother. She whispered something to Anna, but my baby sister, not knowing she was supposed to lie, said quite clearly, "Did Rezia come home?"

Next came the dull thud of an ineffectual spank through layers of clothing, then Anna's healthy lungs let loose a full-voiced bellow that faded as Greta carried her into the dining room.

CHAPTER TWENTY-SEVEN

I watched the colors in the room gradually darken as the daylight waned. Greta brought a candle and a tray of food in when St. Stephen's bells chimed the hour of six. I was far too hungry to ignore the meal, wishing I could leave it aside and prove to them that I would not be manipulated, but if I didn't eat something I would not have the strength for what lay ahead. I sat up and drank the soup and ate the bread so quickly I had to stifle a loud belch. I turned around and pretended to be asleep again just in time to avoid having to speak to my mother when she came in to check on me. All the time I was planning my escape.

I would have to dress in something of my mother's. I could pull on a day dress and a long, concealing cloak. I hoped her shoes would fit me, because a quick glance around showed that mine had been taken away.

Fortunately my mother's room had a small balcony she rarely used, as it looked out over the kitchen courtyard three floors below. I had discovered once when I was much younger that, due to the fact that the house had been constructed so that the apartments on one side were half a floor apart from those on the other, I could clamber from one such balcony to another on the building and make my way undetected to that courtyard. At the time, I had merely wanted to help myself to some freshly baked cakes. I couldn't remember precisely how I'd managed it. When Mama discovered what I'd done, she punished me severely, and the doors to the balcony had remained locked. But I knew she kept the key in the nightstand drawer, although I never attempted that feat again.

Assuming I was able to get out this way that evening, I would have to decide where to go first. Who could I trust? I did not want to expose Mirela to any more danger, and it would take too long to get out to the camp anyway.

I'm not certain why, but the stern, disapproving face of Herr von Eskeles kept encroaching on my thoughts. What could he do? Perhaps he was the only person I could think of who would have no reason to deceive me about the Lodge and Herr Bachmann and Mozart, since nothing about him connected him with it or with any of the others, aside from his being Jewish. But I knew I would be barred from seeing him, and in any case it would be quite shocking for me to go uninvited to their house.

I could go to Danior. Yet something told me that Danior had betrayed me to someone, possibly Mozart himself, although I could not imagine why he would have done so. And Alida was in no fit state to do anything except await the arrival of her baby.

If only I knew how to contact Zoltán without alerting Danior. Perhaps he, of all people, would believe me and help me. He was staying with Danior and Alida though, and if I went there I would not be able to keep my activities secret from the rest of them. If I could but write a letter to Zoltán. Then I could ask him to meet me somewhere. But where?

I wished with all my heart that I had not turned Herr von Eskeles against me. There was something about him that reminded me of my father. Or perhaps it was simply that I knew my father would have frowned on my decision to deceive them. Whatever it was, I regretted not having access to this kind, cultured family.

By the time I heard my mother fetch her dressing gown from the room and retire to pass the night in my little alcove—having sacrificed her own comfortable bed for me—I had only the barest beginnings of a plan worked out in my head. Somehow I couldn't think clearly in that room. I could smell my mother's powder and perfume and sense her presence. And because I had avoided that chamber as much as I could since my father died, I still associated the space with him. Lying in their bed took me back to early childhood when I had truly been ill with a fever, and as far as I recall Papa did not leave my side, even bringing the Amati in and playing for me as I recovered my strength. I think I was only a little older than Anna was now, perhaps three, and the two-week stretch of being confined to my parents' room had faded from my memory, becoming no more than a comforting blur—until this time of being confined there again, if only for a matter of hours.

Once the apartment was truly quiet and I could hear even Greta snoring in her alcove off the parlor, I slipped out from under the covers. I would have to find my way around without a candle.

The cold wooden floor shocked my warm feet and awakened the rest of my body as the cold traveled upward. I tested out my strength on my injured leg and was relieved to discover that my forced rest had eased the pain considerably. I could walk on it almost without favoring it at all, although I knew I would still have to be careful.

I felt for the dress I knew was in my mother's armoire, one that she never wore if she was going out because it was plain and unbecoming, and found her sturdiest pair of boots. The dress and the boots fit well enough, and the cloak—again, an old one reserved for walks in the country in Esterhaza and therefore never used in Vienna these past two years—was as generously concealing as I had hoped it would be.

Staying on tiptoes, I crept to the bedside table and eased the little drawer out. To my surprise, it was now full of letters where, being on my father's side of the bed, it had once contained only the key and notebook where Papa used to write down things he thought about music when he was wakeful at night. I wondered what Mama had done with that little book, and what were these letters she now kept there. I had no light by which to examine them, but something told me they were from Herr van Swieten.

Fortunately, the key was still there, at the very back of the drawer under the letters. I hoped that scrabbling around for it did not make too much noise. I was also relieved that the lock still worked, and that the doors opened with only the smallest creak.

The balcony was smaller than I recalled, but I had been much younger the last time I attempted such an escape. I peered over the edge to the unlit courtyard, illuminated only by the slightest spilling over of light from apartments whose inhabitants were wakeful into the night. I hoped that none of these would see me scramble like a squirrel from ledge to balcony. It seemed a very long way down, and the distance from one balcony to another appeared greater rather than smaller than I remembered.

But I had started, and I meant to continue. I crossed myself and said a silent prayer to St. Cecilia, reminding her that if she spared me, I could praise God with beautiful music, even if I would never be allowed to perform in a cathedral. I hoped the intention would suffice.

I gathered my skirts up and tucked them in, but I wanted to leave the cloak to hang free so that it would shield me from being identified in case anyone happened to wander out to the courtyard to piss. It made the climb more awkward but I felt it was essential.

My descent started with swinging my leg over the wrought iron railing and finding a purchase for my toes on the scant edge that protruded beyond it. I steadied myself, then crouched low, clutching the balusters and screwing up my courage to reach my right leg out to the railing of the balcony on the apartment next door, the one below being too far to reach directly even if I hung fully extended from the bottom of my mother's balcony.

I could not do it. In fact, I could hardly remember how I had managed the climb when I was small. I feared that if I put myself so utterly off balance I would fall to the ground and be killed instantly. I was on the point of climbing back over the railing and admitting defeat when I recalled something from that time long ago. I hadn't had to leap from one balcony to another. I think that was something I accepted as true from my Papa's laughing description of my monkey-like behavior. I remembered that, set into the wall at regular intervals as if designed to allow someone to climb out, perhaps in case of fire, were iron grips. All I had to do was reach the first one and ease myself onto that ladder that was almost invisible from far away. The first step would be the hardest.

I saw an iron handle a short way from my perch and stretched out my hand to grasp it. I could touch it with my fingertips, but I wouldn't be able to get a grip on it without letting go of the railing. I would have to take a leap, although not as dangerous a one as I would if I had had to get from one balcony to the other. And this way, I stood less chance of being seen from within as I made my way down.

After carefully judging where I would have to put my foot so that I would not end up hanging off the building with only the feeble strength of my arms to prevent a fatal fall, I took a deep breath, reached out, and pushed myself off the balcony so that I could grasp the iron ring.

My right hand slipped, but my left hand—the hand made strong on the fingerboard of the violin—got a firm hold. I thought at first I would not be able to grasp with both hands, but on the third try, I managed to get myself established on the iron grips.

As I descended slowly, discovering that not all of the grips were equally securely fixed into the mortar between the stones, I planned my route out through the alley that ran next to the building and to the main road. There would be lamps still lit, but I could hurry between shadows and remain largely hidden. I knew that my ultimate destination had to be the Lodge again, and once I was in that part of town, concealment would be simple since the street lamps were spaced farther apart and in many cases never lit—or extinguished by those who desired the darkness as soon as the lamplighter had gone on his way. I could find my way there again, and probably enter the building unseen.

But that would accomplish nothing. This time, I had to bring someone with me, someone to witness all that occurred and—and what? If Abraham Bachmann had not been murdered, what could I complain of? There was the matter of the huge cat. Yet I had been trespassing on private property. I could hardly make a complaint without exposing my own foolishness.

I was so relieved when my feet felt the cobbles of the courtyard and I stood on safe ground that my knees shook. My head swam a bit, as if I had stood up suddenly after lying down for a long time. And I still had an ache in the leg with the gash, although not nearly as severe as it had been. But I had come to a decision that gave me new confidence. Just before I reached the bottom of my perilous climb, I realized that the person I most needed with me and who I could trust above all others was my brother.

Toby would understand as no one else could why I so wanted to get to the bottom of these strange events. He had once told me that the apprentices knew how to get out at night and sometimes went off for a bit of revelry without Herr and Frau Goldschmidt knowing. I could most likely get behind the luthier's workshop and knock on the window of the room where the apprentices slept, and Toby would be able to find a way to get out without disturbing the others.

I took a few deep breaths, said another silent prayer, and then ran silently and unevenly toward the alley that would lead me out onto the street.

CHAPTER TWENTY-EIGHT

The streets were exceptionally quiet. A light mist had begun to fall, soon coating my cloak with tiny drops that clung to the fuzz of woolen fibers too small to be seen otherwise. I gradually became accustomed to the ache in my leg and steeled myself to ignore it as I dashed from one dark alcove to another toward the street where Herr Goldschmidt had his shop.

As I fully expected, the iron grille over the storefront had been pulled across and locked, and not a glimmer of light showed through any of the windows. I had to go several shops down to find the alley that would lead to the back, and when I did, I found it almost blocked by discarded bits of wood and rusty metal. I took care to climb over it all, making as little noise as I could, hoping that anyone who heard me would think I was an amorous cat looking for a mate.

Despite trying hard not to, I caught my mother's dress on a protruding nail and tore it beyond repair. Now I would never be able to hide my midnight excursion from her. Perhaps, once everything was straightened out, it wouldn't matter.

From the back, the workshops in this row of artisans' establishments looked indistinguishable from one another. I had to rely on counting—three shops from the alley. The windows at the back were shuttered. I crept up and tried one, which was fastened from the inside, then moved to the next, judging that two of the windows let into the back of Herr Goldschmidt's. I prayed that the second of the two would yield.

Fortunately, the shutter on that window was not secured. I had doubtless happened on that very exit my brother had mentioned to me before, which seemed so obvious that I imagined the Goldschmidts were well aware that their apprentices sometimes escaped after hours.

I peered in, the only light a dull glow from a grate where the fire had nearly died away. Three cots were fitted into a room barely big enough to hold them, with just enough space to walk around between. I could hear the gentle snoring of exhausted young men. No revelry for them that evening, apparently. The window, too, was unlatched, and I opened it a crack. The wood creaked, and one of the boys stirred and turned over. Not Toby, I thought. The shape was not like his. But which one was he?

A quick inspection of the sprawled bodies soon made it obvious. Toby was the one who had grown too tall for his cot. A telltale, stock-inged foot protruded from the end of the one farthest away. I had knit-ted those socks for him myself. I bent down to the ground and found a pebble, not too big, but large enough that Toby would feel it when it hit him, and tossed it over the apprentice who lay on the nearest cot. It landed with a soft thud on Toby's back. I heard him groan and wanted to shush him, but I was afraid that would wake up the others. I waited patiently for him to turn so that he could see me.

He did turn, but in doing so he sent the pebble I'd thrown tumbling to the floor. Both of the other young men then squirmed and yawned. One of them sat up and rubbed his eyes. "What's that?"

Toby saw me just before I ducked down below the level of the window sill. I hoped he understood that I wanted him not to let the others know I was there.

"Nothing. I had a dream. Go back to sleep."

He had understood. I waited, as he did, for the others to breathe slowly and evenly again. Toby was so quiet that he nearly startled me into shrieking when he appeared at the window. I gestured to him to come out. He signaled that I should wait while he got his coat. Toby definitely had a practical streak that I sometimes lacked.

Soon he had crawled through the window and stood by me, yawning silently. The way he had done it, without a misstep and without making a sound, made me think he was well versed in this manner of exit in the middle of the night.

I motioned him to follow me a safe distance away from the workshop before I started to explain. "You remember the symbols I asked you to find out about?"

"I did. I was going to tell you on Sunday when I came home."

He remembered. It was real. The tiny shadow of a doubt that had crept in when Mama and Herr van Swieten insisted I had been delirious with fever for the past few days vanished in an instant. "How long have you known? And you were going to wait until Sunday to tell me! You just don't know what could have happened by then. But now I know anyway."

"So what do you need me for? Why are we out here in the cold? If Herr Goldschmidt discovers me missing I'll be whipped." A shiver shook his frame as if he were a sapling in a breeze, whether because of the chill autumn night or the idea of a thrashing, I didn't know.

"I'll smooth things over, I promise. I need a witness, someone everyone else will believe. So you're coming with me."

"Where to?"

"First, we need to find a policeman."

Toby stopped dead. "A policeman! I think you'd better know what I found out first. Then you might think twice about getting a policeman."

"We'll worry about that later. This is too important." I grabbed his hand and pulled him along. Toby had grown strong.

"No! Wait at least and hear what else I have to say."

Toby planted his feet and refused to take another step. "All right, but be quick about it."

"We've had a strange project lately, not making an instrument, but planing large boards and staining them dark, making sure they will fit together tightly. Really, Rezia, I felt as if we were making a coffin!"

His words were chilling. "That is odd, truly, but we have no time to discuss it right now. Please come with me."

This time, he relented. I was relieved. Mirela might be quick-witted and able to use her charms to disarm others, but much as it angered me to admit it, I felt I had a better chance of being taken seriously if I had a man with me. No one need know how young he really was. If he didn't stand too directly in the light or say anything with his still boyish voice, his height made him appear much older than he was. It was only when one saw his smooth cheeks, downy hair, and spindly legs that he looked like a little boy. The work making violins had given him strong shoulders and arms.

I hoped that the guard at the station would be the same one who had called after me before, when I was on my way to the Burgtheater. I had a feeling he knew things, and that we wouldn't have to do too much explaining. He might also know the whereabouts of Captain Bauer, whom I wished to avoid at all costs.

For once, things turned out as I wished. Sergeant Hirsch was there—asleep, but there. And he was alone.

I motioned Toby to remain outside and I crept through the open door. On the table at the guard's elbow was an empty tankard of ale that had tipped and spilled its last drops on the floor. The fellow's pipe lay on its side nearby. It had long ago gone out and emptied its dead, white ash onto the table next to the tankard. The guard had stretched out as far as it was possible in an upright wooden chair, his legs straight out in front of him, hands folded over the bulk of his stomach, head tipped over the chair back. His mouth yawned wide, and a drip of spit clung to its outer corner, threatening to continue its course down his cheek with every breath he exhaled.

But it was the inhaled ones that resounded in the tiny hut. My primary object was to disturb the fellow's sleep in such a way that it would not appear obvious to him that I had seen him in this undignified condition, and at the same time so that he would not be frightened into making a loud exclamation that would bring others running.

The only strategy I could think of was to stand where I was, turn my head to the side, and clear my throat politely. This had no effect, being barely loud enough to be heard above the fellow's raucous snores. So I coughed. Nothing. I coughed again, louder.

"What are you doing in there?" hissed Toby from the dark just behind me.

"Shh!" I said.

Hirsch did not awaken at those sounds either, but something made him stir, and he bumped into the table, sending the tankard clattering to the floor. This jolted him out of his sleep. He sat upright and immediately began talking.

"Yes, yes, quite right! Best to be vigilant at all times."

I tried to pretend I had only just walked in. "As I was saying," I began. "I need the assistance of a policeman, and you had been so kind to me the other day that I thought immediately of asking you." I smiled and willed a blush into my cheeks, trying to exert that power Mirela seemed capable of wielding so expertly.

Apparently I had some success. The guard stood and bowed to me. "It is ever my wish to oblige a lady."

"My brother and I—my older brother—" I swept my hand vaguely in the direction of the door, "would like to know what you know, beyond those facts you were so good as to share with me yesterday, Sergeant Hirsch."

"How come you to know my name?" I saw his eyes gradually register recognition. "Oh, it's you. Fine time of night to be looking to stir up trouble. Because that's what you'll be doing if you insist on bringing the captain's activities out into the open."

"What captain?" Toby had stepped into the small office which, although lit only dimly, was sufficiently illuminated to reveal that I was escorted not by a burly older relative, but by a gangly youth several years my junior.

"Don't you have a Mama to keep you safe at home?" Hirsch said.

"Whether I do or not is none of your affair," I said. "We may be too late already. I heard them say 'tonight' just before I went under."

"Please tell me what is going on here," Toby said, "and I demand to know what captain!?" I had never heard him so emphatic. His tone pulled me up short, and I realized that I had barely listened to what he had to say, let alone told him the reason why I had dragged him out of a sound sleep in the middle of the night possibly to face danger.

Before I could collect myself to answer, Sergeant Hirsch replied to Toby. "A captain, my lad, with connections and power, whose influence extends throughout the empire. My suggestion would be to give up this entire project and go home. It's no concern of yours, and I should be grateful of being able to return to my duties of waiting in case any unfortunate citizen is set upon by robbers or Gypsies in the dead of night."

All the while he was talking, instead of sweeping us out of the door and pushing us away, the old guard began to gird as if for a battle. He put on a stout leather belt from which hung a short sword. He opened a cabinet and took out a pistol and a powder horn, looking over the pistol with a practiced eye before tucking it into a loop on the belt and hanging the powder horn within reach near it. Then he put on his coat and settled his tricorn more securely upon his head.

Without addressing another word to us, the old fellow gestured for us to leave the small station ahead of him, closed and locked the door, and then strode off purposefully in the direction of the quarter where the Lodge was located. Toby and I stood where we were, watching him become brightly illuminated and then fade to shadow as he passed two street lamps. After the second one he turned and whirled around smartly, as if he were in the midst of a military drill. Silently still, he beckoned us to follow him.

Toby and I exchanged a quick look before hurrying to catch up to him. He turned as soon as we reached him and continued to walk, not addressing another word to us.

"So, what else did you want to tell me?" I asked Toby, feeling a little contrite for not allowing him to talk previously.

"I was wondering if you heard a word I said," he said, jabbing me sharply in the ribs. "As I said, I found out that the symbols you showed me had to do with a secret brotherhood of men. They mostly do good, making charitable contributions to certain causes. But that wasn't the interesting part of it all."

"Well? Then what is?" I realized Toby was enjoying making me wait to find out what he had to tell me.

"You know I told you about the black box or coffin we had to make? We also had a most extraordinary sale the other day. Three violins and two violas."

"Is that so unusual?"

"It was unusual because one person bought them. They were ones we had already made, obviously, but very fine nonetheless. I did a lot of work on one of them."

I pondered this event silently for a few paces. "Who would purchase several instruments at once?"

"I said, Herr Goldschmidt sold a violin that I worked on!"

"Oh, well done Toby, but please answer my question."

"It would have to be someone with an orchestra. Or someone who worked for a princely house with an orchestra. Godfather Haydn might, for instance." Toby said.

"Yet it wasn't Haydn, was it." I didn't really ask. I knew that Toby would have said if it had been. And in any case my godfather hadn't yet returned from Esterhaza.

"It was someone I had never seen before. And nor had Herr Goldschmidt." Toby thrust his hand into the pocket of his breeches and pulled out a scrap of paper. "I copied his name from the ledger book when Herr Goldschmidt wasn't looking. I'm not quite sure why, but it seemed so odd. I heard him say he needed the instruments for something that was to occur on this very night."

Toby gave me the paper and I paused beneath a street lamp to read it. Oddly, although I was deeply shocked by what I saw written there, somewhere in my heart I realized that I had known who it would be all along. The name Toby had copied so carefully was none other than Graf Adelbert von Bauer.

CHAPTER TWENTY-NINE

Hirsch stayed about three paces ahead of us the entire way to the poor quarter of the city. I had been concentrating so hard on following him, wondering what on earth would happen next, that at first I failed to notice that instead of being the darkest, dingiest neighborhood in Vienna, this run-down area was in fact increasingly brightly lit as we approached.

We stopped just before the corner we would have to turn to reach the building where I had witnessed the strange ceremony, and where Mirela and I had been temporarily imprisoned. I began to feel as if the world had turned itself upside down. Instead of quiet and secrecy, I heard voices nearby, chatting and laughing, as if we were approaching the Redoutensaal on the night of an assembly ball, except that the light tinkle of ladies' laughter was missing. To make the image complete, an elegant carriage pulled by four smart, sleek bay horses with a postilion seated on the lead horse and two footmen standing on platforms at the back drove across ahead of us.

"What in the name of heaven . . ." I muttered.

"It's as I expected," whispered the guard, and a slow smile turned the corners of his mouth up. "Thor—I mean, the captain—was right."

"Right about what?" I asked. I pretended not to notice his slip, but tucked it away in my mind for later.

Before he could answer me, a loud fanfare blared from the direction of the Lodge. "It would appear that someone important is arriving," Sergeant Hirsch said.

"Toby." I turned to my brother. "Am I awake? Do you realize where we are?"

"We're both awake, and I don't believe what I'm seeing either," he said. "The last time I was here I had to deliver a message for Herr Goldschmidt, and there was hardly a soul around."

"You've been here before?" I asked.

"Only once. But it was enough to convince me not to venture to this place again."

It all began to fit. The instruments. Captain Bauer. Mozart. The Bachmanns. This was the inauguration of the lodge, and that is why there had been so much secrecy, why no one wanted me sticking my nose in and asking awkward questions. But what was Hirsch's connection with it all? What did he have to do with Thorwart?

The sergeant motioned us to flatten ourselves against the wall as another coach rolled by, this one encrusted with gold and pulled by six white horses in rich, brass-studded harnesses. The coach had large windows so that onlookers could peer inside.

"My God!" whispered Hirsch. "He said it would . . . but I didn't believe . . ."

I recognized the emperor in his green Hussars' uniform, staring straight ahead as though he were going to a state occasion. A small detachment of armed cavalry followed behind the coach. I was so distracted by wondering what on earth the emperor could be doing in that quarter at that hour that I would not have even thought to look at them, but Sergeant Hirsch stepped suddenly backward and nearly knocked me over. His face was as pale as if he had seen his own ghost ride by. "I shall be called upon . . ."

He never finished his whispered comment, but I saw what I thought was the cause of his panic. At the very end of the detachment, on a dappled gray horse that tossed its head and flattened its ears at every sound, sat Captain von Bauer. Stranger still, seated on the nag Dobra, wearing a long black cloak that hid everything but her hands and face, was Mirela. She was the only woman I had seen, and she hung well back from the others, as if she did not want her presence to be noticed.

I doubted it was Mirela who frightened Hirsch, and so assumed that it was the appearance of Captain Bauer. After my experiences with him recently, I could understand if I had been frightened out of my wits by him. But Sergeant Hirsch's reaction seemed disproportionate to any danger the captain would pose to him—if indeed that had been the cause.

The sergeant collected himself and took hold of my arm and Toby's, drawing us down an alley away from the bustle of the street. "We must act quickly, or all will be lost," he said.

"Why? What is it?" I couldn't stand it any longer. I had no intention of blindly following this police guard around and possibly letting my own opportunity slip by to discover what had really happened and why it involved all these people I knew.

"There is no time to explain everything. I'll just say that I have been keeping very close watch on the Count von Bauer because of his political leanings. I have reason to believe he is an ardent anti-royalist."

"But he is a count!" I exclaimed. The sergeant put his hand over my mouth and pulled me further into the shadows.

"If we are discovered—disaster." Sergeant Hirsch put as much feeling into his whisper as he could, then took his hand away from my mouth and bowed an apology. "There is no time. You had best remain here. No—" He paced the two short steps of the alley's width several times, then stopped abruptly and took hold of Toby's shoulders. "You look like you could run fast. Go back to the Hofburg, to the guard at the entrance to the palace itself. Tell him Hirsch needs reinforcements, and that I'm near the Leopoldstadt gate, by the abandoned prison."

It never occurred to me to question the sergeant's instructions. In fact, it was not until Toby was quite out of sight and I found myself alone with this old—but by no means unfit—armed man that I had a moment's hesitation concerning the wisdom of blindly following him. I had no doubt that I would be able to outrun him. But I remembered that he had a pistol tucked into his belt, a sword hanging at his side, and a dagger sheathed inside his right boot, obviously to serve in case of emergency.

"What next?" I asked, trying hard not to let on that I was in the least bit nervous about the turn that events had taken.

"We'll wait for the last of them to enter." He took hold of my arm, not roughly, but I sensed that if I tried to run he would be able to stop me quite easily.

"While we're waiting," I said, "Perhaps you can explain what's happening exactly. Why is the emperor here?"

"He thinks that if he gives his approval to this unauthorized Lodge, setting itself up to admit Jews and the like, that he will achieve his goals of reform and prevent any potential uprising or rebellion on the part of the poorer classes. It's America, you see," he said, shifting his weight but not releasing my arm, "It's got all the royal families in Europe scared enough to soil their breeches—if you'll excuse the crude language, *Fräulein*."

"I don't understand why there is danger," I continued. I had gotten myself this far. I may as well see the thing through to its conclusion and know the worst. "The Austrians love the emperor. He is very popular."

"The danger, Mademoiselle, does not come from the mass of the people. They are too stupid to know what is best. No, it takes an individual of vision and determination to see what lies ahead. The emperor, Fräulein, may well be assassinated tonight, if all goes as . . . they . . . have planned."

"Who are 'they?'" I asked. "Is one of them the captain?"

Hirsch shrugged. He was beginning to infuriate me.

"He should be stopped!" I exclaimed. "To assassinate the emperor—that is the worst crime imaginable." I could not imagine what would drive anyone to do it? And more, how could this fellow, whose duty was to protect the people and institutions of Vienna, do no more than to send a young boy back to the Hofburg for reinforcements if he was aware of such a danger?

Suddenly, I was struck with a terrible thought. "If you knew all this, why did you not bring all the guards and police with you here?" And why, I wondered, were we still standing there, not going anywhere or trying in any way to prevent this catastrophe?

Hirsch tightened his grip on my arm. I took a step backwards. He would not let me go. Still, his eyes had a kind expression, like someone's papa or uncle. "Don't run, Fräulein. You will not escape. You have gotten too close already to uncovering our plans. Just be calm, and all will soon be over. Then you can go back to your life, and Austria and Hungary will be free to govern themselves instead of having a corrupt and inbred family tying them to the rest of the corrupt ruling families of Europe. Change, my dear girl, is coming, whether the people know they want it or not."

Sergeant Hirsch's hand gripped my arm more and more tightly as he spoke, and the expression in his eyes hardened. The tips of my fingers began to tingle. "You're hurting me," I said. "Let me go!"

"I'm sorry. But it's for your own good. Would you not rather men of talent and ability were free to live as they liked than be part of a system of patronage that forces them to fawn and scrape to the wealthy just to earn a crust?"

Hirsch seemed to have forgotten that I was a girl, and not only that, but he could hardly realize that I would have given anything to be a part of that world he thought was so terrible, accepted as myself even if I had to work hard to achieve it. It was much worse to have to pretend I was something I was not all the time. Even then, I was grateful enough that I had been able to earn money performing, wherever those opportunities came from. I certainly didn't want our emperor to be killed and have someone claim it was for my own good! Joseph II was an honorable man. He had seen justice done in my own family's case. "I think you should let me go," I said, trying to pull my arm from Sergeant Hirsch's grasp.

"No, I think I should not. You can create no more mischief if I keep you here. You have interfered enough already."

At that, the sergeant with the no-longer-kind eyes wrenched my arm behind my back and took hold of my other arm. Before I knew it he had tied my wrists together. "You're mad!" I yelled.

He clamped his hand over my mouth. It tasted of the tobacco in his pipe—and gunpowder. I opened my mouth and bit down hard, kicking my heel up as swiftly as I could at the same time and aiming for where I believed his crotch would be. Luck would have it that I connected, and he doubled over in pain, both hands releasing me and grabbing his tender parts.

I staggered out into the street. It's surprising how difficult it is to balance well enough to run without the use of one's hands. I didn't know what I should do, but I thought I had better try to find someone trustworthy to warn.

Although now lined with coaches, the street was devoid of people. Everyone, it seemed, had gone inside the Lodge. I could hear sounds of music. Not just singing or chanting, as I had the other day, but an orchestra. And they were playing Mozart's music. I would have known it anywhere. Was he there too? Surely he had not conspired to assassinate the emperor! Herr Bachmann had not accused him. Unless...

No, it was too fantastic. The late hour, my strange, drugged night, must have given me visions. I wished that Toby would come back to reassure me that I was not still in the midst of a nightmare. But if he did, and approached Sergeant Hirsch—I would have to warn him. I must get to him before anything happened. I reminded myself that Toby was bigger and stronger than he had been two years ago, when I had inadvertently led him to captivity in my uncle's basement, yet I couldn't bear to think of it. I would have to act.

I kept to the shadows as much as possible, scurrying between hiding places so that I could get the best view of Toby's approach. A lone sentry guarding the massive door that led to the space where the Freemasons held their rituals turned toward me and I ducked into the shadows just in time. I prayed that Hirsch would not recover soon enough to use his pistol against me.

Toby, come back before the sergeant comes looking for me! I thought. I squirmed and pulled, working my fingers around to pick at the knotted rope that pinned my wrists together. But at such an awkward angle, my fingers had no strength. I became so frustrated that I felt the tears gather in my eyes, and knew I was close to drawing in my breath in stifled gasps, which would tell Sergeant Hirsch exactly where to find me. I made a desperate effort not to cry, and it suffocated me. I doubled over.

"Ssshh!" said a voice behind me. At first I thought it must be that Hirsch had stolen up on me and I opened my mouth preparing to scream. But then I felt a gentle touch on my hands and the shock of cold steel between my wrists. "Be very still. This will only take a moment." The whisper was familiar, and as soon as I realized the knife had been set to work slicing through the rope that bound me, I felt my knees weaken. Without looking around, I knew that it was Zoltán. In a few moments, my hands were free. I turned and fell into his arms, trying to deaden the sound of my sobs.

"There is no time to be fearful, Rezia. We must act now."

He said "we," I thought. "How is it you are here?"

"Toby came to get me."

"But he was supposed to get the police!" I whispered, my panic now rising once again.

"When he went looking for help, the guards had never heard of a Sergeant Hirsch and refused to believe him. He realized something was terribly wrong and came directly to find me and Danior."

"Is Danior here too?"

"Yes. But he was already, and I fear he is not in a position to help us." Zoltán looked in the direction of the great, abandoned prison, brilliant light seeping out of the cracks and fissures in the stone and wood.

"Of course! He is playing."

"As are the rest of the orchestra from the Arnstein's that night, except for you."

For a moment I felt hurt that I had not been included in such an important concert. Then I realized why. This was meant to be the creation of a great brotherhood of all men. Men! No women—or girls—allowed. I felt angry enough to want to wash my hands of it all, let them perform their silly rituals and let the emperor take care of himself. But I soon realized that was childish of me. The safety of the emperor should be my first concern.

"What do you know?" I asked, deciding to swallow my pride.

"I only know what Toby told me this evening, and some hints dropped by Danior and Herr Mozart. I have little patience for these assemblies of well meaning but misguided men. But if, as Danior said at one time a day or two ago, this group would truly be open to all—including Jews and Gypsies—then I would not interfere, regardless of whether it was legal or not.

"When Toby came and said you were here with a Sergeant Hirsch, that you had had some run-ins with Captain Bauer and that something had been said about a plot to assassinate the emperor, I knew I had to do something."

"What do you know of Captain Bauer?"

"I know his story, that he wanted to marry a Jewish woman and was disinherited because of it. I always felt sympathetic to him, knowing my own father's history."

"But would he really try to assassinate the emperor over such a private disappointment?" I had long thought ill of the captain, yet after Hirsch had proven himself to be so different from the character I assumed, I wondered how much I had misjudged Captain Bauer.

"Who can say? But I admit, what little I know of the captain leads me to believe him unlikely to commit so heinous a crime."

"Whoever is plotting, we must prevent them, or at least warn the emperor. I know a way in," I said.

I led Zoltán to the alley and showed him how to peer into the magnificent hall. We stood very close to one another as I lifted the shutter and we looked in at the level of the raised floor of the grand chamber. I could not see the orchestra, but I could see Mozart seated at the clavier, nodding and smiling. They were playing brilliantly. I wished I could simply stay there and listen.

The other men stood in rows, with only the emperor seated on an ornate, gilded chair. He wore his simple military uniform, but in his hands were golden implements, a trowel and another tool I did not recognize, except that it formed part of the symbol I had seen in several places. I now knew that the symbol signified the brotherhood of the Freemasons. Among those in the audience were the Baron Van Swieten, Adam Arnstein, and Herr von Eskeles.

Captain Bauer stood to one side. Unlike the others, his attention was not focused on the glorious music. He appeared distracted, his eyes darting around. At one point he pulled a pocket watch out and frowned at it.

"We must get in," Zoltán whispered, his breath warm on my ear. I shivered with pleasure and felt the blood rush down below my stomach. I would rather have stayed just like that, so close to him I could feel his heat. But we had no time to waste.

"Down here!" I said, showing him the hatch that led into the cellar. "But there is an animal here, or was."

"I've come prepared," said Zoltán. He pulled a length of rope from under his cloak.

"I fear you might not be able to get close enough to tie it up if it is loose," I said.

Zoltán moved his cloak aside to reveal a pair of pistols and a dagger tucked into his belt. I gasped. He put his finger to my lips.

I slid in first, hoping that the huge black cat would at least be tied up at the other end of the cellar. Zoltán followed me. We stood still to adjust to the feeble light, which was brighter than it had been the last time I found myself in that place.

There must have been thousands of candles burning above. The slits around the hatches in the floor gave a steady, dull light to the space, and I could see all the way to the opposite end. There was no big cat. Only a large, oblong box attached to the ceiling in the middle. I was certain such a thing had not been there before.

"Do you know what that is?" Zoltán whispered to me.

"I have no idea. It wasn't here before. But wait!" Of course! The black boards Toby had helped prepare at Herr Goldschmidt's workshop. Here they were. I quickly told Zoltán what Toby had said. "But I still don't know what it is for."

We made our way cautiously to the box. It was made of planks carefully fitted together so that almost no air would get through. We reached it and walked all the way around it. Zoltán ran his hands up and down the wooden boards. "What are you looking for?" I asked.

"A latch. Something. I cannot understand why else this would be here. It must be meant to contain something." He felt underneath. "Ah," he said. "It appears to open from the bottom."

"Why open from the bottom when it is so close to the floor?" I asked. Before Zoltán could give any kind of answer, the music above us stopped. The floor creaked and groaned as hundreds of people shifted their weight, some standing and walking. No applause followed the performance, just throats clearing and surreptitious coughs.

A booming voice immediately above our heads made me jump and I let out an involuntary shriek. I hoped the loud voice had covered it sufficiently.

"Brothers. We are gathered here to consecrate our new lodge, under the watchful eyes of God and the emperor."

A cheer went up and nearly deafened me with its reverberations through the floor not far above my head. I glanced at Zoltán, only then noticing that he was so tall he could not quite stand upright in that space.

"Can you feel underneath the box to open it? Your hands are smaller than mine," Zoltán said.

As the voice of the master continued to boom above, I knelt down in the dark by the box and felt with my fingers for the latch Zoltán had told me about. I soon found it, and easily tripped it. A hatch fell open, two doors fanning outward like gates and reaching all the way down to the floor. "What is it?" Zoltán asked.

"The chamber appears to be empty," I answered, reaching my hand up as far as it would go inside. "I think I could crawl into it and get a better look."

"No!" he whispered hoarsely.

"Too late," I said. I don't know quite what possessed me, perhaps a wish to impress Zoltán with my courage, but I squeezed myself underneath and into the narrow opening until I could stand up. I found myself in a completely empty, man-sized container. If I stood on the sides that remained by the open hatch doors beneath me, my head brushed the ceiling. What an odd contraption, I thought. I didn't like it in there, and started to step out again. In the process I must have tripped some mechanism, because the hatch by my feet snapped shut. I was well and truly trapped. At least Zoltán was outside. He would release me. Then I remembered that he could not reach to work the latch. Now what? I thought, fighting against tears and cursing my blind stupidity.

CHAPTER THIRTY

"Rezia! Are you all right?" Zoltán called.

"Yes. Fine. There's nothing in here. Wait—" My head had bumped into another latch above me. I felt in the absolute dark for the mechanism and traced the outline of a hatch over my head. "That's odd," I murmured.

"What's odd?"

"If this leads to the floor above, there should be light coming through, but it's absolutely dark."

"There must be something up above."

All at once I realized. "The emperor! They're going to—"

Before I could finish my thought, I felt the mechanism of the latch being pulled. I gently traced around with my fingers and found a wire, no doubt rigged up so that someone outside of the box could open the latch. I realized what was happening just in time to squeeze myself aside, as the hatch opened into my nose and a man slid suddenly down from above. As soon as he passed the hatch, it snapped shut again.

"*Gottverdammt!*" the emperor exclaimed. "I command you to release me!"

To my utter astonishment, I now stood literally nose-to-nose with Emperor Joseph II of Austria. I was glad it was dark so he would not see me blush. "Forgive me, Your Imperial Majesty," I said, my knees flexing automatically as if to curtsy, but of course there was no room.

"Rezia! I have to hide now! I'll bring help!" My heart sank as I heard Zoltán run off to I knew not where.

"Who are you!" demanded the emperor, "What do you think you are doing?"

"Please, your Majesty, I can explain—"

"I shall have you and your accomplice horse-whipped and racked when I get out of here!" The emperor's voice was becoming hoarse. I could feel the heat of his body, and I worried that panic would make him ill.

"Please, Your Majesty, I am as much a prisoner as you are. We came to try to foil a plot against you."

"A plot? I don't believe you!"

"I know it sounds crazy, and I don't completely understand, but my friend outside will return with help. Now we must be quiet. No one must know that I am in here with you, for they surely did not expect it."

I was standing close enough to the emperor to feel his pulse beating wildly. I knew it was not my place, and I could well be punished for it later, but I leaned forward to whisper in his ear and at the same time took hold of his hand, "Please, Sir, we must remain calm. I will do anything in my power to prevent harm from coming to you."

He said nothing, but did not shake off my hand. I thought I discerned a slowing of his pulse. I noticed that the emperor was very little taller than I was. I had always seen him either from a distance or seated, and at those times he looked very grand—certainly taller than he actually was.

I heard stealthy footsteps approach, and a scrabbling sound as of someone feeling the outside of the box. A voice whispered, "Just unlatch it from the ceiling."

"Down at your end," said the other, and before I realized what was happening we were no longer upright. Someone had loosened the box from the ceiling and tipped it on its side, so that I found myself lying directly on top of the most important and powerful man in Austria, and possibly in all of Europe.

"I'm so sorry!" I whispered. I listened hard to hear a voice, anything that would give a clue as to what was happening. But the people who carried us did not say a word. It was impossible to know what direction they were taking us. I only prayed that Zoltán had hidden himself well and would follow—with help.

A change in the quality of the air seeping through between the boards indicated to me that we were no longer in the cellar and had emerged into the outside. I took a deep breath. The space was very small for the two of us.

"Heavy for a small man, *nicht war?*" said a quiet voice very near my ear but outside the box. It was quiet, but I recognized it immediately: Sergeant Hirsch.

"Ssshhh!" came the response.

"I don't understand all the secrecy now. We've got him, and he won't likely survive his dunking."

Dunking! I felt the emperor's body stiffen beneath me, and both of our hearts commenced pounding. They were planning to throw us in the Danube! I prayed for Zoltán to come to our aid, and fast.

"He's not putting up much of a fuss in there," whispered Hirsch again.

"Probably passed out. He was never particularly brave." The other voice spoke in a normal tone, and I gasped. It was Captain Bauer.

At the same time, the emperor gave a violent jerk that nearly made Captain Bauer and Sergeant Hirsch drop us. "

"Ah, so he remains quiet for his own reasons. His vanity is piqued, however!"

All manner of foul thoughts swirled in my head. How could he? How could the captain be in league with this insane sergeant? And worse, how could Mirela trail after him, and not have discovered such a thing? Could she be involved in this terrible affair? I wished I had taken more direct action to expose his activities when I had the chance. Now—I thought I might never have a chance to do anything.

I tried to breathe deeply to still my own panic, concentrating instead on figuring out exactly where we were going. After being jolted around for several minutes during which I tried hard not to feel the all-too-obvious contours of the emperor's body, we were tipped upright again. "Shall we tell our esteemed emperor why he is about to die?" said Sergeant Hirsch. He had obviously recovered from my blow, and he didn't wait for a response from Captain Bauer. "I think I'd like to see his face when we tell him that the era of his family's tyrannous rule is coming to an end."

I heard a scraping sound as of a bolt being drawn just behind the emperor's head. I hadn't had time to notice before, but the makers must have taken care to leave a small peephole there. I was suddenly struck with an idea. Without pausing to explain, I took hold of the emperor's shoulders and pushed him down so his face was at the level of my chest. It never occurred to me in that desperate moment to be embarrassed or ashamed, although later I was horrified at the thought of our emperor with his nose pressed into my chest. At first Joseph II resisted, but I pushed harder, and then I think he understood my plan. Let Captain Bauer and Sergeant Hirsch look in and see me, not the emperor.

The hatch opened just behind where the emperor's head had been moments before. I drew myself up to my full height and adopted a haughty expression.

"Good evening, Gentlemen," I said, forcing my voice not to quiver.

The shock on Hirsch's face would have been comical had the situation not been quite so dire. "You!" he yelled.

"Who did you expect?" I said, feigning that I had not heard the hushed conversations about the emperor.

"Not you, certainly," said Captain Bauer, elbowing Hirsch aside. "I am very sorry to have to do this, Mademoiselle—or should I say Monsieur. You can have no idea what you have meddled in." He was—not surprisingly—angry.

"What have I ever done to you?" I asked. I wanted to keep him talking, to give Zoltán time to find us, hoping that he would have alerted the imperial guard by now.

"You did not heed my warning! This is a much larger matter than you can possibly know."

"Did Mirela know of it?" I asked, deciding that I might as well die knowing the truth as not.

"Mirela? Who's that?" asked Hirsch. "If she knows, we'll have to—"

"Enough, Hirsch. Let me deal with this. Mirela only knew what she had to for the plot to work."

"And yet it did not work, did it!" I yelled, knowing that in fact it had, but wanting at least to make him think everything had failed miserably. The captain put his face up close to mine and was perilously near to seeing the top of the emperor's head. He looked as though he wanted to say something to me that Hirsch would not hear, but I was so angry, I gathered what spittle my dry mouth could muster and spat at him with all my force.

"*Scheiss!*" he yelled, and as he took out his handkerchief and wiped his face, he snarled "Seal it!" to Sergeant Hirsch. I had a brief glimpse of the sergeant's paunchy face with the watery blue eyes before the small opening was shut again. I imagined that he looked a little sorry, but perhaps I merely wished it so. I did not want to be completely wrong to have trusted him initially. He did not look like someone who would plot against the emperor. The captain, on the other hand, appeared entirely untrustworthy, and had behaved so almost from the start of our acquaintance.

Chains clanked and the box was buffeted as no doubt we were being trapped more securely inside it. They laid us down again, this time thankfully so that we were lying side-by-side.

"Who was that? What is happening?" The emperor's whisper was more a command than a question.

"His name is Captain Bauer. Perhaps you know him as Graf von Bauer."

"Bauer . . . Yes, I recall the name. His father was much angered when he refused to wed to please his family. Something about wanting to marry a Jew. My mother hated Jews. I do not, but I don't quite know what to do about them. Still, I always thought of Bauer as an honorable—and a brave man."

I let him chatter on as we were tossed back and forth and eventually lifted up and placed down again, but not on the ground. I had the distinct sensation of being rocked in a boat, and the smell of rotting fish through the boards of our claustrophobic prison was very strong.

"Take her out to the middle and wait for my instructions," the captain called. "Remember, take no action until I say!"

The captain had stayed on the shore. His voice faded as we rocked more and more, and a chill wind whistled between the planks. Desperation made me bold. I decided I had nothing to lose. Sergeant Hirsch could not be as unsympathetic as the captain. I started knocking on the crate. "Sergeant! Sergeant! Don't do it! You will lose your own life surely when you are found out."

"Who will find out? Not that I am not sorry. It really wasn't necessary for you to die, Fräulein. If you had only stayed out of the way."

"But it isn't just me! The emperor is in here."

"Lying will do you no good now. Besides, the captain is watching, and he will shoot me if I do not do as he says."

I nudged the emperor, not really caring if he threw me in prison later. "Say something! He does not believe me!"

"What is your rank and company Sergeant?"

It seemed an odd thing to ask, I thought, when our lives hung in the balance. But it silenced the sergeant at first. And when he spoke he sounded different. Incredulous and tentative. "The twenty-fourth. Sergeant. Retired . . . By God, it worked!"

"I command you to release us from this—place," the emperor said, with such distaste in his voice that I wondered if my nervousness had made me stink.

"I cannot, I am afraid. At least, not if I wish to live, Your Imperial Majesty."

"But your friend, the captain, does not know I am here." As he eased into the role of commander, the emperor relaxed. I admired him for being able to do so under such dangerous circumstances. "And you will surely be found out if you do not. Do you think they will blame him? A noble? It is you who will suffer a terrible death for this crime."

"Since when, Your Majesty, do you have such concern for the lower ranks?"

"I have always made it my business to ensure that those who serve me are well and fairly treated."

"I'm afraid that simply won't do." I heard the chains around our wooden sarcophagus rattling. I thought I also heard the sound of a key in a lock. Perhaps the sergeant was doing what he had done at the police station, saying something he thought anyone listening might expect, but acting otherwise. The chains continued to rattle.

"What the devil are you doing!" The voice came from a distance, possibly the shoreline. "You'd better come back in. I hear people coming. There's no time!"

"Just making it fast!" yelled back Sergeant Hirsch. "There is time! There must be time!"

"Cease now! You vowed to be led by me, and I say return immediately!"

"I am afraid the plan is now what I decide, since I am here and you are there," Hirsch said, and started muttering under his breath. "He thinks he's different, but really he's just like the rest of them . . . the meek shall inherit . . ."

These were not reassuring words. I heard more rattling as the chains were moved, but it was clear now that Hirsch was either unable to or had no intention of removing them.

"I said, Hirsch, come back!" shouted the captain, sounding still farther away. "Come back or I shall have to act."

All at once we were jolted as Hirsch began to drive holes into the box, grunting with the exertion. He was not trying to free us, I realized. He was simply trying to ensure that we would sink all the more quickly. I screamed with all my might, "Help! Help! He's trying to kill us!" I had little hope of achieving anything, but I was determined not to go without a fight.

A moment later, the odd, distorted sound of a gunshot over water rang out. The sergeant gave a startled gurgle, and his bulk crashed onto the box we were in and set the small boat to rocking violently. Another shot rang out a moment later. This one must have hit the side of the boat, because water began to seep in, slowly at first, then faster and faster.

"We must break out or we will drown!" I said and began pounding with all my might on the box above us.

"I have a knife hidden in my boot. Perhaps . . ." The emperor tried to bend down, but there was no room for him.

"Let me try," I said, panicking as the water crept up so that my right arm and the emperor's left were now fully covered. I gulped some air and prayed, contorting myself until I could feel the top of the emperor's boot, hoping it was the one with the hidden knife.

It was. I took the knife out and began prying at the boards, trying to open the space between them as the water came up to my ear and I had to turn my head. At least it was not winter, and the water still had a little of summer's warmth in it.

No use, I thought. Soon the water would cover us completely, and the chains would make us sink to the bottom of the river. I don't know why, but I pictured the emperor's gilded coffin, lying in state in the Hofburg, and off in a side chapel there would be me, crowds filing past, hushed, wondering at the story of my misadventure, which I hoped Zoltán would make sure everyone knew, so that they didn't think I was somehow dallying with the emperor! Perhaps my mother would get a pension. That was when the tears started. Might as well cry, I thought. The emperor would not be able to tell in all this water.

Finally just our noses had room above the water line when we turned our heads, but our sinking had slowed. The wood of the boat must have added more buoyancy to us, despite the heavy chains. Without it we surely would have plunged to the depths immediately. I said a prayer, and prepared to die by excruciating degrees.

CHAPTER THIRTY-ONE

But I didn't die. Instead, I felt the wooden casket being lifted up out of the level of the water, and voices, all talking at once so I could not make them out. The water drained fast, and the emperor and I took great, relieved gulps of air.

"Careful! The emperor is in there!" "Wedge the rope under further." "Should I chop it open?" "No! They will be hurt." "Let's hope they're still alive."

"We are! We are alive!" I shouted and pounded on the sides of the box.

A cheer went up. I felt a bump. All the water had now drained out, and I knew we were on dry ground. Despite realizing that I would emerge covered in bruises, soaked to the skin and probably scraped to bits, I experienced the kind of euphoria that I was accustomed to feeling when I played the violin in a performance, and lost myself in the music so completely that I forgot who I was. This time I forgot where I was, forgetting the emperor in the glorious certainty that I would not die that day.

The wood at my left side splintered, and within moments someone had pried the casket open.

It was still night, but the glare of dozens of torches made it feel like day after being locked in the pitch dark box. I blinked and raised my hand to my eyes to shade them, at the same time accidentally hitting the emperor on the nose. "Oh, Your Majesty! How can I—"

Two groups of people reached down and lifted us out, setting us on our feet. I looked down at my sodden dress, folded my arms across my breasts and fell to my knees. "Forgive me, Your Majesty," I said, now unable to stop tears. I couldn't look up to see who was in the crowd surrounding us.

"For what?" The emperor's voice sounded kind. He knelt down in front of me and lifted my chin. "It seems that I owe you my gratitude, not my blame."

He held out his hand for mine and pulled me to my feet. I dared to look at him, and saw that despite his soggy uniform, he somehow managed to retain the air of command that must have been so ingrained in him from birth that he didn't even have to think about it. He waved his hand to the crowd. "Let all here witness that I shall bestow the Cross of Valor on this lady, this—what is your name, Mademoiselle?"

Oddly, I had until that moment assumed that he would remember me from the incident with my father's murder and Danior's wrongful imprisonment two years before. But of course, why would he? He had much more important things to worry about. "Theresa Maria Schurman," I answered, with something like a curtsy.

"Schurman . . . Schurman . . . I don't know why, your name is familiar. However, at the next opportunity I shall call you to court to receive your honor."

"But Your Majesty," I said, suddenly realizing that the matter was not concluded. "What about the Graf von Bauer? Has he been caught?"

"Ah, yes. I shall see that my guard is instructed."

"But—he just killed a man! Sergeant Hirsch! And what about us? About what he did to us? His intention—"

"His intention, yes. But you see, all is well. We are safe. And you must not take things at face value. I believe, in fact, that if Bauer had not shot Sergeant Hirsch, we might not be here now."

He looked around. I followed his eyes, and only then did I notice that our rescuers consisted primarily of Gypsies, that we had been set ashore quite near the Roma camp. It appeared that the entire camp had come out to aid in the rescue, except, I noted, Mirela. Another group of men who were not Romany stood over to one side. This group, I was astounded to see, consisted of Zoltán, Mozart, van Swieten, and Herr Bachmann—looking a good deal healthier than he had when I last saw him although still pale, and altogether changed from our first introduction on the road from the Augarten.

And then I saw something that sent a shock straight through me. In a wooden cage, pacing up and back, its eyes catching the torch glow, was the big, black cat from the lodge. The one that had scratched a painful gash in my leg. I shivered.

"The young lady is cold," the emperor said. "Someone fetch a blanket and get her home."

The emperor must have been just as cold, but before I knew it, someone threw a fur wrap around me, and I was bustled into a carriage. As soon as the door closed behind me, the driver slapped the reins on his horses' backs and we lurched into motion. The carriage turned around and curved right past the knot that included Zoltán. I moved to the side and pulled down the window, leaning out as I passed him. "Zoltán!" I cried.

I thought he had not heard me, but just as I leaned back into my seat, ready to let exhaustion and confusion stream down my face in the form of more tears, I heard rapid footsteps and Zoltán's voice calling out, "Halt the carriage!"

I quickly wiped the evidence of my distress off my cheeks. The coach rocked as Zoltán stepped on the board and yanked the door open, diving in to sit opposite me and knocking on the roof of the carriage simultaneously. We cannot have paused more than an instant.

"Will you please explain to me what just happened? Will there be no trial, no inquiry? Will Captain or Count von Bauer, whoever he is, not be punished for nearly killing the emperor, and me for that matter?" The words tumbled out of my mouth.

"Rezia, try to be calm. I am sorry you suffered such danger. If all you say is true, the captain should be punished severely—imprisoned, or at least banished."

"But?"

"But there is more to it than that. What do you know about what was happening in the lodge?"

"I know it had to do with the brotherhood of the Freemasons, so you need not pretend with me about that." My voice had an angry edge, but I felt I was justified.

"I spoke to Van Swieten and Mozart. They were trying, you see, to redress a terrible wrong. They did not realize that they had played into the hands of the very people they had tried to foil."

"You mean Captain Bauer?"

"No, not Captain Bauer. He worked for—it was someone much higher up, who has his dirty work done by his own mouches."

"I would think, after all this, that you would just tell me."

Zoltán passed his hand across his eyes, and circled it around to cup his chin. I thought he was growing impatient with me. *Why?* I wondered, *after all I had been through!* At last he spoke. "The attempt to establish a more just system of preferment has now failed, although the assassination of the emperor was averted. No one must know what occurred this night. We are all sworn to secrecy. No Jews will be admitted to this powerful group of right-thinking men. All will continue as it had before. The guilty will be punished. Just not in the courts. The attempt to assassinate the emperor has sullied our efforts, and we have lost the leverage we had with the people we most needed."

Zoltán reached out to take my hand. Any other time, I would have yearned for his touch, I would have wanted him to hold me. But I jerked my hand away. I hated being treated like a child. "I thought I could trust you! What about that monster? That—cat!" I hissed, knowing that I was probably overstepping the line with Zoltán. He was, after all, a baron now.

"It's a panther. Apparently one of the members of the lodge brought it back from India, planning to present it to the emperor for his menagerie. There is to be a public ceremony next week."

So, not even the cat would suffer. I felt powerless. "And Herr Bachmann? Will he return to his impoverished life, no better off for all he has suffered?"

"Mozart is trying to persuade him to convert, so that he can play in the orchestra for *Seraglio*."

"And if he does not?"

Zoltán paused before continuing. "The world is not a fair place, Rezia. I thought you understood that from before."

I could not say anything. I was too deeply disappointed and angry. Before, when there had been persecution and wrongful accusation, all had been righted by the emperor. The Gypsies lived in their camp unmolested, and my uncle had been brought to justice for his crime of sending children to the Hungarian nobles to use as slave labor on their estates. "That's as may be," I finally said, "but will we never know who attacked Herr Bachmann?"

"Herr Bachmann will not speak and name the man. Unless he is willing to do this, we have only what you saw as evidence."

By now, the carriage had reached my apartment. What shall I tell my mother? I suddenly wondered. I had all but forgotten that I'd sneaked out in the middle of the night. She might not even have awakened yet, and no one would know that I had been gone. "My mother must not know what happened this night."

"I will take care of it. We could say that in your delirium you walked out into the street."

"And dressed first? And how did I get my bumps and scrapes?"

"You came over to Alida's house and tripped going up the stairs in your sleep."

I shook my head. "She'll never believe it."

"Van Swieten will back me up. He'll say that the drug he gave you has been known to have that effect."

"I'm glad I did not take his drug!" My frustration mounted. It angered me to have to be explained away by men who hardly knew me. But I saw no other way out, and said nothing more, except a rather cool goodbye to Zoltán after he had "explained" everything to my bemused mother.

"Give the baron back his rug," Mama said.

Only then did I remember that I was wrapped in a warm, soft fur. I reluctantly took it off my shoulders and handed it to Zoltán.

"I'll see that Alida gets it," he said. I couldn't meet his eyes.

"Come, get back into bed dear," my mother said.

"I am not now, nor have I ever been ill!" I spat the words at her. "What made you pretend and lie to me? Your van Swieten is not to be trusted. I hate him."

My mother shrank back from my harsh words. I saw tears sparkle in the corners of her eyes. I regretted what I said, but I was too angry to apologize. I turned and went into my own room to change. It was near enough to morning. I would go to the Palais Esterhazy to practice. To think.

I put on my plain brown dress and simple cap, grabbed my violin, and took a crust of bread from Greta's tray on my way out. Even though I didn't feel like eating, I could not ignore the pain in my stomach.

I hardly remembered how I got to the room in the prince's palace that I was allowed to use. The bustle of the servants preparing for the annual residency of his court in Vienna barely registered in my perception. I was too caught up in my own concerns, and desperate for the comfort of feeling the fiddle come to life in my hands. I took extra time on the most mechanical exercises, slowly going up and down the scales, listening carefully to the pitches, testing my ear. I felt as if it had been years since I had been able to concentrate like that.

I spent hours just playing. I told myself that I should let it all go, just allow the music to embrace me. I played a slow sarabande from a Bach partita, one that Danior had loaned me the music for. Its anguished twists and turns suited my mood. So many voices coming from a single instrument, and my art was in bringing those voices out, so that there would be an illusion of a carefully balanced ensemble, that one player could not possibly be producing such complete music—

I stopped in the middle of a phrase. That was it. That was what I was missing. Captain Bauer—as Zoltán said—could not have been the mastermind. He was too visible. And there were too many things that didn't fit. There was someone else. Someone too powerful to be seen, or at least, with enough power to keep himself hidden.

What individual connected all these people? Who would be worth protecting, for Mozart, Herr Bachmann, Van Swieten, the emperor?

At first, no one came to mind. There was, however, a single thread that bound everyone together. It was music. Van Swieten kept the emperor's valuable library, and perhaps wanted some precious manuscript to come his way. Herr Bachmann wished to perform in front of the wealthy of Vienna, not just on the streets and in the parlors of the rich Jews. The emperor was a talented amateur musician, but he hadn't hosted entertainments at his court yet, instead depending on the state-sponsored operas and the other nobles and aristocracy.

And of course, Mozart. Mozart wanted his opera to be performed at the Burgtheater. Who could make this come about for him? Aloysia Weber? She was popular, but I doubted powerful.

All at once it struck me. It was so obvious, I don't know how I hadn't realized before. Who was the one man who had control of the finances of the opera, and without whose endorsement a composer stood little chance of having his opera performed? The one man whose approval determined the contents of every season at the Burgtheater? This man had very conservative tastes, mindful more of satisfying the aristocrats who came to the Burgtheater to be seen rather than to see. Mostly Gluck and Salieri, with some Italian imports. Mozart, by his own statement, was to audition for him soon and would have to persuade him that he deserved his place alongside the established composers.

It was, of course, Herr Thorwart.

I knew that somehow Thorwart had to be involved. I had overheard him speaking with Frau Weber about Mozart, and he clearly was opposed to Amadé's advancement. But what could he have to do with the Freemasons and the Jews?

There was only one way to find out. It was a Wednesday. There would be an opera that evening. Thorwart might well be in attendance. As director of finance, a box was his to command.

All thought of practicing left my mind. I carefully put away my fiddle, at first in the old case, then I thought better of it. I might gain admittance backstage at the Burgtheater as a young musician more easily than as an unescorted young lady. Quickly I put the Amati in the new case Toby had made for me and changed into my black uniform. What I was planning to do was very brash, but I could see no other hope. That no one might wish me to solve this mystery never entered my head. I only thought they didn't see a way, and I saw it very clearly at that moment.

CHAPTER THIRTY-TWO

After a restless nap on the cot in the room at the Palais Esterhazy, I went to a coffee house to eat a light meal and wait until twilight. I knew one where I could sit in a dark corner for hours and no one would bother me. Once I had downed three cups of chocolate and eaten some bread, I left a few Groschen on the table and went out into the evening.

The streets were crowded with people leaving their work or going out to their dinner engagements. I had to dodge carriages and duck out of the way of overloaded carts headed for the city gates. But I pressed on, determined to see everything through. My bumps from my misadventure in the wooden casket were superficial and easily hidden by my clothing—aside from one scrape on my cheekbone, which could have been caused by a dust-up in a tavern, if all who saw me believed my disguise. And my leg gave me such a familiar pain by now that I was able to ignore it if I chose. I kept the Amati tucked securely under my arm and strode along as if I were late for an important engagement.

Carriages were already stopped in an orderly queue to let out their elegant occupants at the door of the Burgtheater. Foot traffic streamed in too, but by the smaller doors that led up to the balcony or into the back of the stalls. I went around to the stage door and fell in with a group of musicians talking among themselves about the opera—still Salieri's *The Chimney Sweep.*

As we passed through the door, one of the other players cast me a curious look. I turned away, thankful that I had been in that confusing place once before so that I didn't look quite as lost as I felt. I followed the general traffic for a bit, then turned off toward the stairs that led to the offices. As I passed a dressing room where I heard a soprano vocalizing, the door flew open, and a well-dressed man stepped into the corridor and we practically collided with one another.

"Ah! *Sancta Maria!* I am delighted."

The slender man in his brocade coat and velvet breeches bowed to me. I must have looked utterly astonished, because a broad grin spread over his face. "*Ich bin Salieri,*" he said, "And you must be the substitute fiddle player. I am so glad you could come on such short notice, Herr Wurzel. But please, the curtain will rise in just a few moments, and you must take your place."

He gestured back in the direction from which I had come. I didn't know what to say without giving myself away completely. I wracked my brain trying to think of a way to slip out without being noticed, but Signore Salieri was so insistent that I follow him and so obviously grateful that I had come—although I was not the person he expected.

"You said you knew the part, so that is good, although you are in the last desk, I am afraid."

He could not have known how relieved I was to hear it. I might be able to pretend I was ill and sneak away without being noticed.

But I hardly had time to do anything except take my seat, accept the introduction of my desk mate, and tune up my violin. I would be sight-reading, I realized. I had done it often enough, and second violin parts were rarely much of a challenge. Still, I did not welcome the detour from finding Thorwart. Now I would have to wait until a pause, or worse, until after the performance.

Fortunately, I was seated so late that I could avoid the usual small talk, and quickly cast my eye toward the boxes. It was only then that

I realized with a start that, quite without intending to, I was about to achieve one of my fondest dreams. Here I was, seated in the orchestra in the most prestigious opera house in Vienna. Nobody had actually asked me to play. I was there by default. But at least I was there. If only I had been prepared, and could sit back and enjoy it.

The audience quieted. The stage lights were lit. My fellow players sat up a little straighter, waiting for the maestro to come out. His entrance was greeted with polite applause, but no one really cared so much about Salieri himself. It was the singers, the Aloysia Webers that drew the cheers and adoration. That suited me. No one was likely to notice whether a back-desk violinist was there or not.

The overture went by in a blur. My part was easy, but very fast. I prayed I wouldn't call attention to myself with a false entrance, and concentrated harder than I ever had on the actions of the other two musicians who shared my score.

By the time the first pause came, I was sweating profusely. Now, I thought, not only would I appear humble, but dirty and menial as well. But I had no choice. It was now or never. I scanned the boxes again, and saw him. It was unmistakably Thorwart, with his bulky body and large mustache. Seated next to him was a frail blond creature, no doubt a soprano hoping for an audition.

As the musicians filed out to relieve themselves and stretch, I walked casually toward a door that appeared to lead to the audience. No one guarded it on my side, at least. I opened it and found myself in the corridor outside the stalls. Ahead was a stairway that I presumed led to the boxes.

Time to make my move. Hesitation would spoil everything. With my fiddle beneath my arm, I strode as though I belonged there, taking the stairs two at a time until I reached the carpeted corridor above. A liveried usher stood in his place. One or two well-dressed couples had walked out to stretch their legs and chat.

"I have a message for Thorwart," I said to the usher. "His box is. . ?"

The fellow gave me a peculiar look, then shrugged. "That one," he said, pointing three doors down.

I walked up to the door, knocked briskly, then grasped the handle to enter.

"Gott im Himmel!" growled Thorwart, who was now huddled in the obscurity of the back of the box and had clearly just been caressing the young singer.

"Forgive me, Herr Thorwart, but I need to speak to you—alone."

"I'll have you fired!" he said in a fierce hiss.

"I don't think so. The emperor knows I am here." It was a lie, but it did not matter. He couldn't fire me anyway, since I was not actually a member of the orchestra.

Thorwart's face paled. He looked at the singer, whose eyes were as round as the buttons on his waistcoat. "Forgive me, dearest. Perhaps you should take a little stroll. Business, you know." He reached into his pocket and pressed a large, silver coin in the young lady's hand. She looked shocked, but closed her fingers around it nonetheless, and without a word swished by me in her stiff petticoats and pocket hoops. I bolted the box door behind her.

Once we were alone, I did not give Thorwart a chance to speak. "I know about the Lodge. I know about Mozart, and the Jews, Captain Bauer, and Hirsch. And so does the emperor."

Thorwart's face went through several changes of expression before he spoke. First he looked frightened, then angry, and finally, he looked as if he had figured out some private joke, and would dismiss me. "And what do you propose to do about it, young man?" he said.

I had almost forgotten that I was wearing my musician's uniform. "Do? I can inform the emperor that the entire scheme was planned by you."

"And why would I do such a thing? I am indebted to the emperor for my position, and am not trying to rise still further."

"Because you would do anything to keep control of this theater, and prevent the emperor from enacting his reforms that would give the Jews the right to perform and manage."

He gave me a look of pure scorn. "The Jews! I think you'll find that the emperor has too much opposition from people whose help he needs to push his reforms any further."

If not the Jews, I thought, then what? Thorwart smirked at the confusion that must have been written on my face.

"And was the young Herr Mozart also mixed up in this plot you speak of?" Thorwart asked, examining his well-manicured fingernails.

Mozart! Could it truly be? "Mozart?" I asked. "How can he harm you?"

"He can harm me by marrying the one remaining member of my cousin Frau Weber's family who could make an advantageous match."

"You mean—Constanze?"

"Of course."

I felt as if a veil had been lifted off my head and I could at last see clearly. All this had been intended to disrupt the course of true love! Now I was angry. The emperor could have been killed. I could have been killed. Sergeant Hirsch was killed. And a dangerous man was still at large.

I couldn't bear the thought of having gotten so far without some positive result, and so I spoke quickly, before I lost my nerve. "If you value your position, I advise you not to stand in the way of Mozart's marriage. In fact, I think it would be wise for you to ensure that nothing stands in the way of his opera's premier at the Burgtheater as well."

"His opera! Piece of junk, if you ask me. He'll never amount to anything. And why should I do as you say?"

"Because," I said, realizing that I had no good answer for him, "I have the ear of the emperor. And a man was killed today. Another was previously attacked and badly wounded. It would not be difficult to trace these events back to you."

"Killed?" Thorwart said. I was surprised at the effect my words had. The florid color drained from the corpulent finance director's face.

As if on cue, the chandeliers over the stalls began to rise, having been recharged with new candles for the next act. The flickering light played across Thorwart's features. "The emperor himself expects Mozart's opera to be performed," I said, digging myself in even deeper, but deciding I might as well go all the way.

Thorwart lowered his chin and glared at me from under his brows. "Young man, I don't know who you are, but this game has gone far enough. Guards!"

He pushed up on the arms of his wooden chair and prepared to raise his bulk. It was time to take action. I grasped the front of my bag wig and pulled it off in a swift movement, letting my long, chestnut hair tumble down my back. "Do you think the guards would believe you were in danger from a girl, in a disguise that might expose you to ridicule?"

The theater director's jaw dropped open. He snapped it shut. At last, I had managed to render him speechless. From the other side of the door, I heard the young singer's voice and her timid knock. "Herr Thorwart! Herr Thorwart! Is everything all right? Let me in!"

"It's your choice," I said. "Swear you'll smooth the path for Mozart's opera, and stop trying to prevent his marriage to Constanze, or I'll let your young lady in—before I put my wig on."

He worked his mouth and looked as if he wanted to spit on me, but I wasn't afraid. He deserved whatever little harm I could do him. Because of him, the emperor had nearly been assassinated, and I—insignificant though I was—would have been murdered too.

"Oh—*Scheiss!*—Very well."

"Your word, Herr Thorwart?"

"I swear it," he said, sinking wearily back down into his chair, beads of sweat glistening on his forehead in the candlelight.

Without another word, I tucked my hair back into the bag of my wig and rearranged the lambs-wool curls, then slid the bolt back on the box door to let the unsuspecting young singer continue to be seduced by a fat old man with a little power.

Chapter Thirty-Three

Weariness settled on my shoulders like a yoke. Yet I could not bear the thought of going home. It struck me, then, that I had not seen Mirela on the shore of the river when the Gypsies rescued us from the boat. I would go out to the camp, sit with the Romany and listen to their music, rest in the pleasant chaos of Mirela's tent. Find out what happened with the captain, and why she had been at the lodge earlier the night before. I felt she owed me an explanation.

It was dark, but curfew had not yet rung, and so I was able to pass unchallenged through the city gate that led out to the camp by the Danube. The moon had not risen, so as soon as I wandered beyond the glow of the city, I was plunged into inky night. My feet knew the way, though, and I was not afraid. I had faced down all the demons, defied death once already that day. What else could happen?

The camp was subdued when I arrived. No dancing and revelry, only a few of the older Gypsies huddled by a fire that had not been fed recently and would soon go out. I nodded to them, recognizing all of them, and made my way to Mirela's dwelling.

"Mirela! It's me!" I called, just loudly enough for her to hear, not loudly enough to disturb the others. A lamp or candle glowed within, so I knew she was there. But she did not answer me. Instead I heard items being tossed around, something heavy dragging across the floor. My thoughts immediately went to danger, having so recently found myself in dire circumstances, and I burst in through the door of Mirela's hut without waiting to be invited.

What I found surprised me, to say the least. Mirela's hut had been nearly cleared out of all of its contents. No chaos of brightly colored clothing strewn about, no candles other than those needed to see, and all her talismans and bits and bobs she used to impress fortune-telling customers had been removed from their places on the shelves built into the walls. Mirela herself was sitting on top of a wooden chest and bouncing up and down, trying to close it. She had filled it to bursting, apparently, with everything she owned.

"What are you doing?" I asked, so completely surprised I didn't even greet her.

"I'm going away."

"Going away? Is the camp moving?" Although Mirela's Roma community had been in this location for years, they were just as likely to up and move, so I'd heard. But it surprised me that there had been no hint of it—and no one else seemed to be packing up.

"No, I'm leaving camp." She turned toward me. Her expression was unlike anything I'd ever seen in her face before. Instead of wary, she looked... enchanted. Her eyes shone with something that—in anyone else—I might have taken for the haze of love.

"I don't understand. Why? And what were you doing last night? Why didn't you join the others who helped save me and the emperor?"

"I saw you would be taken care of, and I had other business."

"What other business? Why are you being so mysterious? You're not acting like yourself." She was starting to make me angry.

"You should return home before the curfew bell makes it impossible, or expensive anyway."

"Mirela, I demand to know what is going on!"

She at last stopped bouncing on the chest, stood, and approached me. She took my face between her two hands, as I had seen her do with the children in the camp. I wasn't a child. I was about to push her hands away when she said, "I am going to marry the captain."

It must have been a full minute before I could think of anything to say. "He asked you to marry him?"

She shrugged. "Not in so many words. But I know."

"How do you know?"

At that she shook her head in the way I've come to understand as meaning that I'm naive, or stupid, or just slow to understand. "A woman knows. Some things he said. He mentioned he would leave soon and hoped to have me always with him. Besides, I saw it in the cards. And I checked with Kaia, who agrees with my interpretation."

Kaia was the ultimate authority on fortune telling in the camp. But needless to say, I didn't trust her. There was no way Mirela would accept my belief that the prophesies were lies made up to hoodwink unsuspecting customers, so I tried a different approach. "Won't there be trouble in the camp if you marry a non-Roma? Outside of the tribe?"

"If Danior can do it, so can I!" She marched back over to the trunk and hopped on top of it, this time managing to close it completely. "Latch it for me, will you?"

As I fiddled with the stiff latches on the trunk, I continued to prod her about this marriage she seemed to think would take place. "Will you stay in Vienna? Does he have lodgings suitable for a wife? What about children?"

"Details. Right now, all I need to worry about is love."

She looked into my eyes and there it was again. The wily Mirela lay buried beneath a veneer of starry-eyed wonder. What had the captain-count actually said to her? "I'm going to meet him at St. Stephen's tomorrow."

"When?"

"He's to send a message, then I'll know."

"How will I know where to come to see you wed?" She couldn't possibly not want me there.

"Oh, it's not going to be a grand affair. No crowds. Just the two of us. I'll write to you afterwards to say where we're living."

This was all most perplexing. Could she really have fallen so madly in love with the mysterious captain? "Mirela, I fear..." How could I tell her that whatever he told her, I didn't trust Captain von Bauer to make good on his promises?

"You fear what?"

"I'm only fearful that I won't be able to see you as often as I want to, after you are married." I decided that to say more at that point would serve no purpose. I went home, determined to seek out the captain in the morning and confront him—about Mirela, and about everything else.

A fine drizzle beaded on my cloak by the time I arrived at the guard station the next morning. I didn't think I'd find the captain there, knowing now that he hadn't been acting officially as an officer, but that he had some secret purpose instead. I still wasn't certain who he was working for, but he turned up everywhere I'd gone while trying to figure out what had happened to the musician I thought had been murdered.

As I expected, rather than speak with the captain I was obliged to leave him a message—which the guard on duty assured me he would receive.

"He must get this message as soon as possible," I said, searching the man's eyes for an indication that he thought I was serious and not just some lovesick girl following the captain around. I wasn't certain I succeeded.

To my surprise, though, I received a letter that same evening from the captain, and it made me heart sore for Mirela.

Graf Adelbert von Bauer

Vienna, October 25, 1781

Dear Mademoiselle Schurman,

I write these words as I am about to mount and ride to Paris, where I have been given a position with the Swiss Guard, the elite soldiers who guard the person of King Louis XVI of France. I have no plans to return, as my commission here—to prevent the assassination of our emperor, brother-in-law of King Louis, has been successfully completed.

Your information regarding the Gypsy, Mademoiselle Mirela, comes as a complete surprise. I gave her no promises or hints of promises that we would be wed. As you no doubt know, I once before fell in love with a lady outside of my family's acceptance, and both of us suffered for it. I would not undertake such a project again, and wish Mirela every happiness with someone of her own persuasion.

I also wish you, Mademoiselle, success in your musical and investigative ventures. You have many talents, and I hope you continue to exercise them all successfully.

With fond regards, au revoir,

And the letter was signed with an extravagant flourish.

Poor Mirela! I thought. Would he have written to her as well? He said he was leaving momentarily. It was too late for me to go out to the Roma camp that night. I would have to find her first thing in the morning and hope she hadn't already left for St. Stephen's.

The brilliant, autumn sunshine the next morning was small comfort as I made my way to from Roma camp to St. Stephen's. Mirela had already left by the time I got there, no doubt flying ecstatically on the wings of love to meet the captain. My heart felt like lead. The fact that she'd gone already made it clear that she hadn't received word from him.

I saw her from across the square. I had to wait for several carriages to pass before I could make my way to her—which gave me a little time to rehearse what I would say. She spotted me when I was halfway across and started to lift her hand to wave, then dropped it. Even that far away I could see perplexity on her face.

"*Guten Morgen,* Mirela," I said. Stupidly, I thought.

"What are you doing here?"

"I wanted to show you something." I had brought the letter with me, deciding in the end that she wouldn't believe me if I just told her. I'm not sure I would have in her position. I pulled the letter out of my pocket and handed it to her.

She looked into my eyes, not at the letter, as she took it from me. I had to look away.

I only knew she'd read the letter when I heard the paper being crumpled and finally looked up. Mirela had remarkable control of her expressions, something she'd practiced in her fortune-telling business. The only indication that she was disturbed was the slight flaring of her nostrils and an almost imperceptible quiver of her lips. She never blushed, at least not that I had ever witnessed.

"You! You bring me such news? How dare you. I shall return to camp. Alone. I curse you, Theresa Maria Schurman!" And then she spit on the ground at my feet.

Without waiting, Mirela whirled around revealing a flash of a red petticoat and marched away.

She blamed me! Why? I wasn't the one who disappointed her. I didn't make her fall in love with me and then disappear.

I probably should have returned to my apartment and left Mirela to come to terms with the news that she'd been mistaken about the captain in her own way, but I couldn't bear the thought that she now hated me. So I hastened back to the Roma camp.

At first Mirela wouldn't let me in, even though I pounded and pounded on the door of her hut. It wasn't until one of the old women yelled at her to let me in for Christ's sake that I heard her rapid approach and the bolt on the other side being drawn. She didn't open the door, but I took it as a signal that I should let myself in.

The trunk she'd packed so carefully the day before was now on its side, all its contents spilling out on to the floor. Mirela stood with her back to me. Her shoulders shook. She was sobbing, silently. Of course she didn't want anyone to know of her humiliation.

I walked to her and wrapped my arms around her. At first she was stiff, resisting, but after a minute she turned and buried her face in my shoulder. I let her shed her tears all over my best day dress. I decided it would do no good to say anything, and so remained silent until Mirela had cried out her despair.

When she at last regained control over her emotions, Mirela said, "It wasn't a real curse, you know. That I would never do to anyone I loved. Even the faithless captain." She smiled.

CHAPTER THIRTY-FOUR

Mirela went back to her usual mischievous, flirtatious self, as I knew she would, although there was no repairing her relationship with Olaf. But my business wasn't yet finished. I wanted to do whatever I could to ensure that Mozart had his premiere, that the captain's flight did not make Thorwart feel secure enough to renege on his oath to me. I did not trust a man who was capable of putting into motion such terrible events simply for the sake of interfering with Mozart's career. I would call on Constanze and find out if Amadé's opera had been given a performance date, and if they had their permission to marry.

I returned to the house called To the Eye of God and inquired for Mozart's fiancée.

"My daughter is not here. She has run away to stay with Countess Thun." Frau Weber stood and blocked me from entering beyond the door. She looked very unhappy, her hands covered in grease and strands of her gray hair wisping out from beneath her white cap. "She has left all the management of my house to me, the ungrateful wretch. And I'm sure I don't know what cause she has to complain."

It seemed Constanze's mother was less disturbed by her daughter's absence than by her lack of household help. When I thanked her and turned to go, she let the door slam closed.

So, Constanze had some wealthy, influential friends. I had no doubt it was because of Mozart. I wanted to go and find her in her hiding place, but I could not simply drop into so illustrious a house when I was not only well beneath them socially but also a complete stranger. Instead I made my way to Alida and Danior's apartment. There I would beg some paper and write two notes: one to Constanze and one to her sister Aloysia. I would ask them both to assure me that Thorwart had honored his promise to me, and that if he hadn't, to meet me at a coffee house where I would discuss a plan with them to bring the desired results about. I had to admit, Mirela's sham curse, and the illusions that had tricked me into believing so many things that turned out not to be real—my own delusions that persuaded me things were so different from actuality—gave me an idea I thought might work if—as I feared—Thorwart had failed to carry out his promise to me.

"Our man will deliver them for you," Alida said. She reclined on a chaise, her swollen belly looking as though at any moment it might burst. She must have been very uncomfortable, but she smiled sweetly at me and apologized profusely for not rising to greet me.

We chatted companionably while I waited for answers, and I was aware all the time of how fatigued Alida was, and that my presence prevented her from napping.

An hour passed, but I received responses from both sisters within moments of each other. They both confirmed my fears: all had not been resolved. Mozart and Constanze had not been given permission to marry. I kissed Alida goodbye and hurried away to meet the two Weber sisters at the coffee house near the Burgtheater.

Constanze had gotten there before I did, and sat waiting at a small table in a corner, a cup of chocolate in front of her. She was dressed in a very pretty gown, a pale rose damask Caraco and overskirt, with a lace-edged white muslin petticoat and under blouse. Her hair was done up beautifully, and a pink feathered hat perched on top of her head at a jaunty angle. She had removed her gloves and placed them, with her fan, on the little table. She sat up very straight, as if she wasn't quite used to wearing such finery and was afraid of spoiling it.

I felt a little plain beside her, wearing a soft wool day dress with a quilted petticoat and only a little ruffle on the blouse. But I had on a hat that Alida had given me, and it was from one of the finest milliners in Vienna. It was a simple, round straw hat with a wide brim, tied under my chin with a silk bow. It allowed me to feel confident that I wasn't completely out of fashion.

"Aloysia will be late. She always is," said Constanze after she embraced me as though we were close friends. I liked her frank openness and her warm-hearted acceptance of me after so short an acquaintance. I could understand why Mozart would want to marry her.

"But she will come? She said that she would," I replied.

"Yes. Although our godfather has helped her to advance her career, she has no more affection for him than I have," Constanze said.

"Your godfather? I thought he was your uncle." I exclaimed.

"Yes. He is both. And he has guardianship over us since my father's death. Didn't you know? I assumed that was why you wrote to us."

"I didn't know," I said, now suddenly understanding how this man could have such an influence on the private life of a niece. "But I'm very glad—for our purpose alone, that is. Otherwise, I should feel very sorry for you."

Constanze laughed. "He is a troublesome meddler and a small-minded, unimaginative philistine. And he has much too much of an influence on my mother, who has made him draw up a ridiculous marriage contract that I refuse to sign."

"What are the terms?" I asked.

"There's something in it that states that if Wolferl fails to marry me, that he will give my mother a stipend to support her. It's absurd! Oh how I wish godfathers had never been invented!"

"I'm afraid I cannot agree with you. I'm very fond of mine. It's Herr Haydn."

"Oh, you are fortunate. Wolferl thinks very highly of Herr Haydn, and has great respect for his string quartets. I have not yet met him."

We talked for half an hour at least, about Vienna, about what life had been like in Mannheim where the Webers used to live, about her dead papa, and how she wished he were alive to see her married to Mozart, whom he considered a great genius. "Of course, Wolferl proposed to Aloysia first. But he was young and had to make his name. She gave up waiting, and married my brother-in-law Lange, the painter."

Here were yet more revelations. How innocent I was! There was no question that Aloysia was more beautiful than her sister, but I liked Constanze better.

Just then, the famous soprano from the Burgtheater swept into the café, causing all eyes to turn in her direction. That was unfortunate. I wanted our meeting to be as secret as possible. Little chance of that now.

The sisters greeted each other with affection.

"I was just telling Rezia about the horrid marriage contract," Constanze said.

"That is unfortunate," said Aloysia, "but you have not heard the worst of it."

Constanze and I leaned forward, waiting for Aloysia to continue, but she waved over the waiter and asked for a glass of wine and took her time removing her gloves and wrap before continuing.

"There is another condition. I only know because I happened to overhear Wolferl's audition with Thorwart."

"What! What is it, Aloysia? You must say right away." Constanze was on the point of tears.

"He agreed to mount *The Abduction from the Seraglio*."

"What is bad about that?" I asked, thinking perhaps that we would not have to take any further action after all.

"He agreed on the condition that Amadé give up his ambitions to marry you."

Some minutes passed before any of us could speak. "The scoundrel," I said. "But I think we can persuade him to change his mind." I outlined my plan to them, hoping they would both agree to play their parts. "We must leave him no possible way to back out. It's important that both of you," I said, looking deliberately in Aloysia's direction, "keep to your resolve."

Aloysia drew in a deep breath and sighed it out impatiently. "Very well. The public will not like it, though."

"If I have judged Thorwart correctly, the public will not end up suffering in the slightest."

We agreed to meet later that very night, when the evening's opera ended and Thorwart would be wending his way home.

The weather cooperated beautifully. It was a windy, moonless night. Aloysia, who was performing that night, was to be the first to accost Thorwart immediately after the performance. She was going to complain that her throat was sore, and that she did not think she could sing for the remainder of the week. Then she was to say that a Gypsy had seen her in the street and uttered a curse, about her voice, saying that if a wedding in her family did not occur very soon, she would never sing again.

Of course, there was a chance Thorwart would not believe her. That's why I had Constanze stationed a little way outside the theater's stage door, dressed all in white and with a gauzy veil over her face. She carried a candle, and would stay just far enough away so that she would appear wraith like and insubstantial. I had told her to say, "I see you. I see you with those innocent young girls. The emperor would not like to hear of your immoral dealings. Redeem yourself by doing what is best for your sister's family."

The coup de grace would be delivered by me. I had gotten myself up like a Gypsy, which I well knew how to do because of Mirela. I took my most colorful clothes and scarves and draped myself with the strings of beads that Mirela had given me over the past two years, and waited in the shadows a short way beyond where Constanze was hidden. When I finished with him, I was certain Thorwart would drop all conditions, allow Mozart to present his opera and to marry Constanze. If the attempt to found a Lodge that would admit all men whatever their background or religion, and that would give Mozart his opportunity to break into the closed musical world of Vienna had failed, at least we could do whatever we could to give him another chance to make his name in our most musical city—at the side of the woman he loved.

The night had turned cold. I drew my shawls around me as the wind drove eddies of dried leaves through the streets. Although it was colder, the clear, moonless sky reminded me eerily of the night little more than a week before when I witnessed the attack on Herr Bachmann. I thought about all the deception around me, how nothing had been as it had seemed to me, and I felt sad. I supposed that was the way life truly was. After all, my father had been so much more than he had appeared to me on the surface. That he was better and nobler even than I guessed was fortunate. My uncle had proven the opposite. And now I had seen once again that people can be worse, that they can hide terrible secrets in their hearts and yet seem honorable and good to most of the people they meet each day.

I don't know how much time passed, but the sound of boots hurrying along the cobbled street interrupted my reverie. Something about the heavy irregularity of the tread made me suspect this was Thorwart, hurrying home after his encounter with Constanze. I glanced out of my hiding place and saw the theater director's bulky form rushing along, intermittently illuminated by the glow of a street lamp. I waited until he was too close to me to run back in the other direction, then stepped out of my hiding place into the pool of light from the nearest street lamp. I held up my hand as I had seen Mirela do when she cursed me, and called out in the deepest voice I could manage, "Thorwart! You are accursed!"

I had planned an entire tirade of nonsense words mixed with the few Romany phrases I had learned at the camp, but I had no need of them whatever. The sweating, panicking Thorwart fell to his knees in front of me, his hands clasped in supplication.

"No! Please! I'll do it! I said I'd do it! *The Abduction* will be presented at the Burgtheater as soon as it can be! And Constanze can marry! I withdraw all objections!"

Aloysia and Constanze must have done their jobs extremely well, I thought. Of course, Aloysia was accustomed to acting on the stage, and Constanze had a great deal to gain. This was altogether satisfactory.

"I release you!" I said, "So long as you keep your promise. Otherwise, beware!"

I skittered away from the fellow. His blubbering weakness embarrassed me. But it did not matter. My scheme had worked. Now, I had only to wait and see if all came to pass as I wished.

I headed home to my bed, feeling that I had indeed done everything in my power to redress any wrongs that may have resulted because I had leapt to conclusions before I knew the entire story. It was a bitter lesson, and one I never wanted to have to learn again.

When I arrived at our apartment, to my surprise my mother was still in the parlor, waiting for me. It was just before curfew so not very late, but normally she retired to her room as soon as little Anna was in bed.

"Theresa, I need to talk to you," she said, casting only a quick, disapproving eye over my strange clothing.

"A costume party, at Danior's," I said, answering her unasked question.

"Very well. You tell me so little of what you are doing that sometimes I think I should say just as little to you about my own life."

She stood and paced up and down across our parlor, twisting her hands together. "What's wrong Mama?" I asked, worried that perhaps she was ill.

"You know I told you that. . . Herr van Swieten. . . you know, we were . . ."

She couldn't string the sentences together. "What is it Mama? Just tell me. I promise not to be shocked or upset."

"Well, I suppose you wouldn't be. You didn't want us to marry anyway!" At that, she collapsed into her customary chair near the stove, took out her handkerchief and dabbed at her eyes with it.

I rose and knelt by her side, taking her hand. "You didn't really love him, did you Mama?"

"What does love matter!" she said, pulling her hand out of mine.

I reached for it again and took it firmly. "It does matter. Did he tell you he could not marry you?" I asked, "Or did you tell him?"

She turned her large blue eyes to me. "Oh, Theresa, I miss your father so! I thought that being married would make me less lonely. But then, when I really thought about it, imagined leaving this apartment where we had been so happy, and having to get to know all the . . . habits of someone new—I just couldn't."

I breathed a sigh of relief. I was afraid Herr van Swieten had found out something about me and told my mother that he could not marry her because of it. Once I realized that was not the case, I felt sad. For my mother, mostly, but a little bit for me. It might have been a good thing to have the advantages of such a connection. "But I am here, and

Anna. We can be company for you. I promise I won't be away from you as much from now on." Although I had not anticipated making this promise, I felt it was the least I could do.

"Your father's daughter," Mama said. "I can no more prevent you from doing what your heart dictates than I could prevent him. I only hope you do not come to such a tragic end because of it."

"I will try not to," I said, and laid my cheek on her hand.

We stayed like that for a moment or two, until suddenly she stood from her chair and walked over to the table. "Oh, I almost forgot. A letter came for you today."

She fetched the letter and gave it to me. I recognized the writing immediately. It was Zoltán's. I felt myself go hot and my hands tremble a little. "I'm tired Mama. I shall go to my room."

"It's from that Hungarian violist, isn't it?" she said, a little smile on her lips and her eyes a bit brighter than they had been. "The one who is now a baron?"

I blushed. "Yes, I think so."

"You go and read it in private. I shall trust you to tell me if there is anything I should know."

I kissed her and left her alone. My heart was pounding by the time I had closed the door to my room and lit a candle so that I could read the letter. I broke the seal so quickly that the paper tore a little. What could Zoltán be writing to me?

My dear Rezia,

I hope you are recovered from your ordeal the other night. It grieved me to see you so shaken and distressed. You behaved very bravely, and the emperor owes you his thanks.

I heard from Danior about the business with Captain von Bauer. Poor Mirela. But she will no doubt bear it well. The cap-

tain's mission had been to foil the ring of ultra-conservative nobles and merchants who were putting pressure on the emperor to reinstate the restrictions on the Jews that he had just lifted. It was a dangerous, double game. Even I did not know exactly what he had planned, and was as surprised as you to find the trap beneath the floor of the lodge. You had stumbled on everything while he was in the midst of his most important initiative. But here, as far as I can make them out, are the facts of the case:

It was sergeant Hirsch who attacked Bachmann, and who intended to drown the emperor, although he most certainly was in someone else's pay—not Captain Bauer's, of course, who was on the side of the right all along. The captain suspected someone very high up, but had not been able to make the connection. He'd been hoping to be able to flush him out of hiding by catching Hirsch at it. Only then would the accusation be believable.

The emperor, deciding to err on the side of caution, told Bauer to stop his investigation and go to Paris, where his help was needed to protect the king there from growing unrest. Now we may never be able to prove the other man's involvement at all, the one who was too high up and powerful to be suspected. Hirsch was a little mad, in the end. And he's dead so cannot tell his tale.

When Hirsch started to make holes in the wooden casket that contained you and the emperor, the captain did the only thing he could to prevent disaster. He shot him. Captain Bauer saved your life, Rezia.

Still, I cannot help admiring your actions. You are your father's daughter. I loved your father, and I have feelings for you that cannot be adequately conveyed in words.

My business is now done here, and I shall be returning to my estate in Hungary in a few days. Would you do me the honor of meeting me before I go? Tomorrow, at noon, at Danior and Alida's? I need to know something, and I can only ask you in person.

With fondest regards, Zoltán of Varga

The captain saved my life? I had gotten just about everything wrong—except for the business with Thorwart. Was he truly the powerful person behind it all? It seemed likely, especially considering his response to my accusations. Yet I wondered, as Zoltán had, if we would ever know.

I felt so stupid, so naive. But there was nothing more I could do about it now. And Zoltán wanted to see me. Tomorrow. I was tired, but how would I sleep? I undressed, blew out my candle, and lay in bed, wide awake. What should I wear? I must do something with my hair. Perhaps my mother would let me wear her pearls?

My dreams that night were a strange mixture of joy and sorrow, hope and despair. I saw my father playing the violin in a quartet with Zoltán and Danior. The captain had Mirela on his arm, but he pulled away from her, even though he was smiling at her.

And my mother wore black again, and carried little Anna in her arms, walking up and down, up and down, on the small stretch of the Bastei that looked toward the Augarten.

CHAPTER THIRTY-FIVE

I awoke too early on the day I was to go and see Zoltán. Even Anna was still sleeping soundly, and I could hear Greta snoring in her cubicle off the parlor. I quickly pulled on a simple skirt and bodice, hose, and my stout boots. I crept through the parlor, took my cloak off the peg by the door and let myself out into the dawning autumn morning.

The mist still lay over a sleeping Vienna, but the dark sky had already brightened in the east. I hoped and dreaded what Zoltán was going to say to me that day, and I needed to think. The city gates would soon be open and the streets flooded with merchants and peasants from the suburbs, selling the vegetables and grains from their harvest along with their fattened pigs, bringing their tanned hides and dyed cloth into their stalls on the busy streets. I needed quiet, anonymity, somewhere to think. So I went to the Bastei.

The sentry nodded to me as I climbed the stone steps up to the top of the broad city wall. On one side, the city lanes and buildings stretched out before my gaze, intermittently blanketed with patches of fog, a few wisps of smoke rising like curls of hair as people lit their kitchen fires. I was overwhelmed with a feeling of love for the very stones and roof tiles. Vienna was my home, especially now, since Papa had died and we no longer journeyed to Esterhaza with the prince's court. I knew its byways and customs so intimately that I felt as if the city itself were a member of my family.

On the other side lay the suburbs, more sparsely built, and petering out to fields, farms and forests. The silvery Danube snaked its way through everything, leading off into the distance, deep into Hungary. The mist shrouded my far-off view, hiding it from me as if preventing me from seeing into the future. Would Zoltán ask what I thought he might? A deep thrill passed through my body. I shivered, although the air had already warmed a little as the sun now painted orange streaks along the eastern edge of the sky.

If Zoltán asked, I would have to decide whether to leave my family, my home, my city. I would have to trust him to care for me and supply everything that I needed in my life. Most of all, I would have to trust him to let me continue to make music, and be as independent as I could be without placing myself beyond the pale.

Could I trust him? He had deceived me, just as everyone else had. He had kept matters from me even though I had stumbled blindly through the maze created by the complicated charade, and ended up figuring out almost everything that was going on. I was sorry that Mirela, too, had been deceived by the captain. I had misjudged her ability to fall deeply in love. But I still had hope that Constanze, Aloysia, and I had together ensured that Mozart's opera would be performed at the Burgtheater, and that Constanze and Amadé would be able to marry at last.

I was lightheaded from lack of sleep, and my stomach rumbled. A cup of chocolate and a soft roll would soon await me at home. Without having come to any clear conclusion, I descended the stairs from the Bastei and wound my way through the now bustling streets to our apartment. The porter nodded to me—the man was so accustomed to seeing me come and go at all hours that he barely turned a hair.

Greta had lit the stove and laid the plates for breakfast. She was probably down at the kitchen warming the rolls. Anna called out from her room, "Mama! Greta!"

I went in and helped her use her little chamber pot, then dressed her in a smock and apron and brushed her soft curls. She chattered away merrily. I don't know why her sweet voice sent a shaft through my heart.

Mama came out of her room wearing her peignoir and nightcap. "Have you been out already?" she asked, yawning.

"I went for a walk," I said.

"Was it the letter?"

I paused, deciding just how much to tell her. I could not show her the letter, because it told of the conspiracy I had discovered and in which I had become embroiled. "Yes. Zoltán wants to see me at noon, to ask me something."

Her eyes grew large, and all vestiges of sleep vanished from her face. "There is no time to waste! Greta!" she called out loudly. Our housekeeper ran up the stairs and into the apartment, alarmed at the tone of urgency in my mother's voice. "Fetch Frau Letchinsky. She must do Theresa's hair. And Theresa, you must wear my pearls, and I have some new gloves and a fan, too."

"But Mama—" Clearly she had jumped to the one conclusion she could imagine. It was the same one I suspected, but I still dared not hope—or fear it.

"No buts, young lady. For once you will do exactly as I say."

I gave myself up to her, and spent the next several hours being primped and prodded and dressed.

I managed to persuade my mother that I didn't need to take a Fiaker the short distance to Danior and Alida's apartment. She insisted that I carry a parasol, though, and wrap a veil around my head so that my hair would not be destroyed by the autumn breeze. She waved from the doorway as though seeing me off on a long voyage, and I supposed that in some sense she was—if what she and I both suspected came to pass.

By the time I reached Alida's apartment, my heart tolled as loudly as the bells of St. Stephen's, and I felt faintly sick with anticipation. The porter let me in and I climbed the stairs. The maid admitted me and took my cloak and veil. "You look beautiful, Mademoiselle Theresa," she whispered. I smiled at her. "But there is so much of a to-do this morning. The lady Alida is unwell. Her time has come, and she is indisposed in her room. You are to come into the parlor anyway."

I had expected to find Danior, Alida, and Zoltán in the parlor, thinking perhaps Zoltán would suggest we take a walk around. Of course, I had forgotten that Alida could not control when her baby would arrive.

So I was not really surprised—and perhaps a little relieved—when only Zoltán was there to greet me.

"I should have met you somewhere else, but I could not think where," he said after he had kissed my hand in greeting. I felt his fingers tremble slightly. Neither of us sat, as if deciding how to arrange ourselves was too momentous a decision to undertake.

"Rezia," he began, then stopped. "Theresa, I should say. You are no longer a little girl." He lifted his eyes from studying the pattern on the carpet, and the look in them was so intense I had to turn away. "You must know. I feel that you do. My life in Hungary is incomplete and lonely."

"Surely there are plenty of beautiful Hungarian heiresses to entertain yourself with," I said, not knowing quite why.

"I don't want to be entertained. I want to be loved. And to love in return. Do you think. . . you could ever. . ."

He had moved gradually closer to me and I could smell his characteristic scent: the odor a man gives off combined with freshly cut hay, the leather of his boots and the faint polish of his buttons. I lifted my eyes, and found myself no more than a few inches away from his.

Before I knew it, the distance closed between us, and our lips met in a gentle kiss. Weakness washed over me, and I swayed a little. Zoltán took hold of my arms to steady me, then grasped me to him, kissing me hungrily, his tongue pushing past my teeth. I dropped my fan and gloves and wrapped my arms around his neck, wanting to be as close to him as humanly possible. I lost all sense of time and space. We could have been standing on the moon, thousands of years from then.

When we pulled ourselves apart, I felt I was no longer the same person. Only music had ever affected me so deeply before.

"Theresa," he whispered.

"Call me Rezia, as you always do," I said.

He smiled. "Rezia. Will you—"

"I—I don't know," I answered, not even allowing him to finish the question. What was I saying? It had been my dream. But something held me back. "I would have to move to Hungary. Which would mean leaving Vienna, and not being a violinist anymore."

"We would have chamber music! You could still play in our home, among friends. And your family could come too. There is room."

"Mama would never leave Vienna, and Toby is here."

His smile faded, and he looked so sad. I kissed him lightly. "I'm not saying no forever. I just need more time."

He nodded. Did he understand? Would anyone? I wasn't even certain I understood. But I had been given a taste of what a truly independent life was like, and I wasn't entirely ready to give it up.

"Shall I walk you home?"

I put my arm through his and pulled him toward the door. "Let's just go for a walk. I want to tell you what I hope to do in my life, make you understand that I love you, but I can't marry you, not yet."

We walked around the Bastei for hours. We agreed to wait a year and then marry, without placing any restrictions on each other in the meantime. My mother was disappointed, but I felt a combination of relief and joy. It may be the highest ambition of most girls like me to marry well and have a family. But I expected more from life. I counted on Zoltán to understand—and respect—my desire. If he did not, then he wasn't the man I thought he was.

At that moment, though, I felt I could trust Zoltán with my heart.

Epilogue

July 16, 1782

It was a splendid occasion. The Burgtheater was filled to capacity with the most illustrious nobles and wealthy citizens of Vienna. Alida had come out for the evening for the first time since the birth of her healthy baby boy, and looked more radiantly beautiful than ever.

Alida and Zoltán sat in a box with my mother, Toby, Herr van Swieten, and Mirela. Alida had persuaded Mirela to wear something more suitable than her usual Gypsy garb, and she looked stunning. It had taken a few months, but she eventually forgave me for being the bearer of such ill tidings about the captain. But I suspected the captain had better beware of her intentions, knowing her as I did.

As for the other matter, with Sophie von Eskeles—Danior persuaded them to receive me, and I was able to explain myself. Although the old man accepted my apology with formality, Sophie had leapt about with joy, eager to hear all about my performing as a young man. I pretended that I had given up the practice when I saw the alarmed look on Herr von Eskeles's face, but I think Sophie saw through me.

An expectant hush descended on the company as the musicians took their places for the overture to Mozart's *Abduction from the Seraglio.* When the maestro himself strode out and bowed before seating himself at the keyboard, a cheer went up from the audience.

The orchestra consisted of the best musicians in Vienna. Danior led the violins, of course, and Herr Bachmann—who had succumbed to necessity and converted from his religion—was the principal flutist. The remaining members of the orchestra were the best of the best. And me? I sat bursting with happiness in the last desk of the second violins. Zoltán had had a new uniform made for me, and Mirela had helped to arrange my unruly hair so that it would not be visible in the bag wig. Thorwart knew, of course, but could do nothing. He had been relieved of his position, pensioned off. I had hoped for worse, but I had learned to be content with that. Needless to say, he did not attend the premiere.

There I was. Not only playing at the Burgtheater, but in Mozart's first opera for Vienna, with Catarina Cavalieri and all the biggest opera stars singing. Aloysia could not perform—she had a prior engagement, and in any case, the real Constanze would have been none too happy at the idea of her sister playing the role of Konstanze. The irony would have been too fresh.

Whatever had gone on behind the scenes, I was in heaven. It was an unforgettable way to end my involvement in this conspiracy that had wound through so many different parts of Viennese society.

More people knew that I'd been deceiving the musical world of Vienna, but somehow I still had invitations to perform not as Theresa, but as Thomas. But for that evening, I was neither Theresa nor Thomas. I was the music I made and the music that surrounded me. Whatever else happened in my life, I would have had this one, perfect experience. I hoped my papa was looking down from heaven and smiling. I was his daughter in so many ways, and intended to continue not only playing the violin, but fighting for justice in any way I could.

6. 20

AUTHOR'S NOTE

This sequel to *The Musician's Daughter* continues the adventures of the fictional violinist Theresa Maria Schurman in Haydn's Vienna. While the drama around Mozart's marriage to Constanze and the first performance of *The Abduction from the Seraglio* is based in fact, all other events in this mystery are purely fictional—including the manner in which the drama is resolved.

What is not fictional are the restrictions imposed on Jews at the time in Vienna, and the traditions and regulations that did not allow women to perform in orchestras. In fact, until 2003, the Vienna Philharmonic did not permit women players, other than as harpists. Soloists were an exception, of course.

The belief that it was unladylike for women to play certain instruments persisted through the eighteenth and nineteenth centuries. Leopold Mozart would not permit his daughter Marianne—known to her family as Nannerl—to perform on the violin, despite the fact that she was a brilliant violinist. She was relegated to accompanying her younger brother on the clavier while he played the violin.

Theresa will continue to play this forbidden instrument, however, and become involved in dangerous escapades in upcoming books. Stay informed of new releases at susanne-dunlap.com, follow me on Facebook at SusanneDunlapAuthor and on Twitter and Instagram at susanne_dunlap.

9 780578 565972